Praise for the *New York Times* Bestselling Magical Cats Mysteries

Final Catcall

"Kelly hits a home run. The book's plot is spectacular. There is a new twist, along with a new suspect, around every corner. With the addition of romantic tangles, this makes for an excellent addition to the already outstanding series."

—*Romantic Times*

"Owen and Hercules are a delight."

—Kings River Life Magazine

"The author is brilliant in not only writing character portrayals, but in creating a mystery complete with twists and turns that will keep the reader trying to figure it all out. . . . I absolutely could not put it down."   —Socrates' Book Reviews

Cat Trick

"Match two magical kitties with an extremely inquisitive librarian and a murder or two and you have all the makings of an extraordinary mystery series . . . a captivating cozy!"

—Escape with Dollycas into a Good Book

"The characters are likable and the cats are darling."   —Socrates' Book Reviews

"Small-town charm and a charming cat duo make this every cat fancier's dream."

—The Mystery Reader

continued . . .

Copycat Killing

"I've been a huge fan of this series from the very start, and I am delighted that this new book meets my expectations and then some. . . . Cats with magic powers, a library, good friends who look out for each other and small-town coziness come together in perfect unison. If you are a fan of Miranda James's Cat in the Stacks mysteries, you will want to read [this series]."   —MyShelf.com

"This is a really fun series, and I've read them all. Each book improves on the last one. Being a cat lover myself, I'm looking at my cat in a whole new light."   —Once Upon a Romance

"A fun whodunit. . . . Fans will appreciate this entertaining amateur sleuth."
                              —Genre Go Round Reviews

"This charming series continues on a steady course as the intrepid Kathleen has two mysteries to snoop into. . . . Readers who are fans of cats and cozies will want to add this series to their must-read lists."   —*Romantic Times*

Sleight of Paw

"Kelly's appealing cozy features likable, relatable characters set in an amiable location. The author continues to build on the promise of her debut novel, carefully developing her characters and their relationships." —*Romantic Times*

Curiosity Thrilled the Cat

"A great cozy that will quickly have you anxiously waiting for the next release so you can spend more time with the people of Mayville Heights."
—Mysteries and My Musings

"If you love mystery and magic, this is the book for you!" —Debbie's Book Bag

"This start of a new series offers an engaging cast of human characters and two appealing, magically inclined felines. Kathleen is a likable, believable heroine, and the magical cats are amusing."
—*Romantic Times*

A
MIDWINTER'S
TAIL

A MAGICAL CATS MYSTERY

SOFIE KELLY

AN OBSIDIAN MYSTERY

OBSIDIAN
Published by the Penguin Group
Penguin Group (USA) LLC, 375 Hudson Street,
New York, New York 10014

USA | Canada | UK | Ireland | Australia | New Zealand | India | South Africa | China
penguin.com
A Penguin Random House Company

First published by Obsidian, an imprint of New American Library,
a division of Penguin Group (USA) LLC

First Printing, October 2014

ISBN 978-0-451-41471-7

Printed in the United States of America
10 9 8 7 6 5 4 3 2 1

For "The Chief"

ACKNOWLEDGMENTS

As always, many people helped along the way as this book went from idea to reality. Lynn Viehl and Janet Koch provided encouragement and laughter. My agent, Kim Lionetti, shared her wisdom and support with good humor. Jessica Wade, my very talented editor, found all the leaps in logic in the story and, as usual, made the book better. Her very capable assistant, Isabel Farhi, kept us both on schedule. As he has since the Magical Cats Mysteries began, Tim Sletten, retired Red Wing, Minnesota, police chief, answered my questions and was a good sport when I twisted his answers to suit the story. And last but never least, Patrick and Lauren could both always be counted on for back rubs, coffee and lots of love.

1

"I look like Fred the Funky Chicken's mother," Rebecca said. And because she was so kind, she immediately added, "And it's not that I don't like bright yellow chickens . . ." Her voice trailed off.

"You just don't want to look like a giant version of Owen's favorite catnip treat on your wedding day," I finished. Owen was one of my two cats. Rebecca, whose house backed on mine, kept him supplied with catnip chickens, which he loved, much to the annoyance of his brother, Hercules, who didn't get the attraction of catnip or neon yellow chickens.

I held the phone out to Roma so she could see the photo of Rebecca in the potential wedding dress, a buttercup yellow ball gown with a huge skirt of chiffon feathers. Rebecca was dwarfed by the dress. I was several inches taller, and I could see that it would have engulfed me, too.

"It's not you," Roma agreed. "But don't worry.

We'll find you something." Roma was one of my closest friends in Mayville Heights and a very positive person.

"This wedding is turning into shredded wheat," Rebecca said, fingering the soft blue scarf around her neck.

I smiled in sympathy across the small table at Eric's Place, our favorite restaurant. I knew Rebecca would have been happy to elope.

Roma frowned and looked from Rebecca to me. "Excuse me?"

"Shredded wheat," I repeated. "The more you chew on it, the bigger it seems to get."

Roma laughed and reached for her coffee. "Rebecca, I promise we'll find you a dress that has nothing to do with breakfast cereal or giant yellow birds."

Rebecca smiled across the table at us. "I don't know what I'd do without the two of you." She smoothed a hand over her silver-gray hair. She'd cut it herself—Rebecca had been a hairdresser for more than forty years—into a little gamin pixie that showed off her beautiful cheekbones and her blue eyes.

Rebecca Nixon wasn't just my backyard neighbor, she was also the first friend I'd made when I'd come to Mayville Heights to supervise the renovation of the town's library. In a couple of weeks she was going to marry her childhood sweetheart, Everett Henderson. And she still didn't have a wedding dress.

I handed the phone back across the table to her.

She looked at the photo again and gave a soft sigh. "Ami means well," she said. "It's just that she seems to have caught wedding fever from Everett."

Ami was Everett Henderson's only grandchild. She'd been close to Rebecca, whom she lovingly called Rebbie, for most of her life and she was overjoyed about the wedding. Rebecca and Everett had waited close to fifty years to be married, and Everett was determined to give her an elaborate celebration—whether or not she wanted it. And she didn't.

I reached over and laid my hand on Rebecca's arm. "My offer still stands," I said, raising one eyebrow at her. Several months ago when Everett had been talking about having the wedding in The Basilica of St. Mary in downtown Minneapolis—which technically wasn't possible since neither he nor Rebecca was Catholic—I'd jokingly told Rebecca I'd be happy to help her "kidnap" Everett and elope. "I have a full tank of gas in the truck and I'm betting Roma has a roll of duct tape in her bag."

"I do," Roma said. "But if you're planning on making a wedding dress, you should know there's only about half the roll left."

"You know, I bet Maggie could make you a wedding dress out of duct tape," I said, reaching for my coffee.

Maggie Adams was my closest friend in Mayville Heights, along with Roma. She was a mixed-media collage artist and potter; plus she taught tai chi. Mayville Heights had a thriving artists' community. Maggie was the current president of the artists' co-op and the most creative person I'd ever met. She'd made an incredibly realistic, life-size replica of Minnesota Wild hockey player Eddie Sweeney as part of a display for last year's Winterfest celebration, and it had indirectly led to Roma's current relationship with the real Eddie Sweeney. I had no doubt that Maggie could make Rebecca a wedding dress out of duct tape, or recycled newspaper, for that matter.

"If I don't find a dress soon, I may have to get her to do that," Rebecca said. She glanced down at the image of the funky chicken ball gown one more time and then tucked her phone in her purse. "Although I don't think it would go with Everett's plans."

"If the wedding is still too elaborate, tell him," I said.

Roma nodded in agreement. "Everett would marry you on an iceberg in the middle of the Bering Sea. He loves you. He just wants you to be happy."

Rebecca had told me once that while she'd dreamed of being married to Everett, she'd never thought about the actual wedding. She didn't care about flowers or food. Everett, on the other hand, wanted a celebration. He wanted the whole world to know how he felt about his bride, although you only had to spend a minute or two with both of them to see it. They made me believe in happily ever after.

"I know he would," Rebecca said, tracing the rim of her coffee cup with one finger. "But all this . . . hoopla is important to him. He already agreed to scale his original plans back for me. I know he wants me to be happy, but I want him to be happy, too."

"I know what you mean," Roma said softly. She got the starry-eyed, slightly goofy look on her face that told me she was thinking about Eddie.

Over at the counter, waiter Nic Sutton looked our way and gestured at the coffeepot. I nodded. He reached for the glass carafe and headed in our direction.

"Thanks, Nic," I said after he'd refilled our mugs.

"Could I get you anything else?" he asked. We'd made short work of three of Eric's pecan sticky buns. I was tempted to have another, but in a couple of hours I was going to have to squeeze into a very formfitting dress, so I shook my head.

The library was hosting an evening fundraiser at the Stratton Theatre for our Reading Buddies program, which paired kindergartners with fourth and fifth graders to help foster a love of reading and improve their actual reading skills. The stage had been dressed to resemble a French bistro, with several local businesses providing elegant desserts. In a wonderful twist of coincidence, Eddie Sweeney's college roommate was the leader and saxophone player in a jazz quartet, Jazzology. They were providing the "atmosphere." Eddie was very generously—and quietly—covering their expenses.

"Roma, do you have plans for tomorrow night?" I asked as I added cream and sugar to my cup. I'd taken Friday night off to relax after the fundraising gala, but I was happy to give that up to help Rebecca find a dress.

"Paperwork and pizza," she said, tucking her sleek dark brown hair behind one ear. "But I'm open to a better idea. Or any other idea."

I smiled at Rebecca. "Let Roma and me take you shopping tomorrow night. Here in town or maybe over in Red Wing."

"Please," Roma added. "I don't want to do paperwork all night."

A smile stretched across Rebecca's face. "Thank you. Yes. I don't think I can do this without help."

"I'll drive," Roma offered. She looked at Rebecca. "I'll pick you up about quarter to seven." She glanced at me. "And then we'll come get you."

I nodded. Roma's SUV was a better choice than the three of us squashed onto the front seat of my old truck.

The front door of Eric's Place swung open then and Lita Clarke stepped inside, pushing back the hood of her jacket. The red wool reminded me of the autumn leaves on the maple tree in Rebecca's backyard. I felt a little twinge of sadness. I was going to miss Rebecca when she moved into Everett's downtown apartment.

Lita smiled when she caught sight of us, stamped her feet on the mat by the door to shake the snow off her boots and then headed over.

"Kathleen, I'm glad I caught you," she said. She

pulled off her black woolen gloves, took an envelope from her purse and handed it to me. My name was written on the front in her tight, angular script. "Everett wanted you to have this."

I lifted the flap of the envelope. There was a check inside made out to me. I looked uncertainly at Lita. "What's this for?" I asked.

"For tomorrow," she said. "Everett said he knows you'll take Vincent Starr out to lunch after his presentation and he didn't want you to use your own money."

Everett knew me well. I *was* planning on taking the rare-book dealer to lunch after his presentation at the library Friday morning.

Vincent Starr was an expert on American literature and children's books. We'd met when Abigail Pierce, one of my staff at the library, found a rare and valuable early edition of *Alice in Wonderland* in a box of books donated for the library's fundraising yard sale my first summer in town.

Vincent and Abigail had stayed in touch. For the past month he'd been working at the Walker Art Center, in Minneapolis, curating a collection of late-nineteenth-century children's literature that was going on display at the art museum. He'd agreed to come and give a talk about rare books. Abigail, who had been to one of Vincent's lectures, promised he was an entertaining speaker. He was also a big supporter of projects for children's literacy and he'd offered to come to the Reading Buddies fundraiser to mingle and talk about books.

I reached for my purse and tucked the envelope

inside. "Please thank Everett for me," I said to Lita. "And thank you for delivering it."

"Oh, you're welcome," she said, peeling off her other glove and stuffing them both into one of the pockets of her duffle coat. "I was coming out anyway. Our coffeemaker died and Everett doesn't work well uncaffeinated."

"Neither do I," I said with a grin.

Out of the corner of my eye, I saw Rebecca roll hers. She thought I drank a bit too much coffee. I thought there was no such thing as too much coffee.

"Is everything set for tonight?" Lita asked.

I nodded. "Everything's ready," I said. "Wait until you see the stage. You'll think Maggie and Ruby somehow transported a Parisian street to Minnesota."

I had my fingers crossed that the gala would raise enough money to expand Reading Buddies. The program had turned out to have benefits I had never anticipated. I'd seen the little ones blossom under the attention of the older kids, and many of the older ones had developed a strong sense of maturity and responsibility toward their little students.

"Everyone's looking forward to this," she said, loosening the red-and-black scarf at her neck. She smiled. "I better get back to the office. If you need anything, call me there or on my cell."

"I will," I said, returning the smile.

"See you tonight," Lita said to all three of us before heading for the counter, where Nic had just started a new pot of coffee.

I watched her weave her way around the tables

and wondered if Lita would show up alone, or with Burtis Chapman. Lita and the burly "entrepreneur" had been quietly seeing each other for several months. I'd only figured it out because I'd seen them in a close moment in the library parking lot. Lita and Burtis were very different. She'd worked for Everett for years. Burtis had a number of small businesses. Rumor had it that some of them danced on the edge of being legal.

I was surprised that they had managed to keep their relationship quiet. It wasn't easy to keep a secret in Mayville Heights; the town was so small. And in Lita's case she seemed to be related, one way or another, to pretty much everyone in town.

"Rebecca, how long has Lita been Everett's assistant?" I asked.

"Ever since he came back to Mayville Heights for good," she said. "Lita was very young when she was married—and divorced. She wanted to stay here and raise her girls, and Everett needed an assistant who knew the town as much as he needed someone who was organized and efficient. That was Lita to a tee."

"Is it just my imagination or is Lita pretty much related to everyone in Mayville Heights?"

Roma laughed as she set down her mug. "It's not your imagination."

Rebecca leaned back in her chair, nodding in agreement. "Her mother's family and her father's family were the first non–Native American settlers here. Only the Blackthornes have been here longer. Half the town is cousin to Lita on her father's side and the other half is related through her mother. I think the only people she's not related to are the Chapmans, and that's just because Chapman men tend to marry women from somewhere else and bring them back here." She laughed. "Which is a good thing or we'd all be our own grandparents."

"What about you?" I said. Across the room Eric had just come out of the kitchen carrying a large stainless steel thermos.

"We're cousins about half a dozen times removed through our mothers," Rebecca said. "On the Hale side of the family."

Roma glanced at her watch. "You know that Oren and I are second cousins."

I nodded.

"Well, we're cousins with Lita somehow on the Villier side of the family, her father's ancestors." She reached for her scarf on the back of her chair. "As much as I'd like to sit here, I should get back to the clinic."

Out of the corner of my eye, I saw the door to the café swing open and a well-dressed woman step inside. I knew immediately that she was, as my friend Harry Taylor would put it, from away. She was wearing beautiful high-heeled, black leather boots. They seemed molded to her long legs—no room for a pile lining for warmth—and the very high heels weren't practical for navigating snowbanks. I'd learned that the hard way my first winter in town.

I looked down at my warm, lace-up footwear.

My boots might not have been trendsetters, but my feet were warm and dry.

I glanced at the woman again. She had the collar of her elegant coat turned up against the side of her face, and her shoulders were hunched as though she was cold.

Rebecca turned her head, probably to see what I was looking at. She put one hand, palm down, on the table and some of the color seemed to drain from her face.

"Oh my word," she said softly. "It can't be."

I put my hand on the older woman's arm. "Is something wrong?"

She let out a breath. "I'm not sure."

Roma shot me a worried glance. "Rebecca, do you know that woman?" she asked.

Rebecca nodded. "I do," she said. "That's Dayna Chapman, Burtis Chapman's wife."

2

"Dayna Chapman?" I repeated. "Burtis Chapman's *wife*?"

"Yes," Rebecca said, her gaze locked on the woman making her way toward the counter and Lita. "Ex-wife."

Two frown lines appeared between Roma's eyes. "Rebecca, are you all right?" she asked.

Rebecca shook her head and turned back toward us. "I'm sorry," she said, reaching up to give Roma's hand a squeeze. "Seeing Dayna was a little like seeing a ghost for a moment. She hasn't been back here in more than twenty years."

"I wonder what brought her back now," Roma said as she shrugged on her jacket.

"I was thinking the same thing." Rebecca's eyes darted over to the counter again where Lita, still holding the thermos Eric had brought from the kitchen, was now talking to Burtis's ex-wife.

The normally unflappable Lita was uncomfortable with the conversation, I realized. I could tell from the rigid way she held herself, shoulders stiff under her heavy jacket, back as straight as a metal signpost.

"I'd better get going," Roma said, pulling on her gloves. "I'll see you tonight. I think it'll be fun."

"I hope so," I said. "If you talk to Eddie please thank him again for me."

"I will." She smiled at Rebecca. "Thank you for the coffee break," she said, and then she headed for the door.

I reached for my own coat, noticing that Rebecca had darted another glance in Dayna and Lita's direction. "You know, don't you?" I said.

Rebecca focused all her attention on me. Her blue eyes searched my face. I waited for her to ask, "Know what?" After a moment she smiled and said, "How long have you known?"

"Since the fall."

"Lita is a good person," Rebecca said, pulling on her hat, a soft rose cloche. "This last year is the happiest I've seen her in a long time."

Burtis and Lita had been a couple for the last year? How had they managed to keep that quiet?

"I like Lita," I said, patting my pockets for my gloves. "And I like Burtis."

It was true. The library renovations, which had originally brought me to town, would have been a lot more frustrating without Lita to answer all of my questions. And I considered Burtis a friend. We'd gotten to know each other after I discovered the body of Roma's biological father, Tom Karlsson, out at Wisteria Hill, the old Henderson family homestead.

"I can't help wondering what she's doing here now," Rebecca said, reaching for her purse and the check.

"Maybe she's here for the fundraiser or Vincent Starr's lecture tomorrow," I said.

"It's possible," she said, but the tone of her voice said she didn't really think so.

I leaned over and gave her a hug. "Thank you for this."

"You are so welcome," she said with a smile. "Thank you for offering to help me find a wedding dress."

"When is Ami coming?" I asked, putting the strap of my own bag over my shoulder.

"The day before the wedding, as soon as her exams are finished."

Everett's granddaughter was studying music at the Chicago College of Performing Arts. She was Rebecca's maid of honor.

"I'm looking forward to meeting your brother," I said. Rebecca's older brother, Stephen, was going to walk her down the aisle. Their other brother had died several years ago. "What's he like?"

Rebecca laughed. "Our mother always said that Stephen and I were as different as chalk and cheese, but I think you'll like him. He used to spend a lot of time at the library. He loves books."

"Now I have two reasons to like him."

"What's the other reason?" she asked, cocking her head to one side, the gleam in her eye telling me she already knew the answer to her own question.

"He has excellent taste in sisters," I said.

She nodded. "I've been telling him that for years."

I grinned at her.

"I'm glad Stephen is coming to the wedding," Rebecca said, "but I really don't need to be 'given away.' For heaven's sake, it's not like I'm an old chest of drawers that someone found in the attic." She sighed. "But the tradition is important to Everett."

"When my mother and father got married—the second time—I walked her down the aisle," I said.

My parents had been married, divorced and then remarried after figuring out that living without each other was worse than living *with* each other.

"The minister asked, 'Who brings this woman to be married?' and I said I did."

"I like the sound of that," Rebecca said.

I didn't add that at one point a couple of my parents' friends had floated the idea that I put my hand on my mother's hugely pregnant abdomen at the front of the church and answer the minister's question with "her children do," since the twins, my brother, Ethan, and sister, Sara, couldn't speak for themselves.

Mom and Dad knew that I was already cringing with embarrassment over the incontrovertible evidence that they'd been "seeing" each other, unbeknownst to everyone including me, and let the suggestion sink without comment.

"I know you wish Matthew could be here," I said.

Matthew Nixon was Rebecca's only child, but he was a geologist looking for oil deposits in northern Canada. Rebecca nodded, brushing a strand of hair off her face. "I do," she said. "But it's just too far and getting out of Izok Lake isn't easy this time of year."

She leaned over and patted my cheek. "But I have Ami and you and Roma and all of my friends. And did I tell you that darling Ruby is going to make a video of the ceremony so I can send it to Matthew?"

"That's a great idea," I said. Ruby Blackthorne was a good friend and a talented artist. I glanced at my watch as I pulled the sleeve of my jacket down over my heavy woolen gloves.

"I'll see you tonight," Rebecca said, her grin giving me a glimpse of the young girl she once was. "Roma's right. It's going to be fun."

"I hope so," I said. "I'll see you later." I raised a hand in good-bye to Eric, who was still at the counter, and headed out.

It was cold outside. The air was sharp and dry, but it wasn't snowing and there wasn't a cloud in the deep blue sky arcing overhead. I walked quickly back to the library, my breath making me look like a train engine chugging along the sidewalk.

Mary Lowe was at the front desk when I walked

in. Since it was December she was wearing one of her many Christmas sweaters. This one was white and a deep forest green with a couple of reindeer heads grinning at me, one on either side of the quarter-size green buttons. There was a little bulb at the end of each reindeer's nose that glowed red thanks to a battery pack in one of the sweater's pockets. The sweater made me smile every time Mary wore it. She smiled now and handed me a stack of messages. I sorted through them. Nothing was urgent.

"How was your coffee break?" she asked.

"Delicious," I said. "I think Eric has perfected his sticky buns."

"That sounds good," she said, reaching back to set four picture books on one of the book carts. "Abigail is shelving and Susan is setting up for tomorrow in the conference room."

"If you can handle things here for a little longer, I'll put my coat in my office and give her a hand."

"Go ahead," Mary said. "It won't get busy until school lets out and all the kids in Anne Stinson's history class show up because they finally figured out that she wasn't joking when she said they have to use 'real' books to write their term paper." She laughed. "The same thing happened last year."

"Mia will be here to help," I said. "She was in that class last year." Mia was our co-op student from the high school.

Mary held up a hand. "I almost forgot. Burtis brought over one of his big coffeemakers and four dozen coffee cups for tomorrow. He said if you need more cups to give him a call."

One of Burtis Chapman's businesses was large tent rentals. He could also supply booths if you were having some kind of trade show, or dishes for a wedding reception. He was loaning us the coffeepot and cups Mary had mentioned. I wondered if he knew his ex-wife was in town.

Mary narrowed her gaze at me. "What is it?" she asked.

I gave my head a shake. "Nothing."

"That's not your 'nothing' face," she said. "Don't worry about tonight, Kathleen, or tomorrow, for that matter. You've thought of everything."

"It's not that," I said, loosening the scarf at my throat. "I was actually thinking about Burtis. When we were at Eric's, his ex-wife came in."

"Dayna Chapman just walked into Eric's?"

I nodded.

Her eyebrows rose and her mouth pulled to one side. "Well, that's a surprise."

"Rebecca said she hasn't been back in twenty years."

Mary nodded. "It's been all of that." She gave me a wry smile. "You know, there was a lot of loose talk when Dayna left."

I pulled off my scarf and stuffed it in my jacket pocket. "What do you mean?" I asked.

She patted her gray curls, fixed firmly in place with the heavy-duty hair spray she favored. "One day she was here. The next she was just gone. You know how people are."

"People actually though Burtis might have done something to his wife?"

"He does have a reputation."

The phone rang then. I gestured in the direction of the conference room with the message slips Mary had given me. "I'm just going to take a quick look."

Mary nodded and reached for the receiver.

The coffeemaker was set up on a long table in front of the windows. Burtis had arranged the cups and saucers in neat rows. He'd also brought spoons and a large, insulated stainless steel carafe that we could use for hot water for tea.

Burtis Chapman was built like an oversize hockey goalie. I'd heard all the stories and rumors about his being the area bootlegger and running some high-stakes and very illegal poker games. And I'd found him intimidating before I got to know the man. But now that I did know Burtis, I also knew he was an ethical man. It was just that those ethics were part of his own personal code, which sometimes put him at odds with the rest of the world. I was surprised that anyone who really knew the man would ever have thought he'd have done anything to his ex-wife.

I walked back over to the desk. Mary had started checking in a stack of picture books.

"Mary, did you know Dayna Chapman?" I asked.

"Not well," she said, turning to put another book on the half-full cart behind her. "Nobody really did. She wasn't in town that long." Her eyes narrowed. "Why do you ask?"

I shrugged. "I only got a quick look at the woman, but—"

"She didn't look like Burtis's type," Mary finished. She didn't miss much.

"I shouldn't make assumptions," I said.

"You're not. Burtis and Dayna were a classic case of opposites attracting." She straightened her sweater so the reindeers were nose to bright red nose. "I wonder why she's back here now, after all this time."

"Maybe she missed her kids, or Mayville Heights." I held up both hands. "Maybe after so many years she missed Burtis."

Mary gave a snort of laughter. Then her expression grew serious. "You know, no one really knows why that marriage ended. Burtis wasn't talking and no one was ever foolhardy enough to ask him."

She took a small, square picture book from the pile at her elbow. A handful of Cheerios bounced onto the counter from between the pages.

"At least it's not peanut butter and marshmallow fluff," I said with a smile, and headed for the stairs.

I returned all the phone calls and sent a couple of texts. Everything was running smoothly. Vincent Starr was checked into a beautiful bed-and-breakfast within walking distance of the library and the Stratton Theatre. Abigail, who had found the edition of *Alice in Wonderland* that had originally brought us into contact with Vincent, was taking him to dinner before the gala at the Stratton.

Maggie and Ruby Blackthorne had done an incredible job of turning the Stratton Theatre into a Parisian bistro and managed to do it under budget. I'd walked over before lunch and I'd found myself at a loss for words at the sight of all their work. Mags and Ruby had donated all their time and managed to borrow most of the design elements.

The rest of the afternoon was busy. As Mary had predicted, nearly every student from Anne Stinson's history class showed up after school and stood, bewildered, annoyed or a bit of both in front of the nonfiction section. The seniors' reading club arrived en masse to register at the last minute for Ruby's bookmaking workshop on Saturday, and Thorsten delivered three cartons of old first- and second-grade readers that he and Oren Kenyon had found in a cubbyhole at the community center. Vincent Starr had offered to look at the books to determine if they might be worth anything. The community center needed a new roof and I was hoping there might be something valuable about their old books.

We closed the building at four thirty because of the fundraiser. I double-checked the conference room before I left and made one more trip back up to the staff room to make sure we had everything we needed for morning.

Susan was waiting for me by the front door, bundled into her red, down-filled coat. "Everything's done, Kathleen," she said. "I put a few more chairs in the conference room and ran the vacuum around in there."

"You are an angel," I said as I hurried across the floor to her.

"Yes, I am," she replied, grinning at me. "Now let's get out of here. I have to get home and make myself even more beautiful than I already am."

I set the alarm, locked the doors and we headed for the parking lot. It was cold, but it wasn't snowing and the sky was clear overhead.

"It's going to be a great night," Susan said. She'd pulled the brim of her hat down and turned the collar of her coat up, so all I could see was her eyes, sparkling behind her black cat's-eye glasses.

"I hope you're right," I said. "I'll see you later."

She made a sweeping gesture with her right hand. "Prepare to be dazzled."

A bit of snow had blown onto my windshield. I brushed it off before I slid onto the driver's seat of my truck. The truck was old and an ugly brown color, like the bottom of a mud puddle, but it ran well and it had a great heater. Harry Taylor Senior had loaned me the truck and then given it to me outright after he'd found his daughter, Elizabeth. I had retrieved some documents that had helped the old man in his search for her, and the truck was his way of saying thank you.

I drove up Mountain Road thinking I'd warm up the last of the chicken noodle soup I'd made on the weekend for supper. That would give me a bit of extra time to spend with the cats before I had to get ready for the gala. Owen and Hercules had been out of sorts the past couple of days. If I hadn't known better, I would have said that they were miffed because they weren't going to the gala. The boys, brothers I'd had since they followed me home, weren't exactly your everyday, run-of-the-mill house cats. Sometimes I had to remind myself that they weren't people, either, even though they seemed to think they were.

I parked in the driveway and headed around the house to the back porch, mentally going over everything I needed to do before I headed back down the hill to the Stratton.

My foot was on the bottom riser of the porch stairs when I heard it. Exactly what the noise was, I wasn't sure. All I could tell was that there was some kind of god-awful sound coming from my kitchen.

3

I knew it was stupid to go inside when I didn't know what was in there, but Owen and Hercules were in the house. It sounded as though there was some kind of injured animal inside with them. I hesitated, and then I heard what I clearly knew was a yowl from Owen.

Fumbling with my keys, I got the porch door unlocked and dropped my purse and briefcase on the bench under the side window. I grabbed the broom that I'd used that morning to clear a dusting of snow off the steps. I had no idea what was in my kitchen or how it had gotten into my house, but whatever was terrorizing my cats was about to meet the business end of that broom.

I heard another yowl from Owen and I wrenched the kitchen door open and launched myself into the space, swinging the broom like a pirate's cutlass.

Detective Marcus Gordon turned from the stove, waving the wooden spoon in his hand at me. The radio was playing softly in the background. Marcus was singing along to Aerosmith. Not at all softly. And not at all remotely on key, either.

"Hi," I said, a little stunned.

Owen was perched on one of my kitchen chairs, bobbing his gray tabby head along to Steven Tyler. The cat seemed to be joining in on the chorus, or maybe he was singing harmony. I wasn't exactly sure. He glanced over at me, still brandishing my broom like a sword, and there was what seemed to me to be a self-satisfied gleam in his golden eyes. I knew what that was about.

I looked at Marcus again. He was wearing jeans and a white T-shirt. The ends of his hair were damp, which meant he'd probably been in the shower just a short time ago. My shower maybe? I thought about that for a moment and then I had to force myself to pay attention to what was happening in my kitchen.

"What are you doing?" I asked. I could see that he was stirring something that smelled wonderful, but I had no idea why all six feet plus of handsome him was at my stove. Or why one of my new dish towels was clipped to the front of his T-shirt with a couple of clothespins.

Marcus smiled. "Making supper." He gestured at the table. "I hope it's okay."

For the first time I noticed that the table was set for two—place mats, napkins and a fork and large spoon at each place. I'd given him my spare key so he could pick up the tablecloths I'd ironed the night before and deliver them to Maggie and Ruby at the Stratton this morning. There was no way I could lay them down in my truck and not get them wrinkled again.

"Of course it's okay," I said. I pointed to the dish towel. "I like your apron."

He flushed. "I had a shower before I came over. I didn't want to get sauce on my shirt."

He seemed to notice the broom then for the first time. "Were you planning on cleaning the kitchen?" he asked.

"Um, no," I said, realizing I didn't really want to tell him I'd mistaken his singing for some animal attacking my cat. "I, uh, guess I don't need this after all." I leaned the broom against the wall by the door, then crossed the room and kissed him. I still felt a little bubble of happiness every time I did that. There had been a time I'd believed Marcus and I would never be a couple. There'd been a time I would have sworn that I didn't *want* to be in a relationship with him. He'd made me crazy sometimes. He *still* made me crazy, but he also made me very, very happy.

I dipped my head over the pot. "You made spaghetti sauce," I said. "It smells great."

Owen meowed his agreement from his perch on the chair.

Marcus gave the sauce another stir. "Actually, I thawed spaghetti sauce," he said. "Hannah made a big batch before she left."

Hannah was Marcus's younger sister. She was

an actress and she'd been in town in September as part of the New Horizons Theatre Festival.

"Thawing is good, too," I said.

Marcus leaned over to turn up the heat on a pot of simmering water. "I'm about to put the pasta on," he said. "You should have time for a shower."

"All right," I said. "Are you sure there's nothing I can do to help?"

He shook his head and a lock of his dark wavy hair fell onto his forehead. "Owen and I have it all under control."

The little tabby meowed enthusiastically at the sound of his name.

There was a spot of something on Marcus's chin. I licked my thumb, reached up and rubbed it away. For a moment I'd considered kissing it away, but I was pretty sure that would have led to a lot more kisses and I really did need to have a shower.

Reluctantly, I pulled my gaze away from his gorgeous blue eyes. Owen was watching me, his gray head tipped to one side. I stopped to give him a scratch under his chin.

"Cats do not eat spaghetti," I whispered sternly.

He made a face and shook his head. I knew that meant he was planning on wheedling at least a taste out of Marcus.

There was no sign of Owen's brother, Hercules, in the living room. Upstairs in my bedroom I noticed the closet door was open just a little.

"You can come out now," I said, peeling off my sweater.

After a moment the closet door opened and a furry black-and-white face peered around the edge.

"I think they've stopped singing for now," I said.

He scrunched up his face in an expression that looked a lot like a grimace. I bent down and scooped up the little tuxedo cat. He shifted in my arms, put a paw on my shoulder and looked at me with his green eyes. "Yes, I heard them," I said. "I thought something had gotten in here and was torturing you two."

He dipped his head for a moment as if he was trying to tell me that it *was* torture for him.

I sat down on the edge of the bed. "You know that was payback from Owen, don't you?"

Hercules immediately turned and looked at the iPod dock on the table by the bed. The cat shared my love for Barry Manilow. Owen didn't. Somewhere in his feline brain, singing Aerosmith along with Marcus—if you could call that noise singing—was his way of getting a little revenge for all the times he'd had to listen to Hercules and me do our version of "Copacabana."

"Don't worry," I said. "I'm going to scrub the kitchen floor this weekend."

Herc's black-and-white face snapped up and it seemed to me that I could see a calculating gleam in his green eyes. I often did the floors to *Ultimate Manilow*.

I gave the cat a kiss on the top of his head and set him down on the floor. Then I grabbed my robe and headed for the shower. Five minutes later I was sitting on the edge of the bed again, rubbing my hair with a towel. Hercules was back in the closet. More than once I'd opened the door to find him just sitting on the floor, staring thoughtfully, it seemed to me, at the clothes hanging there.

"I've already chosen what I'm going to wear," I said.

After a moment I heard a muffled meow from inside the closet, followed about thirty seconds later by what sounded like something falling over.

"I picked the shoes, too," I added.

As I got up to get my comb, Hercules came out of the closet, a dust bunny stuck to his left ear. He swiped at it with a paw, shook his furry head and stalked away. Either he was insulted by my lack of interest in his kitty fashion skills or he'd caught a whiff of the spaghetti sauce.

I pulled on jeans and a long-sleeved T-shirt and stuffed my bare feet into my slippers.

"Perfect timing," Marcus said as I stepped into the kitchen. He was just about to drain the pasta, with two pairs of cat eyes, one gold and one green, watching his every move.

"What can I do?" I asked.

"Nothing. Just sit." He inclined his head toward the table.

I pulled out my chair and sat down while he plated our spaghetti and spooned the sauce over the pasta. There was a small dish of grated Parmesan in front of my place. Marcus must have brought that with him, because I knew I didn't have any. A warm feeling settled in my chest at the thought of him planning all this.

The sauce was delicious—rich with tomatoes, garlic and tiny meatballs no bigger than the end of my thumb.

"Hannah's a wonderful cook," I said, twirling another forkful of noodles.

Marcus nodded and licked a dab of sauce off the back of his fork. "I know. She's been cooking since she was about six." He smiled and his blue eyes lit up. "Whenever she screwed up a recipe, she'd toss whatever she'd made over the fence and the dogs next door would eat the evidence."

I laughed and made a face at the same time. "I'm guessing that probably wasn't so good for the dogs."

"They both ended up at the veterinary clinic, the whole thing came out and my dad ended up paying the vet bills." He speared a meatball with his fork. "Hannah was limited to her Easy-Bake Oven for a long time after that."

Marcus didn't talk a lot about his family. It had taken a long time for him to feel he could trust me and even more important, that I trusted him. That had been a bone of contention between us as we'd danced around a relationship. But not nearly as much as the fact that I seemed to get mixed up in every one of his cases.

In the two and a half months since the two of us had become a couple, I'd been slowly learning about his family. Most of the time, Marcus talked about Hannah, his younger sister, but I'd learned that his mother was a math professor and his father was a lawyer. It was more than I'd found out in the previous year and a half that I'd known him.

"How are rehearsals going?" I asked, thinking that if Hannah's acting career suddenly went south, she could have a future as a chef.

Marcus gestured with his fork. "She said there are some changes that need to be made to the script, but I can tell by the way she talks about the play that she's happy."

Hannah was in rehearsals for a play called *Walking Backwards*, which was going to debut in Chicago and possibly move to New York after that.

Marcus held up one hand. "I almost forgot," he said, pushing away from the table. He crossed over to the coat hooks by the back door and felt in the left pocket of his jacket.

Out of the corner of my eye, I saw two furry faces eye his chair. I leaned sideways so I was in their line of vision. "I know what the two of you are thinking. Stop thinking it," I said quietly.

Owen and Hercules both turned to look at me, blinking in wide-eyed kitty innocence. Marcus came back and handed me a small blue envelope.

"What's this?" I asked.

"Open it and find out," he said.

I stuck my little finger under the flap and tore the envelope open. Inside was a small, square card with a line drawing of a smiling little girl holding a bunch of balloons. It was from Hannah.

Inside she'd written, *Marcus told me all about Reading Buddies and the fundraiser. Good luck tonight, Hannah.* And there was a check.

I looked across the table at Marcus. "She sent it last week," he said, "and asked me to wait to give it to you until tonight."

I liked Hannah, and not just because she was Marcus's sister. "I can't believe she did this." I held up the check.

He picked up his fork. "She's really grateful about how you and your mother saved Hester's Girls."

Ben Saroyan was directing *Walking Backwards.* The play, which had had more than one incarnation, was based on a prize-winning article about Hester's Girls, which worked with teenage alcoholics. The group had lost its prize money when it was discovered that the winning article hadn't exactly been written by the young woman whose name was on the piece. Ben had given my mother her first directing job, and my parents—who were both actors—had put together a benefit for Hester's Girls and raised enough money to keep the program going.

I'd flown back to Boston for a long weekend in November to help with the benefit, although the lion's share of the work had been done by my mother.

Marcus gestured at the check. "Kathleen, that's about to go in your sauce."

I set the card on the table beside me and folded the check on top of it. "She didn't have to do this,"

I said. "I did very little, and my mother loves a chance to get onstage and do Kate to my dad's Petruchio."

He reached across the table for the pepper. "I know exactly how much work you did behind the scenes," he said. "We can argue if you want to, but you can't win this one. It's not a lot of money, but she really wanted you to have it."

He looked over at Owen and Hercules as he sprinkled cheese on his spaghetti. They were watching his every move. "Would it really hurt if I—"

I didn't let him finish. "Yes, it would," I interjected. "You know what Roma said about feeding them people food."

He shot the cats a quick look and all three of them made sour faces.

"I see those cranky faces," I said. "Roma's just trying to keep you and you"—I pointed at the cats, who immediately changed to their faux-innocent "who, me?" faces—"from getting sick. And you"—I pointed at Marcus—"from getting a cup of coffee poured on your shoes because you made them sick."

The three of them exchanged looks again. They looked more sneaky than sorry.

Owen and Hercules weren't just a couple of house cats who thought they were people. They had abilities that no one but me knew about. For all I knew, they didn't have the digestive system of a regular cat, but I didn't want to take a chance on that and I didn't want Roma—or anyone else—

figuring out that the cats were a lot more than they seemed.

I pushed away from the table, went to the cupboard and got a few stinky crackers for each cat. Stinky crackers were made with sardines, and as long as the boys didn't eat too many, they were okay with Roma.

"You're spoiled," I told them as I set a little pile in front of each cat. They didn't pay the slightest bit of attention to what I'd said. I knew they understood the words; they'd just heard them so many times that I might just as well have kept quiet.

I put my hand on Marcus's shoulder for a moment as I passed him. His blue eyes met mine, and my heart literally skipped a beat. Maggie had tried so hard to get the two of us together, and now I wondered why I'd resisted for so long.

We finished supper and cleared the table, stacking the dishes in the sink. I didn't have a dishwasher—I liked to do them by hand; it was my best thinking time—and I didn't have time to wash them.

"Did you bring your suit?" I asked Marcus.

He nodded. "It's out in the car."

"You can get dressed in the spare room," I said. "I'll be ready in ten minutes."

His eyebrows went up.

I folded my arms across my chest and tipped my head to one side, studying him. "What? You don't think I can be ready to go in ten minutes?"

He looked down at the cats, who were sitting

by the refrigerator. Hercules was washing his face. Owen was eyeing the two of us.

"I have a feeling this is one of those times when I should just not say anything," Marcus said to the gray tabby.

Owen meowed and ducked his head as though he was agreeing.

I looked at the clock on the wall above the refrigerator. "Ten minutes," I repeated as the second hand swept up to the twelve. "Starting now."

I headed for the stairs. I didn't look back to see if he was watching me, or if he was already on his way to get his suit.

Ten minutes later I was standing in the middle of the living room waiting for Marcus to come downstairs, a little out of breath because I'd all but bolted down the steps in my high heels so I could be standing casually by the window. Sometimes Marcus still brought out my competitive side.

Hercules had followed me upstairs and watched with what seemed to me was a bemused expression as I hurried to brush my teeth, put on my makeup and twist my hair back into a loose knot, following the steps Rebecca had patiently taught me the previous weekend.

"So your brother is Team Marcus?" I'd said as I fastened my rose-gold locket around my neck. My parents had given it to me on the day they remarried.

"Merow." Hercules had made a move that almost looked like a shrug.

Owen appeared at the top of the stairs then. He meowed loudly, as though he were announcing a celebrity or royalty, and then started down the steps. Marcus came behind him.

I was at a loss for words. I'd seen Marcus in a tie and sport coat before, but never really dressed up. Never like this.

His dark charcoal suit fit his broad shoulders perfectly. The collar of his snowy white shirt was a perfect contrast to his dark hair, and his tie matched his deep blue eyes. Even his black shoes gleamed.

For a moment I just stared.

"Wow!" I finally whispered.

"I know," Marcus said, and I realized then that he hadn't taken his eyes off me since he looked over and caught sight of me. "You are . . . wow."

He walked over to me, still staring. "I didn't think you could look any more beautiful," he said. "I can't believe how wrong I was."

I felt my cheeks getting warm. "It's the dress," I said.

I was wearing a deep purple dress shot with flecks of silver and black. It had long, close-fitting sleeves and a skirt that flared from the waist to swing at my knees. The neckline was a deep V, a little more revealing than I usually wore, which was why I'd added my locket.

Maggie and Roma had talked me into the dress. They'd also chosen the sheer, seamed black hose and the sleek sling-backs that added another three inches to my five-foot-six height.

Marcus shook his head. "It's not the dress," he said.

I don't know how long we would have stood there just looking at each other like lovers in some cheesy romantic movie, except Owen meowed, loudly and insistently.

I looked over to see him leaning around the doorway from the kitchen. He dipped his head and gave me his sad cat pose.

"Owen's trying to guilt me into giving him a few more crackers because we're going out and leaving him."

"He's probably lonely," Marcus said. "You've been gone all day."

Owen meowed again, sounding even more piti- ful than the first time.

I started for the kitchen and as I passed him, Marcus reached out and trailed his hand down my arm. For a moment I seriously entertained the idea of staying home and kissing him for the next four hours.

But there were people counting on me. I really wanted to expand Reading Buddies, and I couldn't do that without money to buy books for the little ones in the program. So I took a deep breath, ex- haled and went into the kitchen.

Marcus stood in the doorway and watched me while I gave each cat three more crackers and got fresh water for both of them. I gave Owen a scratch under his chin and stroked the top of Herc's head. "I'll be late," I whispered to them before I straight- ened up.

"You talk to Owen and Hercules like they're people," Marcus commented.

"So do you," I said, smiling, as I crossed to the sink to wash my hands.

He gave me a sheepish look. "I know. They look at me like they understand what I'm saying, and the first thing I know, I'm having a one-sided conversation with them."

It didn't seem like a good time to tell Marcus that in my experience the boys understood way more of what was said to them than you'd expect, and no conversation with them was ever one-sided. The cats had an opinion on everything and they were pretty good at making their thoughts very clear. I tried not to say that out loud. I knew it made me sound like the crazy cat lady.

Owen was in front of Marcus. He made a snippy little "murp."

"Oh, sorry," Marcus said, moving so the cat could get past him.

"Are you sure the conversations are one-sided?" I said with a laugh.

I put on my coat and slipped the tiny jet-beaded evening bag Taylor King had loaned me over my shoulder. The teenager had shyly offered the purse after our last tai chi class.

"You know, if you're going to protect yourself from some wild animal making noise in your kitchen, I think you need something bigger than that," he said as we passed the broom, still leaning against the wall by the back door.

He knew! I should have guessed he'd figure out

why I'd leapt into the kitchen swinging the broom like I was Johnny Depp doing Captain Jack Sparrow.

"Have you ever thought about getting a cat?" I asked, partly to hide my embarrassment as we walked out to Marcus's SUV parked out on the street. It was clear and cold, the sky an inky canopy overhead.

He nodded as he unlocked my door for me. "I almost took Desmond."

Desmond was Roma's cat. Actually he was the clinic cat. He was sleek and black and he had the soul of a jungle cat.

It was because of Desmond that Roma had found out about the feral cat colony at Wisteria Hill, the old Henderson estate that was now Roma's home.

"Why didn't you?" I asked as I fastened my seat belt.

"I work a lot of long hours. I didn't want to leave him alone for all that time."

"I can't picture Desmond anywhere but ruling Roma's clinic," I said.

"I saw him back Harry Taylor's dog, Boris, right under a chair," Marcus said as he pulled out onto Mountain Road.

"That's because Boris is an old softie. He looks intimidating but he's not."

Marcus shot me a sideways look. "So you're a dog person, too."

"I like Boris," I said, smoothing the woolen fabric of my coat down over my knees. "But don't tell that to Owen next time you two talk."

"I'll try not to let that slip," Marcus said, a smile pulling at his mouth.

We drove down the hill in silence while I ran over a mental list of last-minute things I needed to do when we reached the theater.

"You've thought of everything," Marcus said quietly.

I looked over at him. He kept his eyes fixed on the road, but he reached over for a moment with his right hand and squeezed both of mine.

"This isn't the first fundraiser I've organized," I said as he turned on his blinker to pull into the main parking lot at the theater. "But it's the first time I've been so nervous."

"So what's different this time?" he asked.

"The kids, I guess." I shifted in my seat. "I know every one of them—the little ones who are learning to read and the older ones who're the buddies. I've seen the moment when the letters on the page become a word and the word means something." I stopped to clear my throat. "I have twenty-seven kids on the waiting list. I want this to work."

Marcus shut off the SUV and looked at me. "It will," he said. He inclined his head toward the theater door and gave me a smile. "Let's go."

The gala was a sellout. By my calculations, even after expenses, we'd already made a little money. What I was hoping for was that the evening would inspire people to make donations to the program. Reality was, I couldn't go to Everett to fund everything.

Susan and Eric arrived about five minutes after

Marcus and I did. Marcus went out to help carry in the desserts from Eric's van while Susan wiped the snow off her unbelievably high heels.

"Wow!" I said as she took off her coat. She was wearing a formfitting sea green dress with strappy heels that had to be at least four inches high. Her hair was down, curling around her face. Eric couldn't help smiling at his wife as he passed her while carrying a large covered tray.

"Wow back at you," she said.

She looked over her shoulder toward the door. "And your detective. Yum!" Her eyes sparkled.

"Susan!" I exclaimed.

She tipped her head to one side and gave me a skeptical look. "Please," she said, making a dismissive gesture with one hand. "You can't tell me you didn't notice that he cleans up really well." She wiggled her eyebrows at me as Marcus came in carrying a large box of something that smelled like cinnamon.

I leaned over so my mouth was next to her ear. "Yes, he does, doesn't he?" I whispered.

She laughed and clapped her hands together.

We stowed Susan's coat in the coatroom and walked through the main auditorium doors together. She took a couple of steps and stopped. "Oh my word!" she said softly.

The stage really did look like a Parisian sidewalk café. I had no idea where Maggie and Ruby had found the wrought-iron chairs and small round tables. The potted trees, branches entwined with twinkling lights, had been rented from a nursery in

Minneapolis. I hadn't even known it was possible to rent trees, let alone do it in December.

The tiny fairy lights continued up the edge of the outside seats on both the right and the left aisles. Curved ramps on both sides led from the floor to the stage. Again, I had no idea how Maggie and Ruby had done it, but they looked like two tiny stone bridges.

"Good Caesar's ghost," Susan whispered softly as she stepped onto the stage and got a good look at the backdrop Ruby had painted. The huge canvas curtain covered the back of the stage from side to side and floor to ceiling. Ruby had re-created a Parisian street scene and Maggie had spent hours with the Stratton's lighting tech, working out the lighting so the huge mural looked its most realistic. I knew what a perfectionist she could be, so I wasn't surprised it had taken that long.

"What can I do?" Susan asked.

"Mingle. Answer questions if anyone has any," I said. "Otherwise, just enjoy yourself."

"That I can do," she said with a smile. "I'd better go see if Eric needs anything."

The next hour went by in a blur. Mary arrived looking very elegant in a rose-colored dress and heels that showed off the great legs she'd gotten from being the state kickboxing champion in her age group.

"Bridget is sending someone to interview you," she said. Mary's daughter was the publisher of the *Mayville Heights Chronicle*.

"Thank you," I said, leaning down to give her a squeeze.

"Kathleen."

Someone tapped me on the shoulder. It was Mia, our student volunteer. The seventeen-year-old looked ethereal in a cream-colored flapper-style vintage dress with a fringed hem, her grape Kool-Aid hair pulled back behind her ear on one side.

"Mia, you look beautiful," I said.

"Thank you," she said. She ducked her head for a moment as her face flushed a little. Then she looked at me again. "I, uh, wanted you to meet my dad."

I held out my hand to the man standing beside her. "It's good to meet you, Mr. Janes," I said. "I'm Kathleen Paulson."

"Call me Simon, please," he said.

Simon Janes had a firm handshake and a direct gaze. He was close to six feet tall, rangy with hair buzzed close to his head and he didn't look anywhere near old enough to be the father of a seventeen year-old.

"Mia's doing an excellent job," I said, shifting my gaze to give the teenager a smile.

"Seriously?" he said. "Or are you just making polite conversation?"

Mia's face flooded with color.

I had the urge to kick the guy in the shins. Not a good way to start the fundraiser, I reminded myself.

"Seriously," I said, letting just a tiny edge of coolness come out in my voice. "She shows up on time, works hard and everyone from the four-year-olds to the senior citizens likes her."

I shot Mia a quick, encouraging—I hoped—smile. "She shows initiative. It's hard to find in adults. It's even rarer in young people without any work experience."

Simon Janes looked at his daughter. If he was chastised at all by my words, it didn't show. "That's good to know," was all he said.

"Kathleen, what can I do?" Mia asked.

I gave her a full-on smile. "Talk to people. Have fun. And make sure you try some of Eric's chocolate pudding cake."

She smiled back at me. "Okay, I will," she said.

Out of the corner of my eye, I caught sight of Brady Chapman standing in the wings of the stage. Maybe Maggie was with him. I turned to Mia's father again. "Thank you for coming," I said. "Please excuse me. I see someone I need to speak to."

He gave a slight nod, and the accompanying smile seemed more amused than polite.

I started toward Brady. Burtis's son was talking to someone and as I got closer I realized it wasn't Maggie; it was his mother. And based on his body language, Brady was upset with her. As I'd backed away, I couldn't help noticing Dayna seemed impatient, forehead furrowed and one hand restlessly playing with the catch on her purse. She reached out suddenly and touched her son's arm. He brushed her hand away.

I crossed the stage toward Rebecca and Everett, who had just arrived, and thought how different Simon Janes was from his daughter. Maybe he didn't just look young. Maybe he was young, which might explain why he'd come across as, well, a little rude.

"Your hair is perfect!" Rebecca exclaimed as I joined them, taking my hands in her own and giving them a little squeeze. "And your dress looks even prettier on you than it did on the hanger."

She was wearing a black evening suit with a slim skirt and a fitted jacket that coordinated perfectly with Everett's dark suit.

"And you look beautiful," I said. I let go of her hands to shake hands with Everett.

Everett Henderson always made me think of actor Sean Connery. They had the same charm with just a tiny edge of ruthlessness.

"You've done an outstanding job," he said, nodding as he looked around.

Eric was set up on one long wooden trestle table. I could smell the chocolate pudding cake keeping warm in a gleaming warming tray. Georgia Tepper from Sweet Thing was at another table with a selection of tiny perfect cupcakes, and Peggy Sue from Fern's Diner was at a vintage sideboard with coffee, tea and espresso.

"Thank you," I said to Everett, "but the credit should go to Maggie and Ruby."

"I'll make sure the right people get the credit," Everett said.

I smiled at him. "Thank you."

Abigail joined us then. She was wearing a simple black dress with a red–and-gold scarf draped at the neckline. But the biggest surprise was that she'd cut her hair.

"Abigail, your hair looks beautiful," I exclaimed.

She beamed at me. "Thank you."

Her auburn hair, shot with streaks of silver, had been partway down her back and usually she'd worn it in a long braid. Now it just brushed her shoulders with a fringe of long bangs swept to one side.

I noticed that Rebecca was smiling, too. "You did this," I said.

She nodded. "Abigail said she wanted a little update. Do you really like it?"

"Yes, I do," I said. Rebecca had helped me grow out my own hair after an ill-advised haircut I'd gotten just before I arrived in Mayville Heights. Unlike Maggie, I didn't have the bone structure for that short a cut.

"Is there anything you can't do?" I asked Rebecca.

Everett smiled and lightly touched her arm. "No, there isn't," he said. Pride was evident in his voice

"Kathleen, may I borrow you for a minute?" Abigail asked.

"I'll talk to you a little later," I told Everett and Rebecca.

Abigail had set up a small table next to the coffee station with more information about the Reading Buddies program. She also had a receipt book and several pens.

"Susan and I are going to take turns being here," Abigail explained. "No hard sell, I promise."

"That's fine," I said. "Thank you for doing this."

"The program is a great idea," she said, running a hand over the stack of children's books she had piled on the table. "I love watching the kids coming in after they've learned to read and picking out books to borrow."

I remembered the check from Hannah. I took it out of my purse. "Would you write a receipt for this and give it to Marcus, please?" I asked.

She smiled. "Of course. Now go mingle and be charming."

I walked around welcoming people. It was fun to see everyone dressed up.

All three of the Taylors had shown up. Young Harry and his brother, Larry, looked like a couple of bankers in their unaccustomed suits. Their father, Harrison Taylor Senior, was striking in a black suit, set off by his white hair and beard.

"Kathleen, my dear, you look beautiful," he said. His blue eyes twinkled and I thought, as I always did, how much he reminded me of Santa Claus.

"And the three of you look very handsome."

"It's good to put this monkey suit on and not be laid out at Gunnerson's," Harrison said.

"Good for us, too, Dad," Harry Junior said dryly.

"Since we're on the subject, don't bury me in this suit," Harrison said. "There's a lot of wear left in it."

Harry ran a hand over his chin. "I've got a tarp in the shed. How about that?"

"Fine with me," the old man retorted.

"This is a party," I interrupted. "Could we please talk about something other than people being laid out?"

"Yes, ma'am," he said, somewhat contritely. I could still see the glint of mischief in his blue eyes.

I leaned over and kissed his cheek. "I'm glad you're here," I whispered.

"My pleasure," he whispered back.

He turned to his younger son. "I see Peggy over there and I wouldn't mind a cup of coffee." He glanced at Harry Junior. "The good stuff," he added.

Harry shook his head as he watched his father and brother make their way across the stage. "There's no point in taking him to the doctor," he said. "He flirts with her while he's there, and then he comes home and does the exact opposite of what she told him."

"I know he's stubborn," I said. "But that stubbornness has gotten him this far."

"That it has," Harry said, nodding. "Sometimes I think it's the reason he's still with us."

He reached into his pocket and pulled out an envelope. "Kathleen, this is for your reading program."

"Thank you," I said. "If you take that over to

Abigail"—I pointed over to the table where she was standing, talking to Vincent Starr—"she'll give you a receipt."

He looked across the room. His father already had a cup of coffee and some kind of cream-filled tart balanced on his saucer. He was talking to Mary and even from this distance I knew he was flirting with her.

"Good thing the old man's as tough as a barbe-cued shoe," he said. He rolled his eyes and started for Abigail.

I turned around to take in the entire space for a moment and found Maggie standing behind me. The sparkle in her green eyes matched the spar-kling clip in her short blond hair.

She grinned at me. "I knew that dress was per-fect for you," she said. "What did Marcus say when he saw you in it?"

I felt my cheeks get warm. "Um . . . wow."

She laughed. "He's right. And he's looking very wow himself."

"He is, isn't he?" I agreed. I looked around and finally caught sight of Marcus standing by the front row of seats on the theater's main floor, talking to Ella King and paramedic Ric Holm. As if he could feel my eyes on him, he turned and smiled at me.

I raised one hand for a moment and then turned back to Maggie. "You were right about him, about us."

"I know," she said.

"You know, you look very 'wow' yourself."

She was wearing a slim, pale yellow calf-length dress that went beautifully with her fair skin and cropped blond hair.

"It's fun to see everyone dressed up," she said. "Have you seen Lita and Burtis?"

I shook my head.

"I almost didn't recognize Burtis when I saw him in the parking lot. He was wearing this wonderful dark gray fedora. Very forties film noir."

"I'm looking forward to seeing that."

"Kathleen, is that one of your book experts talking to Mary?" Maggie asked, looking past me. "She looks familiar."

I turned sideways to see who she was talking about.

"No," I said, slowly. "That's Dayna Chapman."

Her eyes widened. "Brady's mother? Burtis's ex-wife?"

"Yes."

She frowned at me. "What's she doing here? Here at the party and here in Mayville Heights?"

"I don't know," I said, turning back to face her. "I had lunch with Roma and Rebecca and she walked into Eric's. Rebecca said Dayna hasn't been back in more than twenty years."

Maggie nodded, her expression still serious. "I was just a kid, but I remember when she left. You can imagine all the speculation." She gave me a wry smile. "I don't know what Burtis said, or did, but all of a sudden." She snapped her fingers. "The talk just stopped."

I looked back over my shoulder again. Dayna

Chapman was wearing a very simple, but elegant, dark red dress that hugged her tall, thin model's figure. Her hair was pulled back in a severe twist that showed off her long neck.

"She seems very different from Burtis," I said.

"That's probably what did in their marriage."

I thought about Lita: kind, warm and impossible to rattle, in my experience. The cool, unsmiling Dayna was very different.

I realized Maggie was watching my face, green eyes narrowed. "You don't like her."

"I don't even know her," I said, smoothing a hand back over my hair. "But . . . have you ever met someone who you just didn't get a good feeling from?"

Maggie nodded. "We can feel another person's energy, even if we're not aware of it." She gave me a small smile. "You're a very positive person, Kath. I don't think Dayna Chapman is." She touched my arm. "There's someone I need to find. And you probably need to circulate. I'll look for you later." She leaned over and gave me a hug and then she was gone.

I looked longingly in the direction of the cup cakes, but Vincent Starr had just walked in and I wanted to talk to him before the party got any busier.

"Thank you so much for coming, Vincent," I said, walking over to him.

He took my hand in both of his. "Kathleen, this is extraordinary," he said, looking around. He reminded me of an English prof I'd had in college.

He had the same dark hair waved back from his face, although Vincent's was touched with silver at the temples, and the same style of horned-rim glasses.

I smiled back at him. "Thank you. I can't take any of the credit for the décor. It's the work of my friends Maggie and Ruby."

"They're very talented artists," he said.

"Yes, they are," I agreed. I pointed to Maggie across the room talking to Harry Junior. "That's Maggie," I said. "I know she'd love to hear that you like her work."

"I'll be sure to tell her," he said. He let go of my hand. "I'll let you circulate and we'll talk later."

I turned around to discover that the reporter from the *Chronicle* had arrived for the interview. I spent about fifteen minutes with her and then I left her with Rebecca and Everett.

Abigail made her way through the crowd to me. "Susan is at the donation table," she said. "Olivia would like to know if you want her to pass out the chocolates now or after Everett thanks everyone for coming and makes his pitch for money."

I looked around. People were laughing and talking and the jazz quartet was playing. "Now, I think," I said. "If we do it after, we may shift everyone's focus away from the point of the party." I rubbed my left wrist with the other hand. It was aching a little, a sure sign we were going to get snow tomorrow. "Does that sound too mercenary?" I asked.

Abigail made a face. "No. It sounds practical. Reading Buddies is a great program, but we can't keep it going or help any more kids without money. Olivia's chocolates are incredible, believe me. And I don't have a problem with Decadence Chocolatier getting some free advertising from tonight." She patted one hip. "But I want people to think, 'Gee, I want to help those kids,' not, 'Gee, I want to buy a box of these chocolates.'" She held up both hands. "So sue me if that seems mercenary."

I put one arm around her shoulders and gave her a squeeze. "How do you always know the right thing to say?" I said.

She leaned against me for a moment as she scanned the crowd, looking for Olivia, I was guessing. "It's a gift," she said with a grin.

She spotted Olivia then, lifted one hand and nodded. Olivia returned the nod and headed for the wings on the right side of the stage.

"Do you want to hear how much we've made so far?" Abigail asked, straightening up and smoothing the skirt of her dress.

I hesitated and then I shook my head. "No. Tomorrow will be fine."

Abigail frowned at me. "Kathleen, have you had anything to eat or drink yet?"

"I haven't had time," I said with a shrug.

She raised her eyebrows at me. "Don't. Move," she said, stressing both words.

She was back in less than a minute with a cup of coffee and a tiny mint chocolate chip cupcake.

"As of this moment you're my favorite person," I said, taking the coffee cup from her hands.

Abigail gave a snort of disbelief. "I'm your favorite person only until a certain detective makes his way over here."

"Only if he brings me more chocolate," I said as I took a bite of the cupcake. I gave a little groan of pleasure and Abigail laughed.

Olivia, along with Taylor King and Harry Junior's teenage daughter, Mariah, were circulating through the crowd, handing out the chocolate sampler boxes. Olivia had made all the chocolates at cost. Each box held three of her gourmet truffles.

Nic Sutton—who was a full-time artist and a part-time waiter—had crafted all the boxes by hand, again, donating his time. The tiny containers looked like little books with *Reading Buddies* written in gold script on the cover. I wasn't sure if the samplers would turn out to be a good promo item or not. They seemed like a better idea than a brochure about the program that would probably have ended up in everyone's recycling bin in the morning.

I caught sight of Nic moving across the stage. I raised a hand, trying to get his attention. I'd seen him earlier, tweaking the arrangement of chocolate boxes on one of the serving trays, but I hadn't had time to speak to him. I wanted to tell him how beautiful the boxes looked, but he wasn't looking in my direction. He was so intent on wherever he was headed that he bumped into Dayna Chapman. She pushed past him before he had a chance to apologize.

Marcus was still down on the floor, talking to Larry Taylor and police officer Derek Craig now. I caught sight of Maggie, Roma and Brady Chapman at a nearby table. Oren was deep in conversation with Vincent Starr, while Susan stood with her arms around Eric's waist, smiling up at him.

Burtis and Lita were standing just a couple of tables away. Burtis was a big barrel-chested man and he looked even more imposing in his suit than he did in his everyday work clothes. Maggie was right. Something about the cut of the suit did make me think of a character out of an old gangster movie. The effect would be even more noticeable with the fedora, I was guessing.

Burtis was standing close to Lita, so close that anyone who saw them would know they were a couple. That included Dayna, who was only a couple of feet away. The woman gave off an odd vibe.

I watched Olivia offer the tray to Burtis. He handed a box to Lita and then turned and passed one to his ex-wife before he took one for himself. Burtis was making a point, I realized.

"As soon as Taylor's finished on the main floor, I think we can start," Abigail said.

"All right," I said. Time to stop speculating about Burtis Chapman's love life and focus on what I wanted to say about the Reading Buddies program.

Beside me, Abigail was scanning the crowd,

trying to spot Everett, I guessed. Around us people were exclaiming over the little boxes, opening the "books" and trying the chocolate truffles inside.

Everett and Rebecca were sitting at the table next to Maggie and Roma. I touched Abigail's arm to tell her. At the same moment I caught sight of Dayna Chapman putting a hand to her throat. Her face was the same ashen color as the sky before a December storm. She made a sound halfway between a wheeze and a rasp.

She couldn't breathe, I realized. Her legs buckled as her eyes rolled back in her head.

"Abigail!" I shouted as I pushed forward, managing to catch Dayna before she hit the floor.

"Live," she rasped at me.

"It's okay. It's okay," I said. "You're going to be all right."

"P . . . p . . . package," she managed to choke out.

"Oh, good Lord," I heard Abigail gasp behind me.

We laid Dayna on the stage. She wasn't breathing.

Abigail was already checking for a pulse. After a moment she shook her head.

"I'll do mouth-to-mouth. You start chest compressions," I said. I knew Abigail knew what to do. The library staff had taken a CPR refresher course in November.

Dayna's lips were blue and there were raised red blotches on her neck. I swept a finger inside her mouth and started breathing for her, counting to keep the rhythm. Across from me, Abigail kept up with the chest compressions. Under her breath she was singing the Bee Gees song "Stayin' Alive." Our instructor had told us the song was the perfect pace for CPR and we'd laughingly and loudly sung the disco anthem as we'd practiced on our resuscitation dummies.

"Has anyone called nine one one?"

I recognized Ric Holm's voice behind me.

"I did," I heard Lita answer.

Ric knelt beside Abigail. He'd discarded his tie and his suit jacket and pushed back his sleeves. "What happened?" he asked.

"I don't know," Abigail said. "The first time I noticed anything was when Kathleen went to catch her."

"Okay," Ric said. "I'm going to take over for you. You just move back out of the way in three, two, one."

Abigail slid out of the way and Ric moved into place without losing the rhythm of the chest compressions.

"You're doing great, Kathleen," he said. "Ambulance should be here in just a couple of minutes."

I managed to nod as I continued to breathe for Dayna and the seconds ticked away. Behind me I could hear Marcus taking charge, sending someone to watch for the ambulance and moving chairs and tables out of the way.

It probably was only a few minutes before I

heard the wail of the ambulance and then sometime after that, someone touched my arm and said, "I have it, ma'am." It seemed like a lot longer.

I got to my feet and Maggie's arms went around my shoulders.

"You all right?" she whispered.

I nodded. I was too overwhelmed to say anything. I saw Burtis touch Ric's arm. "She's allergic to pistachios," I heard him say, his face ashen. He reached out a hand to me then. "Thank you, Kathleen," he said, his voice raspy with emotion.

I nodded.

Ric leaned over to the female paramedic. I remembered what Maggie had said to me earlier— that we could feel other people's energy whether we realized it or not. There was no energy coming from Dayna Chapman—negative or positive. All the time I'd been doing mouth-to-mouth, there was no sense that she was still there.

The paramedics continued to work on her, but I realized it wasn't going to make any difference.

Dayna Chapman was dead.

4

I saw Ric exchange a look with the two other paramedics. They knew it, too: Dayna Chapman was dead. Still, they continued CPR, got her onto a stretcher and loaded her into the ambulance. Everyone had been silent for the most part, but now people started talking again.

Marcus walked over to me. "Are you all right?" he said softly.

I nodded without speaking.

"I'm sorry, Kathleen," he continued. "The party's over. I need to find out what happened and then send people home."

"It's all right," I said. As important as the Reading Buddies program was, this mattered more.

Brady Chapman came up to us. He was wearing a gray suit with a lavender shirt and a darker purple tie. If he was worried at all about his mother, it didn't show. I wondered if he even realized she was dead. "Larry Taylor is at the front door and Harry is at the stage door. What can I do?"

"It's okay," Marcus said. "You can go ahead and leave for the hospital."

Brady shook his head. "I'm fine. What can I do?"

Marcus studied him for a moment. Then he loosened his tie. "Go to the hospital," he repeated.

Brady didn't say anything, but the muscles in his jaw tightened. I saw Maggie briefly touch his hand. "Go," she said softly.

Brady's mouth moved but he didn't say anything. He just glanced at Maggie and headed across the stage.

"If we give everyone coffee or tea, it will give them something to do while they wait," Maggie said to Marcus. "Is that all right?"

He nodded. "Go ahead."

She looked at me.

"I'm fine, Mags," I said. "I'll get some people to help you."

I scanned the crowd. Mia was standing by Eric and Susan. I beckoned to her.

She made her way over to me, arms folded tightly over her chest. "Kathleen, is that woman going to be okay?" she asked.

"Let's hold a good thought for her," I said, hoping I sounded reassuring. There didn't seem to be any point in saying that I was pretty sure Dayna Chapman was dead. "It's going to be a while before people can leave. Could you start finding out what people would like—tea, coffee, water, anything—and take it to them?"

Mia nodded. "Sure."

"Thanks," I said.

Ella and Taylor King were down on the auditorium floor. I put a hand on Marcus's back. He half turned and gave me a tight smile.

"I'm just going to get Taylor and Ella to help with coffee," I said. "Do you need anything from me?"

"Not right now," he said.

I could see Derek Craig, with a pen and a ringed notebook I was guessing had probably come from Abigail, already taking people's names and numbers.

Marcus swiped a hand over his chin. "I'm sorry about this. You put in so much work for tonight."

I slid my hand up to his shoulder. "It's okay," I said. "We'll figure something out."

He moved a step closer to me and lowered his voice. "It looked like she had some kind of allergic reaction."

I looked at one of the tiny book-shaped boxes of chocolates, discarded on the edge of a table. "I heard Burtis say Dana was allergic to pistachios."

Just then there were raised voices behind us. We both turned around to see what was going on.

Olivia Ramsey was standing in front of Burtis. She was in her early twenties, tiny, no more than five feet without her heels. Her hands were pulled into tight fists and her face was flushed with anger.

"And I'm telling you there weren't any pistachio nuts in any of my chocolates," she said hotly, her voice rising with each word. "I know about nut allergies. I have a reaction to cashew nuts. There weren't any pistachios in my chocolates! There weren't any nuts anywhere in my kitchen!"

Burtis held up one of his huge hands. "Look," he said, his voice still edged with emotion. "I'm not accusing you of anything. I don't know what happened yet and neither do you." He gestured at Marcus. "Let the police figure out what the hell happened."

"Whatever happened wasn't my fault," Olivia insisted.

Dayna's box of truffles was on the floor, one chocolate still inside and intact despite all the uproar. Before anyone could stop her, Olivia bent down, picked it up and took a bite. "See?" She all but spit the word at Burtis.

Then something in her face changed. Her eyes widened and hives began to rise on her hand and her neck as her breathing took on a strained, raspy sound.

Olivia's right hand flailed in the direction of a small red satin purse lying on the table beside her. She knocked it to the floor and it skidded across the smooth wood.

Everett's granddaughter, Ami, was allergic to poppy seeds—just like her grandfather. Ever since she'd learned about the allergy, which had landed her in the emergency room, Ami had carried an autoinjector of epinephrine in her purse.

I grabbed Olivia's bag, yanked the zipper open and rifled through her things. Marcus and Ric Holm already had Olivia on the floor.

The autoinjector was in a zippered compartment at the back of the purse. I pulled it out and handed it to Ric. Olivia's right hand and neck were covered in raised red welts now and I could see how much work it was taking just for her to breathe. She flinched as Ric jammed the needle into her leg.

The effect of the epinephrine was rapid. By the time the ambulance arrived for the second time, Olivia was breathing a lot easier.

Ric came to stand next to me as Olivia was wheeled out of the building. "Nice reaction, getting that EpiPen," he said. He undid the knot on his loosened tie and let the two ends hang free.

"Is she going to be all right?" I asked.

He pulled a hand back over his neck. "I think so," he said. "Her reaction wasn't as strong. I heard her say she has an allergy to cashews. Sometimes there's a cross reaction to other nuts." He looked around the room. "No offense, Kathleen, but worst fundraiser ever." He gave me a half smile. "I should give Marcus a hand."

Marcus and Derek Craig already had their heads together. I wasn't sure if anyone would want a cup of coffee now, but it didn't hurt to at least try. I slipped down to Ella and Taylor.

"Is there anything we can do?" Ella asked.

"There is," I said, rubbing my aching wrist again. "Could you give Peggy a hand with the coffee and the tea? And maybe Taylor could help Mia find out what people would like?"

"I can do that," Taylor said immediately.

Ella nodded. "Do you think Olivia and the other woman will be all right?"

"Let's hope for the best," I said.

I turned around to survey the stage. Ric had a large black garbage bag and he was collecting all the boxes of chocolates. Derek was still collecting contact information.

Marcus had discarded his suit jacket. He was on his cell phone, probably talking to the station. I could see Maggie moving between tables, quietly reassuring people. I should be doing the same, I realized.

It was close to an hour before the majority of the people were gone. I reached back and pulled the pins from my hair and gave my head a shake. My feet hurt and my shoulders ached.

Rebecca came over to me. She and Everett had stayed, talking to people, trying to do a little damage control.

"How are you?" she asked, giving me a half smile filled with warmth.

"I'm all right," I said, pulling out a stray bobby pin. "You and Everett didn't have to stay, but it helped. Thank you."

She reached out and laid her hand against my cheek for a moment. "I'm sorry this happened, Kathleen."

I swallowed hard. "I just hope Olivia is all right," I said.

Rebecca nodded. "I do, too, dear." If she'd noticed that I hadn't said anything about Dayna, she let it pass.

"Everett and I are going to leave now, unless there's anything else we could do for you." She looked over her shoulder to where Everett was standing, talking to Vincent Starr. "We're taking Vincent over to the St. James for a nightcap."

"Thank you," I said. I'd talked to Vincent, briefly. He'd been very gracious. "Would you tell Everett I'll call him in the morning? We need to work on a plan for refunding everyone's money."

Rebecca sighed softly. "Do you really think that's necessary?"

"Absolutely. People paid for a full night of desserts and jazz, not this. I can't keep their money."

"I'll tell him." She leaned over and gave me a hug. "Things will work out, Kathleen," she said.

I nodded. I didn't want to think about what kind of setback this was for the Reading Buddies program right now. The morning would be soon enough. I gave Rebecca a smile I didn't really feel. "I'll see you tomorrow night," I said.

She rolled her eyes. "Of course," she said. "How could I forget?" She gave my arm one last squeeze and walked back over to Everett.

I watched them leave, and then I walked over to Marcus. His tie was askew, his sleeves were rolled back and he'd raked his hands through his hair at least half a dozen times in the past hour.

"Hey, you must be tired." He managed a small smile.

"I wouldn't mind taking these shoes off," I said. I wasn't used to spending so much time in high heels.

"You still look beautiful," he said in a low voice.

I smiled at him and mouthed a thank-you.

"I'm going to be a while."

I knew I couldn't walk up the hill in those heels on the snowy sidewalks. "That's okay," I said. "I'll get a ride with someone."

"How about me?" Maggie said from behind me.

I turned around. "You don't mind?" I asked.

She shook her head and then held up a small cardboard box. "Georgia gave me some cupcakes."

I would have said I wasn't hungry, but then my stomach growled loudly and I realized I was.

"I'll take that as a yes," Maggie said.

I nodded. "Yes." I looked at Marcus. "Call me when you're done. I don't care how late it is."

"I will," he said. He looked at Maggie. "Thanks."

She nodded and put an arm around my shoulders. We got our coats from the coatroom and Oren let us out the front doors.

"I'm sorry about . . . everything, Kathleen," he said.

I pulled the collar of my coat up around my face. "Me too."

It was bitingly cold outside. The clouds were rolling in over the water. That usually meant snow. I ran my gloved hand over my wrist. Once again it seemed to be right about the weather.

Maggie's Bug was in the parking lot. She brushed away a bit of snow that had blown onto the windshield, and then we both got in.

I leaned back against the seat, shut my eyes and exhaled loudly. Then I opened them again and turned my head to look at Maggie.

"I'm sorry, Mags," I said.

She frowned. "Why are you apologizing to me?"

"You and Ruby did such a wonderful job and people barely had time to enjoy all your work."

"What happened to Dayna Chapman—and Olivia—was a terrible accident, Kath," she said, sticking the key in the ignition. "That's all."

She backed out of the parking spot and turned around in the almost empty lot. "Did I ever tell you that I was on the decorating committee for the homecoming dance in high school? It was the first time I ever decorated anything."

"No," I said.

"At least tonight no one threw up over the bridge all over a palm tree."

"Stop trying to make me laugh," I said, even as I was doing it.

She grinned and shot me a sideways look as she pulled out of the lot. "Reading Buddies is a great program," she said. "We'll find some other way to get the money you need. Maybe you can get another grant."

The reading program had started with a grant. Maybe there was some money I'd missed, some thing else we could apply for.

"Dayna Chapman's dead, isn't she?" Maggie asked, her eyes glued to the road.

"I think so," I said.

"May she be welcomed by the light," Mags said softly.

"Do you think Olivia will be all right?" she asked after a moment.

I rolled my head slowly from one shoulder to

the other, trying to work the knots out of my neck. "I think so. Her reaction seemed less severe than Dayna's."

"Was it Olivia's chocolates?" Maggie asked as we turned up Mountain Road.

I shook my head. "I don't know. I know it looks that way, but it could have been anything Dayna ate at the theater—or maybe something she'd brought with her."

Maggie sighed softly. "I feel bad for Brady and his brothers—and for Burtis."

"What's going on with you and Brady?" I asked. I remembered how Brady had looked at Maggie after Marcus told him to go to the hospital. And how she'd brushed his hand when she urged him to go.

"We're just friends," Maggie said as she pulled into my driveway. She looked over at me as she turned off the engine. "Really. That's all it is."

I got out of the car and we started around the side of the house. "I didn't know you and Brady knew each other," I said.

"He did some legal work for Ruby. Then he offered to look at the paperwork for the co-op's grant application."

Maggie had applied for and gotten a grant to start an artist-in-residence program at the artists' co-op store.

I unlocked the back door and she followed me into the porch. "We've had lunch a couple of times, but that's it. There's nothing going on."

I'd seen how they looked at each other. There

was definitely something happening between Maggie and Brady Chapman, even if they couldn't see it or admit it yet.

We stepped into the kitchen and discovered Owen waiting just inside the door.

"Hey, Fuzz Face," Maggie said, leaning down to him, hands in her pockets. Owen's golden eyes narrowed as he looked up at her and he began to purr.

Owen adored Maggie. He would have been the perfect guy for her, if he'd been a person instead of a small gray cat.

I stepped out of my heels and tossed my coat and scarf over the back of a chair. While Maggie talked to Owen I washed my hands and started hot chocolate for both of us.

Hercules wandered in from whatever he'd been doing. He looked at Maggie and Owen and then looked at me and his expression seemed just a bit amused.

I leaned down to scratch the top of his head. "How was your night?" He gave a small "murp" that I knew meant "fine." Then he tipped his head and studied me for a moment before meowing softly.

"Long story," I said quietly as I straightened up. "I'll tell you later."

I got a plate for the cupcakes, put our cocoa on the table and sat down. Maggie peeled off her coat and took the chair opposite me, her furry boy-friend sitting adoringly at her feet.

I reached for a Death by Chocolate cupcake. I

could see the irony, but I was tired and not eating a cupcake wasn't going to change what had happened.

"Ruby and I will get everything cleaned up in the morning," Maggie said, peeling the paper liner off her Maple Crème cupcake.

"You don't have to do that, Mags," I said.

She smiled. "I know that, but it's okay. I have my own little cleanup crew already put together."

I smiled back at her across the table. "What would I do without you?"

"Merow!" Owen seconded his agreement loudly from his station by her chair.

Maggie laughed, and I felt some of the tension in my shoulders begin to melt away. "Well, lucky for you"—she leaned down to make a smiley face at the cat—"and you, since the new contract with the library board has been signed, neither one of you will be finding out anytime soon."

It had taken me a long time to decide whether or not to continue as head librarian here in Mayville Heights or go back to the life I'd left behind in Boston. I'd been originally hired on a short-term contract to supervise the renovations to the library for its centennial. Maggie hadn't exactly been silent or subtle about what she thought I should do. In the end, I'd decided to stay because the little town had become my home. Maggie was here, and Roma and Rebecca, the Taylors and Susan and Eric.

Marcus was here.

I'd discovered that I didn't need to go home. I already was home.

"We're still going out to Wisteria Hill on Saturday to help Roma paint, aren't we?" Maggie asked, breaking her cupcake into three pieces. She moved her hand casually down to her side and dropped a tiny bite of her cupcake on the floor for Owen.

I should have objected—Roma had been very clear about not feeding things like that to the boys—but Owen had sniffed the bit of cake and starting licking the frosting before I opened my mouth.

"As far as I know, that's what Roma's planning," I said. "Eddie's on the road."

Roma's boyfriend, Eddie, aka Crazy Eddie Sweeney, played for the NHL's Minnesota Wild.

Maggie licked a dab of maple icing from the side of her thumb. "So, the three of us can put our heads together while we're working and come up with another way to keep the Reading Buddies program going."

Mags and Roma had helped me work out the details for the fundraiser at this table, I remembered, over a Crock-Pot of beef stew and dumplings, with a furry four-legged Greek chorus in the background.

"All right," I said, leaning back in my chair, my hands wrapped around the warmth of my mug of hot chocolate. "But the dunking booth is still off the table."

Maggie looked down at Owen again, her green eyes sparkling with mischief. "Oh, but that was our best idea, wasn't it, Fuzz Face?" she said.

"Meow!" he said, again with great enthusiasm.

Hercules rubbed against my leg. I lifted him up onto my lap.

"They think they're funny," I said. He made a face, which as far as I was concerned meant he disagreed.

Hercules leaned back against my chest and I stroked his fur with one hand and held my hot chocolate with the other.

I knew Maggie and Roma would help me figure out how to find the money to keep the reading program going. And I also knew that Marcus would figure out what Dayna had eaten that had caused that allergic reaction. Maybe it hadn't been the chocolate truffles. Maybe it hadn't been something at the reception at all. Olivia had been adamant that there were no nuts in her chocolates.

I still felt unsettled, though. I couldn't banish the image of Dayna struggling to breathe, lips rimmed with blue, wheezing and gasping and trying to tell me how much she wanted to live. I couldn't help wondering why she'd been at the party and why she'd come back to Mayville Heights at all.

5

I had an early breakfast with Vincent Starr in the morning at the St. James Hotel. It had already been planned and I didn't see any reason to cancel. He was already seated in the dining room at a table that looked out over the Riverwalk.

He got to his feet and pulled out a chair for me. "How are you, Kathleen?" he asked with genuine concern in his dark eyes. "I'm so sorry about what happened last night. I heard that one of the women didn't make it."

I nodded as I sat down. "Sadly, that's true."

Dayna Chapman was dead, most likely from anaphylaxis. Olivia was going to be fine. The medical examiner's office was investigating, but so far, no one had any idea what Dayna had eaten that had triggered the allergic reaction.

"If you'd like to cancel your talk this morning and head back to Minneapolis, I understand," I continued. "Last night was unsettling for everybody."

Vincent shook his head and stretched his arm along the back of his chair, resting his hand on the empty one next to him.

"It wouldn't change anything, Kathleen," he said. "That unfortunate woman would still be dead. Maybe this morning will be a bit of a distraction for people."

I felt a little of the tension in my shoulders ease. "Thank you," I said. The waitress arrived then with coffee and Vincent began quizzing her about how the hotel's eggs Benedict was made.

We talked about the exhibit Vincent was curating for the art museum over breakfast and I left him nursing his third cup of coffee and charming the waitresses.

Abigail pulled in right behind me at the library.

I turned off the alarm and the two of us went inside. She headed for the stairs and I followed. I put my things in my office and found her in the staff room, starting the coffee.

"So it's going to be one of those days," I said, getting the mugs down out of the cupboard.

Abigail leaned back against the counter. "I couldn't sleep last night," she said. "I kept seeing Dayna Chapman struggling to breathe. I couldn't seem to stop it from playing over and over like some kind of endless movie loop."

"I know," I said, setting the mugs on the table. "It almost doesn't feel real."

"Kathleen, do you think it was the chocolates?"

I shrugged. "I don't know. Olivia was pretty insistent that she didn't use pistachios or any other kind of nuts in those truffles."

"That's because she's allergic to cashews," Abigail said. "People who are allergic to one kind of nut sometimes react to other nuts as well."

"How did you know Olivia has a nut allergy?" I asked, turning to get the coffee cream out of the refrigerator.

"She shares the kitchen space with the Earl of Sandwich and Sweet Thing. Remember? Georgia told me that before Olivia rented space to her for her cupcakes, she told her there couldn't be any nuts in the kitchen. If she wants to make anything with nuts, she does it at Fern's."

Abigail poured me a cup of coffee, got one for herself and sat down at the table.

I pulled out a chair. "So, how do you explain what happened to Olivia when she bit into that chocolate from Dana's box? She definitely had a reaction."

Abigail poured a little cream into her coffee. "I know, but it doesn't make any sense. If Olivia had used nuts in the truffles, why lie about it? It's easy enough to check. And why would she eat one and put herself at risk?"

I added sugar to my cup and stirred it slowly. "You're right," I said. "It doesn't make any sense."

None of what little information I had with respect to Dayna Chapman made any sense. Maybe that was why I couldn't shake that unsettled feeling.

I pictured the woman, collapsing into my arms,

unable to breathe, looking wide-eyed at the tiny box of chocolates in her hand before it fell to the floor. I didn't see how it could be anything other than those chocolate truffles that had caused Dayna to go into anaphylactic shock. If Olivia hadn't used any nuts when she made them, could someone else have accidentally contaminated them?

"Abigail, who packed the chocolates into all of the boxes?" I asked.

"Olivia did," she said. She turned her cup in tiny circles on the table. "Nic dropped off all the boxes and Olivia packed every single one of them. And in case you're wondering, yes, she wore gloves."

"So the chocolates couldn't have accidentally come in contact with any nuts while they were being packed?"

Abigail made a move as though she was going to flip her braid over her shoulder and then caught herself. She smiled sheepishly at me. "Old habits," she said.

She took a sip of her coffee and set the cup down again. "I don't see any way there could have been any cross contamination during the packing. The kitchen was spotless and I didn't see any sign of any nuts. And, Kathleen, I tried all three of the truffles—Chocolate Raspberry, Dark Chocolate and Crème Maple. For what it's worth, I didn't taste any nuts, either."

I nodded. "Okay, so what happened after Olivia filled the boxes?"

"I packed them back into the cartons and took

them over to the theater. The boxes were locked in the front office until it was time to set them out. I can promise you that I washed my hands, and I didn't touch anything except the outside of the cardboard boxes."

I leaned against the back of my chair. "So there was no way the chocolates could have been contaminated during the packing. That just leaves the time they were in the office over at the Stratton."

Abigail brushed a bit of lint off the front of her dark green sweater. "Oh, c'mon, Kathleen. Why on earth would someone sneak into that office and contaminate the chocolates? First of all, what did this mysterious person do? Take a handful of pistachio nuts and rub them all over every chocolate, or just a random selection? Why? What would that person gain? Other than ruining the fundraiser, what would be the point? And who would want to do that? Everyone thinks Reading Buddies is a good idea."

She continued to play with her coffee cup, tracing the design on the side with a finger. "It couldn't have been someone who wanted to hurt Dayna. How many people would have known that she was going to be at the reception last night? She just arrived in town yesterday afternoon, from what I heard." She shook her head. "This makes no sense at all."

"Eliminate the impossible and whatever remains, no matter how improbable, must be the truth," I said softly, more to myself than to Abigail. "Sherlock Holmes."

I nodded. "From the pen of Sir Arthur Conan Doyle, yes."

"So, what can we eliminate?" Abigail asked. "It's not impossible that the chocolates were contaminated at the theater. I don't think it's very likely, but it's not impossible."

"And it's not impossible that they came into contact with nuts in Olivia's kitchen, no matter what she says," I countered. "Maybe this is just the perfect storm of a series of accidents that wouldn't have mattered except Dayna Chapman just happened to be severely allergic to pistachio nuts."

"Maybe you're right," Abigail said. "If we're eliminating the impossible, we can't exactly eliminate that."

I rubbed the space between my eyes, then glanced at my watch. "We'd better get downstairs. It's almost time to open. People are going to be here soon."

"I'll go turn the lights on," Abigail said, rinsing her mug and setting it in the sink. She looked back over her shoulder at me. "Things will work out, Kathleen. It was just a horrible accident. And we'll find a way to get the money we need."

"Thanks for the vote of confidence," I said, handing her my own mug. "I'll just get my keys and I'll be right down."

I headed for my office. Maybe the medical examiner's investigator would be able to figure out why Dana had had the allergic reaction that killed her. Maybe I'd been involved in one too many of Marcus's cases and now I was seeing something suspicious that wasn't even there. Maybe the whole thing was just a set of sad coincidences—improbable, maybe, but not impossible.

I grabbed my keys from my desk drawer and headed for the stairs, trying to shake the thought that while it wasn't impossible that last night had just been a mistake—a very tragic mistake—it wasn't impossible that it hadn't been, either.

Vincent Starr's talk was a huge success. Quite a few people had come from Minneapolis for the lecture, but there were a lot more people from Mayville Heights than I'd expected. Ruby was in the front row along with Nic Sutton, Ella King and Georgia Tepper. Georgia had made her way over to me as soon as she came in through the front doors.

I walked over to intercept her. "I'm sorry about last night, Georgia," I said. "You put in so much work and the cupcakes were delicious."

She shrugged and gave me a half smile. "They were only cupcakes, Kathleen. And I wanted you to know that Eric and I packed up all the leftover food and dropped it off at the Boys and Girls Club. They have a big freezer and pretty much everything can be frozen. They can use it all. They do a hot lunch program over the Christmas break."

"Thank you for doing that," I said. "I feel a lot better knowing the food wasn't wasted."

She looked back over her shoulder to where Susan was standing, talking to a group of women by the checkout desk. "It wasn't my idea," she said. "It was Susan's. I kind of had a feeling she wouldn't tell you."

"I'll thank Susan for the idea. And thank you again for making it happen."

I was surprised to see Lita and Brady sitting together at the end of a row as Abigail and I added another group of chairs at the back of the room. Even from a distance I could see the dark circles under Lita's eyes that makeup hadn't really been able to hide. Brady's face was unreadable. I wondered what they were doing at the lecture. I didn't know either one of them was interested in rare books. Lita liked romance novels and shared Maggie's affection for Clint Eastwood's movies. Brady read a lot of science fiction. It was Susan's favorite genre too. Early in the week they'd had a spirited discussion about the merits of John Wyndham versus Ursula K. Le Guin.

Less than five minutes before Vincent got started, I turned around to see Olivia Ramsey slip into the last empty chair.

Abigail followed my gaze. "That's a surprise," she said softly.

"Yes, it is," I agreed.

Vincent's talk was on what he called the Golden Age of Children's Literature: the late nineteenth and early twentieth century. When the lecture was over Olivia got up and made her way over to me. She was a little pale, but other than that she looked all right. Her blond hair was pulled back in a ponytail and she was wearing a heavy caramel-colored sweater.

"Kathleen, I wanted to say thank you," she said. "They told me at the hospital that you found my autoinjector in my purse. If you hadn't . . ." She shook her head and didn't finish the sentence.

"I'm just glad you're all right," I said. "You are okay, aren't you?"

She nodded, taking in a deep breath and letting it out. "Yes, I am. I'm allergic to cashew nuts. That can trigger a lesser reaction to something like pistachios, and that's what the doctors think happened." She pushed up the sleeve of her nubby sweater. There was a silver-colored medic alert bracelet on her right wrist. "I should be wearing this all the time. I *will* be wearing it all the time now. I thought it didn't look very fashionable, which was stupid on my part."

"I think that's a very good idea," I said.

She swallowed a couple of times. "I'm so sorry the other woman . . . didn't make it. I don't know what happened, but I swear there were no nuts in those chocolates." She was carrying her quilted jacket over one arm and she played with the zipper pull. "I, uh, understand totally if you don't want my help, but if you decide to do another fundraiser, I'd like to help."

"Thank you," I said, smiling so she'd know I meant what I was saying. "I don't know what we're going to do yet, but I appreciate all the work you did. And please take it easy. You just got out of the hospital."

Olivia gave me a tentative smile in return. "I will. I can't use my kitchen right now anyway. The police and some people from the state medical examiner's office are there."

My surprise must have shown on my face.

"I want everyone to know my chocolates weren't the reason that woman died last night. It wasn't my fault." She looked over her shoulder. "I see someone I need to talk to. Again, if I can help with another fundraiser, call me."

I nodded and watched her walk over to Georgia, who was part of a small group of people talking to Vincent Starr, and touch her on the shoulder.

The police and the medical examiner's office were already checking out Olivia's kitchen? I could see Marcus's hand in that. Had Olivia been negligent in some way that could be considered a crime? I really hoped not.

Vincent answered questions for close to twenty minutes. He looked at the box of old readers from the community center and told us they were probably worth a couple of thousand dollars, which would help with their roof repairs. Then Abigail and I took him to lunch at Eric's. Over bowls of Eric's pea soup with ham and carrots, we talked about the morning's lecture. Or rather Vincent talked and Abigail and I listened. He was enthusiastic over a couple of potential finds. It seemed that Ella King might have a first edition of *Live and Let Die*, by Ian Fleming.

"I haven't seen a decent copy of that book in years," Vincent said, gesturing with half a slice of Eric's sourdough bread.

It turned out that Lita had a box of books from

Wisteria Hill that Vincent was equally eager to check out. "I'm hoping there's a copy of *The Birds of America* in that collection," he said, beaming across the table at us.

I'd been worried that Dayna Chapman's death would leave Vincent with a negative impression of Mayville Heights. Clearly that hadn't happened. I was relieved and at the same time I felt a little sad. No one really seemed to be grieving for the woman. I remembered Brady, quietly saying he didn't need to go to the hospital. It seemed that his mother had burned a lot of bridges.

I paid for lunch, although Vincent gallantly tried to pick up the tab.

"Thank you for inviting me to town, Kathleen," he said as we stood outside on the sidewalk, buried in our heavy overcoats, our breath hanging in the frigid air.

He turned to Abigail. "And thank you for all the work you did putting it all together."

"You're very welcome," I said. "We appreciate your coming. We had a bigger turnout than even I expected."

Vincent nodded. "There are several people here in town that clearly know something about rare books. I was impressed with the questions I was asked." He patted the pocket of his heavy dark brown jacket. "I'll be e-mailing more information to several people." Then he smiled. "I'd love to return and do a workshop next time I'm in the area, Kathleen."

I smiled back. "I'd like that as well," I said.

We shook hands and Abigail and I pointed him in the direction of Henderson Holdings. Then we headed back to the library.

"This morning went better than I expected," Abigail said, pulling her scarf a little tighter around her neck.

"I know," I said, stuffing my hands in my pockets and wishing I'd worn my heavier gloves. "We had a great turnout. There were a lot of people who drove from Minneapolis, but there were a lot of people from here in town, too."

She looked at me as we waited to cross at the corner. "I was surprised to see Brady," she said. "Given that his mother . . ." She didn't finish the sentence. Then before I could say anything, she shook her head. "Listen to me. I sound like the stereotypical small-town busybody."

"You don't and you aren't," I said as we turned toward the library. "You're concerned about Brady. That's not being a busybody, that's just being a decent person."

She kicked a chunk of snow down the sidewalk. "My father would never have won any father-of-the-year prizes. I told you how he reacted when I got married without his approval."

I nodded.

"He was the kind of person for whom nothing was ever good enough, especially anything I did, it seemed." She looked past me, out over the water. "I'd like to tell you that he changed as he got older, but he didn't. He was a sour old man and I promised myself that I wasn't going to be like that. I didn't forgive anything he did, but I did spend time with him before he died. Not for him, Kathleen. For me, so I could know I wasn't the same kind of person he was."

"I understand that," I said as we approached the library building.

"Brady's relationship with his mother is none of my business," Abigail said. "She left those boys and that's a hard thing to forgive." She sighed. "But Dayna's dead now and there are no more chances for . . . anything. Swallowing all the feelings that go along with that isn't a good thing."

I thought about Mags, touching Brady's hand and seconding Marcus's suggestion that Brady go to the hospital. I was very glad she'd done that.

As we came level with the parking lot, I spied Burtis Chapman's big black truck in the parking lot with Burtis behind the wheel.

"Abigail," I said. "I see Burtis over there. I'm just going to go talk to him for a minute."

She nodded. "I'll see you inside," she said, and headed for the stairs.

I made my way across the lot, making a mental note that I needed to get Harry Taylor to spread a little more sand around, and Burtis climbed out of the truck when he saw me coming. He was wearing a heavy navy jacket and a trapper hat with earflaps.

"Hello, Kathleen," he said as he came around the front of the truck.

I smiled. "Hello, Burtis," I said. "Were you by any chance waiting for me?"

"Yes, I was. I wanted to say I'm sorry your fundraiser got ruined last night."

I pulled my hat a little farther down over my ears. The air was sharply cold and the snow I'd known was coming was just beginning.

"Thank you," I said. "But it wasn't your fault. It wasn't anyone's fault." I hesitated. "I'm sorry about your wife."

"Dayna hasn't been my wife in a long time, but I appreciate the thought." He studied my face for a moment. "You know about me and Lita," he said. "I know you saw us together, months ago."

My face flooded with color as I realized Burtis must have seen my swan dive down onto the front seat of my truck the day I'd spotted him with Lita, standing this close in this same parking lot.

"I apologize," I said, feeling like an awkward teenager. "I was just . . . surprised. I wasn't spying. I didn't want to embarrass the two of you." I gestured with one hand. "So I decided it was better to embarrass myself."

Burtis laughed. "Don't worry about it, girl. I knew you wouldn't be spreading my business all over town, although I wasn't sure for a minute if you were just trying not to be seen or if maybe you were after a sandwich you'd spied on the floor."

I laughed. "Could we pretend I was going after a sandwich?" I asked.

"Fine by me," Burtis said with a smile. He reached into the pocket of his jacket and pulled out a folded envelope, which he held out to me.

"What's this?" I said, even though I pretty much knew.

"It's for your reading program."

I narrowed my eyes, studying his ruddy face. It didn't look as though he'd shaved since the previous day, and I noticed lines pulling at the corners of his eyes and mouth. Discovering that his former wife was back in town and then having her die in such a public way had to have been difficult for Burtis.

"You already gave me a check for Reading Buddies when you bought your tickets."

His expression hardened just a little. "And now I'm giving you another one."

"Why?" I asked. I still hadn't taken the envelope he was holding out.

"When someone offers you a check, you're supposed to say thank you and take it," Burtis said. There was just a bit of an edge to his voice. He dropped the folded envelope into my pocket.

"You're the last person I would have expected to give me guilt money," I said, meeting his dark eyes with the hint of a challenge in my own.

He gave a loud snort of derision. "Really? Do I look guilty to you?"

"Maybe guilty isn't the right word," I said. "But I do think you feel something—bad, angry frustrated, I don't know—because of what happened last night."

He continued to meet my gaze, never once looking away. "I think what happened last night was a damn shame—for my boys and for your fundraiser." He fished his keys out of his jacket pocket. "I have to get down to the community center. Thorsten is waiting on me."

I touched my own jacket pocket. "Thank you for this," I said. I knew there really was no point in arguing about the money. He'd just do an end run around me and give the check to Lita.

"You should come by Fern's for breakfast," Burtis said. "I haven't seen you there for at least a month. Weekend special this Saturday is the Big Breakfast. Best coffee in town. Don't tell Eric Cullen I said that." One eyebrow went up. "And the conversation can be pretty interestin', too."

"I might just do that," I said.

"I'll keep an eye out for you," he said. He raised a hand in good-bye and walked back around the front of the big black truck. I trudged across the snowy parking lot toward the front steps of the library. I pulled the envelope out of my pocket and looked at the check inside. It was made out for more money than Burtis's original donation.

I didn't know if he really was motivated by guilt or something else. I just knew that first thing Saturday morning I was going to be perched on a stool at Fern's Diner digging into the Big Breakfast and trying to dig up some answers about how Dayna Chapman had died.

6

There were two furry faces waiting for me when I got home and stepped into the kitchen. Two pairs of feline eyes, one green and one gold, looked up at me. I wasn't so gullible that I thought the cats had actually missed me. I'd made fish cakes for supper earlier in the week and I'd cooked a little extra fish for them. I had no idea how they knew that. But they did. For all I knew, they both had X-ray vision that let them see inside the refrigerator. It wasn't totally preposterous, given their other superpowers.

I didn't really know how else to describe the "abilities" Hercules and Owen had, which was part of the reason why I hadn't told anyone—not even Marcus. What was I going to say to him? "Oh, by the way, Owen can make himself invisible, and Hercules can walk through walls?"

Cats can't dematerialize and then rematerialize at will. They can't walk through several inches of solid wall. Except mine could.

It defied logic and reason and I had no idea why or how they could do what they did. I just knew it wasn't the kind of information I should share with anyone.

I put my briefcase and my outside things away and then knelt down on the kitchen floor. Hercules put a paw on my knee and almost seemed to smile at me.

"How was your day?" I asked, and reached over to stroke the sleek black fur on the top of his head.

He yawned. Nothing exciting.

"Okay, how was your day?" I said to Owen, reaching over to scratch behind his ear.

His response was to turn away from my hand, shoot a daggers look at his brother and then glare at the refrigerator before finally looking back at me. He meowed loudly.

It wasn't his "I'm so hungry" meow.

"What happened?" I said.

Owen stalked over to the refrigerator, murping continuously just under his breath. I knew those disgruntled noises meant he was irked about something. He stopped in front of the refrigerator door, sat down and looked at me again. Clearly, I was supposed to know what was wrong.

I looked at Hercules. "What's wrong with Owen?" I asked.

Hercules yawned again, stretched and joined his brother. He stuck one white-tipped paw underneath the fridge, fished around, and then pulled it back again.

I knew that meant that Owen had lost something under the refrigerator and I had a pretty good idea what that something was.

I got to my feet. "Move," I ordered, making a shooing gesture with my right hand. Both cats backed up.

I grabbed the wooden spoon I used for mixing up cookie dough, got down on all fours and managed to retrieve the head of a yellow Fred the Funky Chicken stuck underneath the fridge, sending it skidding across the floor, stopping right in front of Owen.

He immediately put a paw on top of the severed catnip-filled head. It looked to me like the same Funky Chicken head that had ended up under the TV stand earlier in the week. I'd managed to bat that one free with the broom handle.

I got to my feet again. "Remember what Eddie said. It's not enough to have a blistering slap shot. You need some finesse as well."

Roma and Eddie had come for dinner—along with Maggie—just before hockey season started. Maggie had picked Eddie's brain for stick handling tips, while Owen sat at her feet seemingly captivated by the conversation. Mags was a good skater, but as Mary put it, she couldn't hit the broadside of a barn with a puck—or anything else.

Owen made another crabby murping sound, almost under his breath. Then he picked up the Fred head and stalked toward the living room.

Hercules kept me company as I got supper ready. I told him about my day, including what I'd learned from Olivia and Abigail about the boxes of chocolate truffles.

"And Burtis invited me for breakfast," I said. "At least I think he did."

Herc cocked his black-and-white head to one side. I related the parking lot conversation with Burtis.

"I think I'll go," I said. "Dayna's death doesn't make any sense. What are the chances a pistachio nut ended up in the one chocolate she bit into?"

Hercules's whiskers twitched. He might have been considering my question or he might have been enjoying the aroma of a fat, dill-scented fish cake sizzling on the stove.

I slid the hot, crispy fish cake onto the whole grain bun I'd just toasted and added sprouts, Swiss cheese and my homemade tartar sauce.

"Maggie thinks I'm looking for a crime where there is none," I told the cat as I set my plate on the table. "Marcus all but said the same thing." I reached for the dish of plain poached white fish I'd saved for the boys. "I just . . ." I shook my head. "I'm not wrong. You know what Old Harry says: If it walks like a duck and quacks like a duck, you'd better start making the orange sauce. And all I've heard since last night is a lot of quacking that hasn't made me change my mind."

My extended metaphor had gone completely over Hercules's head. But he'd had Harry Junior's barbecued duck on a beer can, so he knew the word "duck" meant something good and he licked his lips. I decided to see that as a vote of support for my side.

Roma and Rebecca picked me up right on time for our shopping trip. Owen had disappeared again, but Hercules gave Roma a soft meow.

"Hello, Hercules," she said with a smile as I pulled on my boots and zipped my jacket.

The cats had never been that crazy about Roma—after all, she was the person who poked them with needles and warned us all not to feed them "people" food. But over the last few months Hercules and Roma had been inching toward a friendship of sorts. Early in the fall I'd gone over the embankment by the water along the Riverwalk downtown. I'd ended up bruised and scraped, and Roma, without being asked, had shown up to make me dinner, throw a couple of loads of laundry in the basement washing machine and feed Owen and Hercules.

"I won't be late," I said to Hercules. I grabbed my purse and followed Roma out to her SUV, where Rebecca was waiting in the front passenger seat. She half turned to smile at me as I slid along the backseat.

"Hi, Kathleen," she said.

I smiled back at her. "Hi, Rebecca."

Roma slipped into the driver's seat and turned to look at me. "Where are we going first?"

"Abel's," I said.

"They're a little expensive," Rebecca said slowly.

Roma and I exchanged looks.

"How much did you spend on your dress the first time you were married?" I asked.

"Nothing," Rebecca said with a smile. "My mother made over a dress that had belonged to my cousin."

"Did you like it?"

"It was pretty," she said. I noticed that not only had she not answered my question, but she'd hesitated before telling me her first wedding dress had been pretty.

"Abel's," I said to Roma. Then I leaned back and fastened my seat belt. "Randy says every woman should feel beautiful in her wedding dress."

"That might have more meaning if I had a clue who the heck Randy is," Rebecca commented, looking at me in the small lighted mirror on the windshield visor.

Roma and I both laughed.

"Randy is a wedding dress expert on a television show, *Say Yes to the Dress*," Roma said as she backed out of the driveway.

Randy to the Rescue was Maggie's new favorite reality show. Since her not so secret crush, *Today Show* host Matt Lauer, had successfully defended his title on *Gotta Dance* and hung up his dancing shoes, Maggie's enthusiasm for that reality show had waned. Then she'd discovered *Randy to the Rescue*. She'd roped Roma and me into watching a couple of episodes of the show, and even the cats had seemed to enjoy it. Randy was a cross between

Tim Gunn and Cinderella's fairy godmother, who dropped in on unsuspecting brides and helped them find the perfect gown. It was a lot of fun, mostly because Randy and the show didn't take themselves too seriously.

"So, what's your wedding dress wish?" I asked.

Rebecca sighed. "I think that's the problem," she said. "I don't know. Every wedding dress I've seen so far looks like it was made for someone who's twenty-five. Not for an old lady."

"You're not an old lady," Roma said. "You don't look it and you don't act it."

"And I don't have the bosom for a strapless wedding dress, either," Rebecca said. "That ship sailed . . . and sank."

It took a moment for me to realize that she was making a joke. Then I saw her blue eyes twinkling at me in the visor mirror.

After I'd stopped laughing I leaned forward on the seat and put one hand on Rebecca's shoulder. "Okay, no strapless dresses. In fact, how about no wedding gowns at all? Let's just find you something you like so you can marry the man who's been in love with you since you were six."

Rebecca put her hand over mine and gave it a squeeze. "That sounds wonderful, my dear," she said.

"Kathleen, have you talked to Marcus today?" Roma asked. "Have they figured out if it was an allergic reaction that killed Burtis's ex-wife?"

"It looks that way," I said.

"The police were at Olivia Ramsey's business most of the day," Rebecca said. "Earl had to cancel his lunch run."

Earl was the Earl of Sandwich, who ran two lunch trucks and shared kitchen space with Olivia's business, Decadence Chocolatier, and Georgia Tepper's cupcake bakery, Sweet Thing.

"So they were looking for what? Nuts?" Roma said, turning right toward Mayville Heights' downtown shopping district.

"That's what Olivia said." I started watching for a parking spot. "I talked to her this morning."

"Heavens! They let her out of the hospital already?" Rebecca half turned in her seat.

I nodded. "Her reaction wasn't as severe as Dayna's."

"I'm sorry that Dayna didn't make it," she said. "But I can't help wondering, why now, of all times, did she decide to come back to Mayville Heights?"

"Maybe she just wanted to see her children," Roma said. A half-ton truck was pulling out of a parking spot just ahead of us and she slowed to let it out so we could take the space.

"Maybe," Rebecca said, though she didn't really sound convinced.

I didn't say anything, even though I'd been wondering the same thing.

It was busy downtown. I wasn't surprised. Even though it was early December, I knew a lot of people were doing their Christmas shopping. Thorsten and his crew had spent the first of the week hanging wreaths and twinkling lights, and the entire downtown looked like a scene from an old Christmas card.

When we stepped inside Abel's, I heard Rebecca sigh softly. Even if we didn't find a dress for the wedding, I wanted her to have fun looking. I thought about the times I'd gone shopping with my sister, Sara, back in Boston, or with Maggie here. I couldn't remember what I'd bought on any of the trips, but I did remember laughing a lot.

I smiled at Avis, the store owner, who was behind the cash register. "We need to look around a little," I said.

She pushed her silver-framed glasses up her nose and smiled back at me. "Take your time, Kathleen," she said. "Let me know when you need my help."

We spent about fifteen minutes just looking, Roma and me pulling out dresses and holding them up for Rebecca's reaction. Very quickly I realized that she didn't like anything with lace or ruffles. Mostly she twisted her mouth to one side or just shook her head. Even so, I managed to come up with five possibilities.

I hung them in an empty dressing room. "Try the first one on and then come out so Roma and I can see you."

"What if I don't like the dress?" Rebecca said.

I put my hands on my hips and mock-glared at her. "Don't make me come back in here and drag you out, because I will." I got a mental image of myself trying to pull petite Rebecca out to the three-sided, full-length mirror. It was hard to keep a straight face.

Rebecca must have been picturing the same thing. "Yes, ma'am," she said gravely, but her mouth twitched with the beginning of a smile.

I went out and sat next to Roma on the bench just inside the dressing room area.

"How did the lecture go this morning?" Roma asked.

"Very well. We had a full house," I said. "And when Abigail and I took Vincent to lunch, he offered to come back at some point for another talk."

"That has to be good," Roma commented, pushing her dark hair behind one ear.

I nodded and rubbed my left shoulder with my other hand. "It is." I didn't have to say "but." Roma heard the word without me speaking.

"I'm sorry about the fundraiser."

"Me too," I said. "We're going to refund all the ticket money. Lita will be mailing the checks on Monday. You should get it by the middle of the week."

"I don't want the money back," Roma said.

"You gave me a donation," I said, firmly, wondering if Maggie would have a couple of minutes to use her long, strong fingers on my shoulder tomorrow. "And Eddie arranged for Jazzology. I'm not keeping your ticket money, or anyone else's for that matter. No one got what they paid for."

"Has anyone ever pointed out that you can be really stubborn sometimes?"

I grinned at her and leaned back against the

wall. "Marcus might have pointed it out—one or two . . . dozen times."

Roma laughed. "Things are good between you two?"

I felt my cheeks get warm and I ducked my head. "Very good," I said, giving her a sideways glance.

She leaned over and bumped me with her shoulder. "I'm glad," she said with a smile. "Sometimes I did wonder if you two were ever going to get it together."

Rebecca came out of the dressing room then. She was wearing the first dress of the five, an inky navy dress with long bell-shaped sleeves and a full skirt.

"I feel like I should be conducting an orchestra," Rebecca said, raising her arm and swinging the sweeping sleeve through the air.

"I like the dress," Roma said.

"But not for a wedding," we both said at the same time.

I gestured toward the dressing room. "Next."

The second and third dresses weren't quite right, either, but when Rebecca walked out in the fourth one I was actually at a loss for words for a moment.

"Oh, Rebecca," Roma said softly beside me.

She looked beautiful. The dress was a soft rose color with long, semi-sheer sleeves, a round neckline and a long, slim skirt. It was simple and elegant and very Rebecca.

"What do you think, Kathleen?" Rebecca asked.

"I love it," I said. "What's important is what do you think?"

She turned to study her reflection in the three-sided mirror. "It is pretty," she said. Then she frowned. "But it's not very fancy. It's not the kind of dress for the wedding Everett is planning."

She held up a hand as if to hold off the words she knew I was about to say. "I know you think I should tell Everett I want to scale way back on the wedding, but it's so important to him. I don't want to take that away from him."

I wrapped my arms around her and gave her a hug. "You really are the nicest person I know," I said. "And we will find you a dress. I promise."

Rebecca tried on four more dresses, but none of them were quite right and none of them looked as beautiful as that simple, rose-colored dress. We left Abel's empty-handed.

"We still have time," I said as we walked back to the car.

Roma nodded. "Why don't we drive over to Red Wing next Friday night?"

"Shouldn't you two be spending time with the men in your lives?" Rebecca asked.

Roma laughed as she unlocked the SUV. "The guy in my life is spending his time with a bunch of smelly, sweaty hockey players. Most of whom don't have any front teeth."

"Hey, mine, too," I said, grinning at her over the hood of the car. Marcus was playing in the annual Winterfest Hockey Classic, and practices had started the previous Monday night.

Rebecca shook her head. "I can see I'm going to have to have a talk with those young men," she said. She tried to look stern but as usual couldn't quite keep the smile from around her eyes.

"So we'll head to Red Wing next Friday?" Roma said, looking from me to Rebecca.

"Yes," I said.

Rebecca hesitated for a moment and then nodded.

Roma drove us home. She dropped off Rebecca first. The older woman undid her seat belt and turned partway around in the seat. "Thank you," she said. "I don't know what I'd do without the two of you. You're angels."

I leaned forward; Roma leaned back. We tipped our heads together and folded our hands under our chins and looked at Rebecca with our most angelic expressions—which probably looked a lot as though our brains had just run out of our noses.

Rebecca laughed and shook her head again. "You're also very silly."

I straightened up and brushed my hair back off my face. "I know I sound like a broken record, but we will find a dress." I held up three fingers. "Librarian's honor."

Her eyes flicked over to Roma. "It's sweet how she thinks I believe that, isn't it?"

Roma laughed. "It is." She leaned over and hugged Rebecca. "I'll talk to you before Friday and we'll decide on a time."

I reached forward and gave Rebecca's shoulder a squeeze. "Come for tea on Sunday," I said.

"Call me," she said. She climbed out of the SUV and waved good night. Roma waited until she was safely inside before she backed out of the driveway.

"Do you really think we're going to find a dress for Rebecca in Red Wing?" she asked.

I adjusted my seat belt a little tighter. "I hope so," I said. "I wish there was some way to persuade Everett to give up on his idea of a wedding extravaganza."

Roma waited for a half-ton and a car to go by before she backed onto the street. "I thought it was the woman who was supposed to turn into Bridezilla, not the groom."

"It's not that Everett is Bridezilla—or Groom-zilla—exactly. It's just that he's got the idea that Rebecca should have the wedding she didn't have when they were young. And he's so happy he wants the whole world to know."

I caught her smile in the rearview mirror. "It's really kind of sweet, when you think about it," she said.

I nodded slowly. "It is. All those years apart and they're still crazy about each other."

"So, why are some couples like Rebecca and Everett when others end up like Burtis and Dayna Chapman?"

"I don't know," I said. "Look at my parents. They were married, got divorced, then got married again. My mother said what she learned was that she didn't want a man she could live with. She wanted a man she couldn't live without."

"That sounds like your mother."

I could see Roma smiling. She'd met my mother earlier in the fall when she filled in as a last-minute director for the New Horizons Theatre Festival.

She pulled into my driveway behind my truck, put the car in park and shifted around to look at me. "My dad says that marriage works as long as you both don't want to pour a bucket of water over the other person at the same time."

I thought about the bumpy path Marcus and I had followed before we ended up together. More than once I'd thought about pouring my coffee on his shoes. I laughed. "I think your dad's onto something."

I gestured to the house. "How about some hot chocolate?"

Roma made a face. "I'll have to take a rain check. There's a German shepherd at the clinic I really need to check on. But you and Maggie are still coming out for lunch tomorrow, right?"

"Absolutely," I said.

I undid my seat belt and slid across the seat. "Thanks for coming tonight."

Roma smiled. "It was fun."

"Somewhere in the state of Minnesota we will find Rebecca a dress," I said. "I'll see you tomorrow."

She waved and I headed around the house to the back door.

Marcus called just after ten o'clock. I was curled up in the big chair in the bedroom reading, with Hercules sprawled in my lap.

"How was practice?" I asked.

"Good. But I ended up going into the boards, headfirst."

I straightened up, disturbing Herc, who sat up as well and glared at the phone. "Are you all right?" I asked.

"I'm fine," he said. "My cheek's a little swollen, and I have a couple of bruises. Brady said it makes me look a little more menacing."

"Brady Chapman's on the team?"

"Uh-huh."

I could hear him shifting in his seat and guessed that he was stretched out on the sofa.

"We needed a goalie. Derek starts college after Christmas. Remember?"

Officer Derek Craig was finishing his degree with the long-term goal of law school. He'd borrowed every LSAT prep book I'd been able to get for him. He was smart, observant and focused. I had no doubt he'd make a good lawyer.

"Did you finish going through Olivia's kitchen?" I asked. Hercules had settled himself again, his head against my chest. I started stroking his fur and he began purring.

"How did you—never mind. We're just about done," he said.

"You didn't find anything, did you?"

"You know I can't answer that."

I could picture him smiling and I could hear it in his voice.

"You know you just did," I pointed out.

He yawned.

"You're tired," I said. "Go have a shower."

"Yeah, I think I'll do that. You and Maggie are going to Roma's to paint tomorrow afternoon, aren't you?"

My hand had stopped moving, and Hercules gave it a nudge with his head. "Uh-huh," I said. "And you'll be here for supper?"

"Ummm, I'm looking forward to it."

That sound, a little like the cats purring, made me weak in the knees. "I'll see you tomorrow, then," I said softly.

"Good night, Kathleen," he said.

I hung up the phone but sat there for a moment, thinking about how good Marcus smelled, how much I like threading my fingers through his dark brown hair and kissing his warm mouth. After a moment I realized Hercules was staring curiously at me.

"Sorry, I just got a little sidetracked," I said. He gave me a look that if he'd been a person I would have called "yeah, right."

I leaned back in the chair and stretched my arms over my head. "I forgot to tell Marcus I'm going to Fern's in the morning to have breakfast with Burtis," I said.

The cat's expression grew even more skeptical.

"I really did forget," I said. I made a mental note to tell Marcus as soon as he arrived for dinner tomorrow night. I really was trying to stay out of his cases. I just wasn't sure if I was going to be able to do it.

I didn't want to get up in the morning. It was so warm and comfortable under my heavy quilt and woolen blanket. It had snowed, but only a little, so I was able to clear everything away with just the broom. Owen came out with me, chasing snow-flakes as I swept them away, jumping around and generally having a good time. Hercules came only as far as the top step. He looked around, shook his head and went back through the door with a sour expression on his face. (Hercules hated snow.) And when I say through the door, I mean literally through it. The air seemed to shimmer, ever so slightly, and he was gone. Seeing that happen still made the hairs come up on the back of my neck and I couldn't help looking around to make sure no one else had been watching.

I fed the boys breakfast, pulled on my down-filled jacket and heavy-soled lace-up boots and grabbed my purse.

"I'll be back," I said.

Hercules looked up and meowed. Owen made a low "murp" and didn't even bother lifting his head from his bowl.

Burtis was sitting at the counter at Fern's when I got there, his huge hands wrapped around an equally huge mug of coffee. I'd never gone to Fern's for breakfast and gotten there before him. I had no idea what time he got up in the morning, but it was clearly very, very early.

I slid onto the stool next to Burtis. The place was empty except for four long-distance truckers sitting together at one of the middle booths.

Peggy Sue turned and smiled at me. "Coffee?" she asked.

"Oh, please," I said.

She poured me a cup a big as the one Burtis had and set it in front of me along with a pitcher of cream and a little metal bowl filled with sugar packets.

I could feel Burtis's eyes on me, but he didn't speak until I'd added cream and sugar to my cup and taken a very large sip. "Morning, Kathleen," he said then.

I leaned my right elbow on the counter. "Good morning, Burtis," I replied.

He looked over at Peggy and held up two fingers. She nodded and went through the swinging door into the kitchen.

"Big Breakfast okay with you?" Burtis asked.

"Yes, thank you," I said. I took another sip from my oversize mug. My fingers were beginning to thaw out.

"I hear your boyfriend didn't find anything over at Olivia Ramsey's kitchen," he said after another stretch of silence.

"I heard the same thing," I said.

Burtis took a long drink of his own coffee. "Dayna and I were just kids when we got married. You probably already heard that."

I nodded. "I did."

"She came here with her parents on vacation. Probably vain of me to say it, but I cleaned up pretty good in those days."

I smiled at him. "I believe it."

He ran a hand over his stubbled chin. "For me, it was just going to be a summer fling. I know that's kind of a shameful thing to admit, but it's the truth."

His mouth moved and I waited without speaking. "She was the most beautiful woman I had ever seen and she looked at me like I could pull the stars down and hand them to her." He looked at me. "That's a powerful feeling, Kathleen."

"I can see how it would be."

"She ran away," he said. "She came back here. And we got married." He turned back to his coffee cup. "Brady came along nine months and a day after the wedding."

Peggy Sue came out then with our breakfasts: scrambled eggs, bacon, sausage, baked beans, fried potatoes with onions and yellow peppers because tomatoes were out of season and two thick slices of raisin toast. We ate in silence for several minutes. When Peggy filled up our mugs again, I set my fork down and shifted a bit on my stool so I could look at Burtis. "You said that Dayna was allergic to pistachios."

He nodded. "That's right. We spent one night in a hotel in Minneapolis. She had some kinda dessert with those nuts on it. She would have died on the spot if there hadn't been a doctor having dinner at the next table."

"She didn't know she was allergic?"

Burtis shook his head. "Dayna was a picky eater. A lot of stuff she'd never tried."

"I don't remember seeing a medic alert bracelet," I said, spearing half a sausage with my fork.

"That's because most of the time she didn't wear one," Burtis said with a snort of derision. "At least not when we were together. Doctor said she needed it and I bought one for her, but she didn't think it looked fashionable." I remembered Olivia saying pretty much the same thing. He reached for his coffee again. "I doubt that changed. She did carry one of those autoinjector things like Olivia Ramsey had. Or at least she used to."

"Who knew about the allergy?"

He shrugged. "Far as I know, nobody outside of me. It's not as common as peanuts. She had a bad reaction to poison ivy one time, though. Doctor said it's the same family."

I used a bit of toasted raisin bread to mop up a few stray baked beans and sauce on my plate.

"Burtis, why am I here?" I asked.

He looked at me and nothing in his face could tell me what he was thinking. I made a mental note never to play poker with the man. He had no tells or tics that I could see.

"Looks to me like you're eatin' breakfast," he said, his tone affable.

"You don't think your ex-wife's death was an accident?" I said. I picked up my fork and finished the last of my potatoes while I waited to see how he'd answer my question.

He let out a slow breath. "I think it's a possibility," he finally said. "And based on the questions your boyfriend has been asking, I think he's leanin' the same way."

I reached for my coffee again. "So you want me to do what? Find out what Marcus is thinking?"

Burtis gave a snort of laughter. "I think I know you well enough by now to know that's never going to happen."

He pushed his plate away, turned to face me and his expression grew serious. "Dayna and me were too damn young to get married. And way too different. A lot of the blame—hell, most of it— is mine. I was gone from sunup to sundown and she had babies and no help. I can't fault her for feelin' overwhelmed and leaving."

I threaded my fingers through the handle of my mug. "All these years, she never came back for a visit?"

"She was unhappy here, unhappy with me. She stayed in touch with the boys: She wrote letters, and she remembered their birthdays and Christmas and such." He sighed. "It wasn't perfect, but what is?"

"So, why did she show up now, after so many years?"

He put his huge hand over the top of his coffee mug. It engulfed the heavy stoneware cup. "I swear, Kathleen, I don't know."

I had a million questions swirling in my head. "Did you talk to her before the reception?" I asked.

He shook his head. "Lita called. Told me she'd seen Dayna at Eric's Place. I called Brady. Then I called the other two at school. I thought she'd show up out to the house. When she didn't, I figured I'd just wait until she did. I'd waited more than twenty years for her to get in touch. I could wait a little bit longer."

"I saw her come over to you and Lita," I said. "At the Stratton. What did she say?"

He picked up his cup and set it back down again. "She said hello. She told me I looked well and she told Lita she liked her dress."

"That's it?"

He nodded. "Yep, that's it."

I pressed my lips together, trying to come up with the best way to say what I needed to say. "Burtis, even if Dayna's death wasn't an accident, it's not something I should be involved in."

"Because of Marcus Gordon," he said.

I ran my finger along the edge of the counter. "Yes, because of Marcus. And because I'm not a police officer."

Burtis's expression didn't change. "That didn't stop you when Mike Glazer died and Harrison Taylor asked you to see what you could find out. Or when that whole side of the hill let go up at Wisteria Hill and those bones were uncovered. You put all the pieces together and figured out how he died and gave Roma some peace about her father."

I turned to face him more directly. "Both of those times are different," I said, narrowing my gaze at him. "Roma is one of my best friends and Harrison and I are very close. Not to mention that Marcus and I weren't together either of those times."

"So you and me? We're not friends?"

It was one of those questions that had no right answer. So I didn't answer it. Instead I said, "Every time I've gotten involved in one of Marcus's cases, it's cost me. He's a good man *and* a good police officer. Let him do his job."

"Marcus *is* a good man," Burtis said. He gave me a half smile. "It surprise you I think that?"

I shook my head and tucked my hair back behind one ear. "Not really," I said. "You're many things, Burtis, but petty isn't one of them."

"I could say the same thing about you, Kathleen," he said. He stretched and reached for his Minnesota Wild cap on the counter beside his plate.

"You and the detective come at things from two different ways. He follows the evidence." Burtis put a hand on his chest. "It seems to me you follow this."

He climbed down off his stool. "I get that you don't want anything to get in the way of what you have with Detective Gordon. I wouldn't take kindly to anyone getting between Lita and me." He pulled on his cap. "You know, Kathleen. If that boy loves you—and a person only has to look at him when you're around to know he does—he isn't going to want you to stop being who you are." He gestured at our plates. "Breakfast is on me."

"Thank you," I said. I'd said I wasn't going to get involved and I meant it, but there was one question I still had to ask.

I put out my hand as Burtis moved past me and

touched his arm. He turned to look at me. "Do you know why someone would want to kill your ex-wife?" I asked.

His gaze narrowed. "That's the problem, Kathleen," he said. "I don't."

7

Ruby's truck was just pulling into the parking lot when I got to the library. I parked beside her and got out of my truck. "Good morning," I said.

Ruby smiled. "Hey, Kathleen, isn't it a beautiful day?"

The clouds were already retreating up the hill. The glimpses of sky I could see were blue, and even though it was cold, my left wrist told me there wasn't going to be any snow for a while.

I smiled back at her. "Yes, it is," I said. I gestured to the boxes on the front seat and the floor of the passenger side of the truck. "Give me something to carry."

She slid a lidded banker's box across the seat and handed it out to me. Then she grabbed another box and her overflowing canvas tote bag.

We headed for the front door. I was happy to see that Harry had been by and spread more sand in the parking lot.

I unlocked the front doors and disarmed the alarm system. Ruby set the carton she'd been carrying on the checkout desk and leaned her bag beside it. "I have one more box," she said. "I'll be right back." She was wearing a neon green quilted jacket with a red-and-white stocking cap. Her sherbet-colored hair poked out in two pigtails from under the edge of the knitted hat. Just looking at Ruby made me smile.

Once she came back with the last box of supplies, I relocked the main doors. I put my things in my office, started the coffee in the staff room for myself—and Susan, assuming she wasn't still on her latest green smoothie kick—and set some water to boil so I could make Ruby some tea. Then I went back downstairs.

Ruby was already in the conference room setting up. Harry had put up three long tables in the inverted U shape Ruby had asked for, and she was already unpacking her boxes.

"What do you need?" I asked

Ruby looked around as she rolled up the sleeves of her denim shirt. "Mary said you have a portable corkboard somewhere that maybe I could use. It's not a big deal if you're using it somewhere else."

"It's in the closet next door," I said. I pulled my keys out of the pocket of my sweater. "I'll go get it for you."

I opened the smaller meeting room, retrieved the bulletin board and wheeled it in to Ruby. Then I went upstairs. The coffee was ready, so I poured myself a cup and then made tea for Ruby. I'd brought a few of the tea bags I kept at home for Maggie—and my mother when she visited.

Ruby smiled when I handed her the tea. "Thank you, Kathleen," she said, bending her head over the cup. "I was so caught up in loading the truck this morning I ended up leaving my tea on the table and I'd only had about half of it."

I looked at the piles of paper, cardboard and fabric she'd arranged on the table in front of her. "This looks like it's going to be fun." I fingered a piece of translucent blue paper shot with what looked like some kind of plant fibers. "What is this?"

"Japanese paper," she said, bending down to take what looked to me like her own handmade paper out of the box at her feet. "It reminds me of the river, late in the summer."

"I wish I could stay for the workshop," I said, leaning against one of the tables with my coffee.

"Bookmaking isn't that complicated," Ruby said. "I could teach you how to make a really simple journal sometime." She held up a sheet of thick, creamy paper flecked with gold. "I could teach you how to make paper, for that matter."

"Really?" I said.

She shrugged. "Sure. Take a look at your schedule and maybe we could do it some Saturday after Christmas." She gave me a sly smile. "That's assuming all your Saturdays aren't taken up by a certain detective."

I was happy to see the genuine warmth in her

smile. Ruby and Marcus had been at odds after her mentor, Agatha Shepherd, was murdered last winter. It had taken some time for them to work their way back to a cordial relationship, but they had.

"I think Marcus is going to be playing hockey pretty much every Saturday between now and Winterfest," I said. "They want to win this year."

The police/fire department team had lost big-time to the boys' high school hockey team in last year's charity hockey game. Marcus and his teammates were—not surprisingly—very competitive. Even though the game had just been for fun, he didn't like being on the losing side. He didn't like losing period, I'd learned, when I bested him at the Puck Shoot, one of the games set up down by the marina during the February winter celebration.

Ruby pushed back the sleeves of the tie-dyed tee she was wearing under her denim shirt. "Is it sexist of me to say it's a guy thing?"

"Um, yes," I said, smiling at her over the top of my cup. "Hope Lind is coaching them this year."

Ruby's eyes widened. "No way!"

"Yes way," I said. "Hope played hockey in high school and in college. She's had the guys doing dry land training drills for a month. And she picked Eddie's brain last time he was here."

Ruby laughed and held her free hand up level with her ear. "Detective Lind is only about this high."

She was exaggerating a little.

"She can skate faster than all of the guys," I said, grinning back at her. "Forward and backward. She's working them hard. I had to rub Tiger Balm on Marcus's shoulders twice last week."

"I'm sure that was a hardship," Ruby teased, raising an eyebrow at me.

"No comment," I said, ducking my head over my coffee.

"Who's going to be their goalie?" she asked, straightening a stack of heavy cardboard that was about to tip sideways on the table.

"Brady Chapman."

Ruby's expression changed and she shook her head. "Do they know yet what happened to his mother? That was so awful."

"I'm not sure," I hedged.

"The police pretty much took Olivia's kitchen apart yesterday. And now she's telling everyone they didn't find anything." Ruby folded one arm across her chest. "I feel bad for Brady, though," she said. "We were just a year apart in school and I think it was hard for him, not having a mother around." She blew out a breath. "And then when she finally does come back, the last words he has with her are angry ones."

I frowned. "You saw them fighting?" I'd almost said, "Too."

Ruby nodded. "The other night at the fundraiser. Brady and Dana were off to the side in the wings having a pretty animated discussion about something. Half an hour later she was dead. I can't imagine how he must feel."

"Me either," I said softly.

"So, what are you going to do?" she asked, bending down to pull a file folder out of her tote bag.

I looked at her uncertainly. "About what?"

She straightened up and waved the folder at me. "Reading Buddies? The fundraiser?"

I shook my head. "I don't know yet."

"You'll let me know what I can do, right?"

"You've already done enough," I protested. "More than enough. That backdrop you painted was incredible. I wish people had had more time to enjoy it."

"Nope, nope, nope, nope." Ruby shook her head. With her two pigtails she looked for all the world like a stubborn toddler. "There's no such thing as doing more than enough." She came over and put one arm around my waist, leaning her head against my shoulder. "I'm serious. If you don't ask me to help when you decide what you're going to do, I will be mortally insulted."

"Mortally?" I said. "Really?" Together we walked out into the main part of the library.

Ruby nodded solemnly. "Yes." Then she smiled, let go of me and turned slowly in a circle. "Maggie said you're getting a second tree. How are you going to decorate it?"

"I want to do something a little old-fashioned," I said, looking at the big open space that made up most of the main floor of the library. "Like an old Currier and Ives Christmas card."

She turned to face me and I could see by the

gleam in her eyes that she had an idea. "Want to use my collection of old Christmas ornaments on the tree?"

"Yes," I said at once. "Are you sure?" I added.

Ruby had a wonderful collection of vintage Christmas decorations from the 1930s to the 1960s.

"Oh yeah. Absolutely. We're not using them on the tree in the co-op store this year. Remember? Maggie had us all make ornaments for the tree that can be sold for Toys for Tots. So I'd love to see my collection on the tree here."

"Thank you," I said. Getting Ruby's Christmas ornaments for the library tree meant I could cross one more thing off my to-do list.

There was a tap on the front door then. Susan was on the top step hunched into her heavy duffle coat, stamping snow off her boots.

I headed for the door to let her in.

"Tell me there's coffee," she said as she stepped inside. Her hat was pulled low on her forehead and all I could see were her eyes above the collar of her red coat.

"What happened to your green smoothie?" I asked.

She frowned darkly at me. "The boys happened to my smoothie. The boys decided to *make* my smoothie." She kicked the snow off her knee-high brown boots. "There's spinach on my kitchen ceiling, and that's my mother's problem since it was her idea to 'involve the boys in meal preparation.'" She made little quotation marks in the air with her gloved fingers.

"Well, the coffee's made and there are tea bags if you'd like a cup of tea." I struggled to keep a straight face. I had a mental picture of Susan's twins trying to make their mother her morning smoothie. The boys were genius-level smart, resourceful and totally fearless. It made life for Susan and Eric very interesting sometimes.

Susan shook her head. "No. I need more caffeine. Lots and lots of caffeine." She pulled off her hat. I picked a bit of spinach out of her updo as she moved past me.

She waved to Ruby and headed for the stairs. She was a woman on a mission. I was glad I'd made a full pot of coffee.

8

The journal-making workshop was just as successful as Vincent Starr's talk had been. I wasn't surprised. Ruby was a natural teacher—good at explaining her techniques in simple terms. When the class was over, five different people sought me out to ask if we were planning more workshops.

Maggie showed up about ten to twelve—dropped off by none other than Brady Chapman. The library closed at lunchtime on Saturdays. We climbed into the truck and headed for Wisteria Hill to have lunch with Roma and help her continue to fix up the place.

"How did Ruby's workshop go?" Mags asked as I started up Mountain Road.

"Really well. All but two people put their e-mail addresses on a list to be notified about more workshops, and they were tourists from out of state."

Maggie clapped her mittened hands together and smiled at me. "I knew people would love her class. I wish I'd been able to get there, but Oren and I spent the morning going over the plans for the changes to the store."

Maggie had gotten a grant to renovate the artist co-op store and add a small space for demonstrations and courses in the summer and fall. Oren was going to do the work.

I glanced over at her. "What did he think about your drawings?"

Maggie pulled off her fuzzy hat and ran her fingers through her blond curls. "He had a couple of suggestions for changes—he thinks we should move the half wall about a foot to the right and he suggested glass block for the other wall."

I tried to picture the sketches Maggie had made for the proposed changes to the main floor of the store. "I do like the idea of using the glass block," I said. "It would let in more light."

"I do, too," Maggie said. "Oren says that costwise it should work out about the same."

We talked about the renovations all the way out to Wisteria Hill. I wondered when Mags was going to tell me that Brady had dropped her off at the library. There was something going on between those two. I knew she'd tell me about it eventually.

As I flicked on my blinker to turn into the driveway of the old estate, I thought about all the changes that had happened since Roma bought the property from Everett. The house and grounds had been empty for so long. I'd always thought the whole place had an air of sadness. Now that Roma was getting ready to live in the old farmhouse, it somehow seemed alive again.

I had a big soft spot for Wisteria Hill. It was where I'd found Hercules and Owen—or to be more exact, it was where they had found me. It was where Marcus and I had become friends— and then more than friends.

Once Roma was living there full-time, she wouldn't need her group of volunteers who made sure that the feral cat colony in the old carriage house was fed and cared for. I was going to miss watching Lucy and the other cats.

Roma waved from the kitchen window as we got out of the truck. This was my first chance to see the kitchen since Oren had finished installing the new cupboards.

We took off our boots in what used to be the old side porch. Now it was a combination mudroom/laundry/storage area.

"Ready?" Roma asked, eyes sparkling.

Maggie and I both nodded.

Oren had done a beautiful job on the new cupboards—not that I'd ever had any doubt of that. Maggie and I had helped Roma steam about a hundred years' worth of wallpaper off the kitchen walls. Before training camp Eddie had patched and repaired them and Maggie and I had spent a weekend helping Roma paint the kitchen a creamy shade of palest yellow. The new kitchen cupboards were a simple Shaker style, painted white, and they went beautifully with the buttery walls and the wide boards of the refinished hard-wood floor.

"Oh, Roma, it's beautiful," I said.

Maggie put her arm around Roma's shoulders and gave her a hug. "It really is," she agreed.

Everett and Rebecca had left Roma the original farmhouse kitchen table as a kind of housewarming present. It sat in the far corner, surrounded by a bank of windows.

"Hey, where did you get the chairs?" Maggie asked, pointing to the corner.

I looked across the room and realized Roma had four new-to-her chairs that looked as though they'd been made to go with the big table.

"Eddie and I found them at a flea market," she said. She smiled at me. "Marcus said he'll spray-paint them black for me in the spring."

"Isn't he a sweetheart?" Maggie said, giving me a saccharine grin. She was never going to let me forget she'd thought Marcus and I were perfect for each other about ten minutes after we'd met.

"Yes, he is," I said, making a face at her.

"So you like the kitchen?" Roma asked. "Really?"

"Very much," I said.

"Me too," Maggie agreed, running a hand over one of the cabinet doors. "The energy of the entire house has changed."

She was right. The lonely feeling the old place used to give off was gone.

Roma had made minestrone soup for lunch and

there were thick slices of brown bread and a wedge of cheddar cheese. We ate at the kitchen table.

"This is Rebecca's brown bread, isn't it?" I said.

Roma nodded. "Yep. She brought it out this morning along with two new shelters for the cats."

Since the cats were feral, they lived in the old carriage house year-round. Harry Taylor Junior had strengthened and added insulation to one corner of the old building, where hay had once been stored. Rebecca and several other volunteers had made warm sleeping shelters for each cat out of large plastic storage bins with straw for insulation.

"How are Lucy and the others?" I asked. Lucy was the smallest member of the feral cat family, but she was its undisputed leader. We seemed to have a rapport. Maggie liked to call me the Cat Whisperer.

Roma looked out the window toward the carriage house. "I'm going to put the cage out for Smokey."

"Why?" I asked.

She shifted her gaze to me. "He was moving a lot more slowly yesterday and he didn't eat very much."

"Is there anything I can do to help?"

Smokey was the oldest cat in the colony as far as Roma could tell. The scar above his right eye and the missing tip of his tail made me wonder what his life had been like before Roma had discovered the cats and taken over their care.

She gave me a half smile. "Thanks. There isn't anything you can do right now. I'll let you know how he is once I get him down to the clinic."

Maggie shot me a look of sympathy and I picked up my spoon again. "What about Micah?" I asked.

Micah was a small ginger tabby that had been wandering around Wisteria Hill since early fall.

Roma broke a slice of bread in half and dipped a piece in her bowl. "She shows up to eat about every second day. But it doesn't matter what I put in the cage; I can't catch her."

Maggie's head was bent over her bowl, but she inclined it in my direction. "You need to use the Cat Whisperer and her sidekick, the Cat Detective," she said.

Roma laughed. "The Cat Detective?"

Maggie smiled. "Marcus is the one who found Desmond and brought him to the clinic, which is how you ended up discovering the cats up here. That makes him the Cat Detective."

"Very funny," I said.

"And Marcus managed to figure out that Micah was a girl cat and not a boy cat, something that had stymied the best veterinary minds in town," Maggie added teasingly.

When Roma first spotted Micah she'd thought the little cat was male. Later, when Marcus and I encountered him, he quickly saw that "he" was in fact "she."

Roma squared her shoulders, and her chin jutted out. "I wasn't wearing glasses," she said.

"That's because you don't need glasses." I reached for the cheese.

She crinkled her nose at me. "I mean my sunglasses," she said. "It was a very bright day."

"Oh, of course," I said, nodding solemnly.

Roma stuck her tongue out at me and then she laughed.

"Seriously," I said. "Would you like Marcus and me to try to catch Micah?"

Roma nodded. "Please. I'm not having any luck and I'm worried about where she's sleeping, especially since it's been so cold."

"Okay," I said, dropping a chunk of cheese into my soup. "Let me know once you have Smokey and then I'll see if we can get Micah for you."

After lunch Maggie helped Roma load the dishwasher and I changed into my old jeans and a long-sleeved T-shirt.

We covered the hardwood floors with cardboard that Harry Junior had saved for Roma from the recycling bins at the community center. Then Maggie settled in with a brush and a small foam roller to paint around the big bay window. Roma started in on the brushwork on the adjacent wall, and I followed her with the roller. This was the second coat and we wanted it to look good.

Eddie, with some guidance from Oren, had stripped and refinished all the wide oak trim and baseboard in the room. Roma had carefully taped off all the wood before Maggie and I had arrived.

"Eddie did a great job with this trim," Mags

said as she worked her brush along the edge of the big window.

"He has more patience than I do," Roma said. She was working on a small stepladder above my head, cutting in with her brush where the wall and ceiling met. "Eventually, he wants to do all the woodwork in the house."

Maggie looked at me and raised her eyebrows. "Eventually?"

"You know what I mean," Roma said.

"It's none of our business," I began.

"But that's not going to stop you." Roma looked down from her perch on the ladder and smiled at me.

"No, it's not," Maggie agreed, her head turned almost upside down as she worked underneath the window.

"Does that mean you and Eddie have talked about the future?" I asked.

Roma continued to paint along the top of the wall. "We have. Well, sort of. It's just . . ." She stopped painting and turned to look down at Maggie and me. "You know that Eddie's been divorced for a long time."

"Uh-huh," Maggie said.

I nodded.

"He has a good relationship with his ex, Sydney's mother."

Sydney was Eddie's ten-year-old daughter from his brief marriage to his high school sweetheart.

"He gets to spend a lot of time with Syd in the off-season, but even so, I know he wishes he had more time with her." Roma sighed softly. "I don't want him to regret giving up the chance to have more children."

I opened my mouth to tell Roma that from what I'd seen, what Eddie wanted was a life with her, but she spoke first, inclining her head toward Maggie. "What I really want to know is what's happening with Maggie's love life."

"I don't have a love life," Mags said, keeping her gaze focused on the stretch of wall in front of her.

"I don't think that's true," Roma said teasingly, shaking her head. She looked at me again, raising an eyebrow. "The night of the fundraiser I saw Maggie and Brady Chapman this close together." She held up her thumb and index finger maybe a couple of millimeters apart.

"It's not what you think," Maggie said.

I leaned my roller on the edge of the paint tray. "You don't know what we think," I said, smiling sweetly.

"Brady had a little grease mark on his tie. I had one of those detergent pens in my purse. All I was doing was cleaning his tie."

I looked up at Roma. "She was cleaning his tie," I said.

Roma closed her free hand into a fist and pressed it to her chest. "Awww, isn't that sweet?"

"I was," Maggie insisted, still focusing on her painting.

"The lady doth protest too much, methinks," I said.

Maggie sat back on her heels and looked over at me. "Brady and I are just friends," she said, enunciating each word slowly and carefully.

"Marcus and I started out as just friends," I said.

Above me on the ladder, Roma cleared her throat.

"Sort of," I amended.

"Eddie and I were just friends at first," Roma offered.

I remembered how Maggie had squeezed Brady's hand at the fundraiser, urging him to go to the hospital. "You like him, Mags," I said.

She couldn't hold my gaze.

"You do!" Roma crowed.

"He's not my type," Maggie said, pulling her painting pail a little closer. "He's so serious and competitive. He wears suits. He's a lawyer, for heaven's sake."

"So?" I said.

"So I like the sensitive type—artists, musicians, guys whose idea of dressing up is putting on a clean T-shirt."

"Brady has a sensitive side," I said. "When Marcus's sister needed a lawyer, he took her case. He's been helping Ruby get the last of Agatha's estate settled and I know he's only charging her for his expenses because the money's all going into art scholarships."

I held up a finger before she could interrupt me.

"And he stepped in to be goalie for the first responder team because Derek isn't going to be able to get back for Winterfest."

"He sounds like a nice guy," Roma said.

"Brady is *not* interested in me romantically," Maggie insisted.

Roma and I exchanged a look, which Maggie caught.

"Now what is it?"

"You've been out of the dating pool a little too long, Mags," I said.

"You really haven't noticed the way he looks at you?" Roma asked.

Maggie was clearly surprised. Then she shook her head. "No. Anyway, things are too complicated right now, with his mother coming back and then dying the way she did."

Roma looked down at me. "Does Marcus know what happened yet?"

I shook my head.

"That was such a bizarre accident," Maggie said, pushing back the sleeves of her gray T-shirt.

"I know," Roma agreed, turning back to her painting. "What are the chances that Dayna Chapman would come back to town and then end up dying from an allergy attack the same day she got here?"

Maggie had glanced over at me and she must have seen something in my face, or maybe it was just the fact that I didn't immediately agree.

"Kath, no," she said quietly.

Roma turned around again and looked down at us. "What is it?" she said.

"You think that Dayna Chapman's death wasn't an accident," Maggie continued, as if Roma hadn't spoken.

"What?" Roma said.

"Why?" Maggie asked.

"I could be wrong," I said, looking from one to the other. "I probably am wrong."

Maggie made a face. "Sure, because you're always wrong about this kind of thing."

"The police are still investigating and so is the medical examiner's office."

"Why would anyone want to kill the woman?" Roma asked. "She hasn't been here in more than twenty years."

"I don't know," I said, leaning over to put more paint on my roller. "And maybe no one did. It just seems like an awfully big coincidence that Dayna would show up and then eat the one thing that could kill her. And Olivia has been so insistent that there were no nuts of any kind in the chocolates she made. At least none that she put there."

"She could just be trying to cover herself," Maggie said.

"Why?" I said. "If she had put nuts of any kind in the chocolates she made for the fundraiser, why lie about it? She hadn't made any promise that they would be nut free. And then she picked up that other chocolate from Dana's box and ate it and had a reaction herself. Not very smart if she knew there were nuts in it. She could have died, too."

Maggie shook her head

"Mags, it doesn't mean I'm right," I said. I turned back to the wall with my paint roller.

Roma had come down the ladder and was moving it to the right. She didn't look at me and I realized she hadn't said a word. My stomach gave a little twist.

"Roma, something's wrong," I said. "What is it?"

She turned to look at me then, leaning against the side of the ladder. "It's just, I was running a little late Thursday night. I stopped to check on that dog I told you about. So I was probably one of the last people to arrive at the Stratton." She let out a breath. "When I came in I saw Dayna and . . . Burtis, just off to the side of the stage. They were . . . talking."

"Talking or arguing?" Maggie asked.

Roma hesitated. "Arguing."

I saw Maggie swallow. She cared a lot more about Brady Chapman than she was admitting, probably even to herself.

"But I saw them later," Roma said, "just before the chocolates were handed out, and everything seemed fine between them then."

I stopped painting for a moment and looked from Roma to Maggie. "Look," I said. "I know the kind of reputation Burtis has around town. I know that not everything he does is on the up-and-up, but he wouldn't kill anyone, especially not the mother of his children. Seriously, would Lita be going out with him if there was any possibility Burtis was that kind of person?"

"Lita?" Roma said.

"And Burtis?" Maggie finished.

So much for me not spreading Burtis's business all over town. Although I'd had a feeling after they'd shown up at the fundraiser together that it was pretty obvious they were a couple, it was apparently not as clear to Roma or Maggie.

"Lita and Burtis," Roma said. "How long has that been going on?"

"A while," I said, working my way across the stretch of wall she'd just moved the ladder away from.

"How did you know?" Maggie asked, hanging her head almost upside down once again as she worked her way along the bottom of the window.

I put more paint on my roller and turned back to the wall. "I saw them together at the library, a while ago."

"Were they holding hands over by the DVDs?" Maggie asked. "I know Lita is a Clint Eastwood fan."

"No, they weren't," I said. "Although I did catch Everett giving Rebecca a kiss over by the magazines earlier this week."

I remembered how the two of them had smiled at each other a bit like two unrepentant teenagers when I walked around the shelves and surprised them. Neither one of them had seemed embarrassed at being caught in a public display of affection.

"That's what I want," Maggie said.

"You want someone to kiss you in the library?" Roma asked.

I was glad the conversation had shifted away from Burtis and his ex-wife.

"No," Maggie said. "I want to be crazy about someone the way Rebecca and Everett are about each other when I'm their age. Or right now, for that matter." She glanced over at me. "Your parents are that way, aren't they?"

"My parents are crazy, period," I said. "And yes, they're still crazy about each other."

We spent the next hour painting and talking about great love affairs and thankfully nothing more was said about Burtis or Dayna Chapman. I tried not to think about what Roma had said, that she'd seen the two of them arguing. I'd meant what I'd said. Burtis was many things, but he never would have deliberately hurt his ex-wife. And he wouldn't have asked me to look into her death if he'd had anything to do with it. Would he?

With three of us working, it didn't take long to get the walls finished. Then we sat around the kitchen table and Roma showed us the rough sketches she and Oren had made for the work she wanted to do outside in the spring.

The sun was low in the sky when I looked at my watch. "I should get going," I said. "Who knows what Owen and Hercules have been doing?"

Roma hugged us both. "Thank you," she said. "It would have taken me the next two weeks to get this all done if I'd had to do it by myself."

"Anytime," I said.

Maggie nodded her agreement. "When you decide what you want to do upstairs, we'll come back."

"Let me know about Smokey," I said as I pulled on my boots at the back door.

"I will," Roma promised.

She waved as we started down the long driveway.

I headed for Maggie's apartment. "I like Brady," I said as we drove down the hill.

"I hope you're wrong," she said.

I knew she didn't mean about liking Brady.

"Me too," I said.

"Could you imagine you and Marcus and Brady and me on a double date?" she said after another silence.

Marcus, the straight-arrow police detective, and Brady Chapman, defense attorney and son of the alleged town bootlegger, breaking bread together?

"That could be . . . interesting," I said.

She laughed. "Uh-huh."

The idea kept us laughing the rest of the way to her apartment.

"Thanks for the drive, Kath," Maggie said. "Give my love to my furry boyfriend."

"I will," I said.

My cell phone rang just as I pulled into my own driveway. I put the truck in park and looked at the screen. It was Marcus.

"Hi," I said. "I'm running a little late, but supper is in the slow cooker."

"I'm sorry, Kathleen," he said. "I'm not going to get there."

I knew what he was going to say before the words came out.

"It looks like Dayna Chapman was murdered."

9

Marcus told me he'd stop by later just to say good night if he could. Then we ended the call and I tucked my phone back in my pocket. At least I had Owen and Hercules for dinner companions.

Except neither cat was anywhere to be seen. They weren't in the kitchen. They weren't in the living room. I went upstairs to change my paint-spattered clothes, and there weren't any cats nosing around in the closet or sitting in the big chair by the window, either.

The bulb had burned out in the ceiling light at the top of the stairs. As I padded down the steps in my sock feet in the dark, I made a mental note to ask Marcus to put in a new bulb for me.

Three-quarters of the way down the stairs, I saw movement just inside the living room doorway next to the bookcases. There was enough illumination from the streetlight outside that I could catch a glimpse of gray fur.

Owen was so focused on what he was doing that he didn't notice me come behind him until I flicked on the light. He started and looked up at me, guilt written all over his gray tabby face.

He was standing on his back legs, one paw on the first shelf up from the bottom of the bookcase. I'd seen him drop whatever he'd been carrying in his mouth on the shelf and put one paw on it. Now he tried to casually rest his other front paw next to the first one. If he'd been able to lean against the side of the bookcase and whistle, I think he would have done that, too.

I looked down at him. "Hello," I said.

"Murr," he said softly, his golden eyes not quite meeting mine.

"What's that?" I asked, nodding my head at whatever he was trying to hide with his front paws.

"Merow?" he said, blinking at me as though what I'd said made no sense at all to him.

I wasn't fooled. "Nice try," I said, folding my arms over my chest. "What's under your paws?"

He lifted a paw, giving me his confused-kitty expression. At the same time he seemed to be surreptitiously trying to bat whatever he was hiding toward the back of the shelf. Sometimes I thought that if Owen hadn't been a cat he could have been some kind of criminal mastermind—Lex Luthor or the Joker, maybe.

"Owen!" I said, sharply.

To his credit he knew when he was caught. He

dropped down onto all fours and dejectedly hung his head. I leaned over to see what he had been trying to hide from me. Sometimes he liked to swipe things from Rebecca's recycling bin, although I was fairly sure there was too much snow on the ground for him to do that now.

A tiny purple mouse lay on its side on the dark wooden shelf.

"What are you doing with that?" I asked sternly, narrowing my eyes and glaring at him.

He kept his head down, and his shoulders seemed to sink just a little more.

The little purple mouse belonged to Hercules. It had been a gift from Rebecca, who loved to spoil the boys no matter what I said to her. She kept Owen in yellow catnip chickens, but Hercules was pretty much indifferent to catnip. He wasn't the only cat who felt that way, I'd learned. Rebecca had found the little mouse at the Grainery where she bought Owen's chickens and other cat treats. Once it was wound up, all you had to do was press down on it and the mouse would run in a circle on the floor, randomly changing direction and occasionally doing a loop or a figure eight.

Roma thought the toy was a wonderful idea, the feline equivalent of a person doing the *New York Times* crossword puzzle or a Sudoku puzzle to keep their mind sharp.

I crouched down on the floor beside Owen. "This is not yours," I said. "You did a very, very bad thing."

He muttered almost under his breath, like a child making excuses for his behavior.

"Were you trying to hide this from your brother?" I asked.

He turned his head sideways a little and one half-lidded eye looked at me.

I sighed in exasperation. It had become pretty clear to me from the beginning that Owen and his brother weren't ordinary cats, even without taking into account their extraordinary abilities. Among other things they seemed to have a nose for, well, crime solving, as preposterous as that seemed. And Owen, at least, seemed to have a bit of a larcenous streak.

I tried to imagine how Marcus would react if I told him that the cats seemed to have helped me every time I'd been connected with one of his cases. Oh no, that wouldn't make me seem crazy.

The problem in front of me at the moment, thankfully, had to do with a lesser crime.

"Owen, you must have five or six funky chickens—or parts from them—hidden in this house," I said. "This belongs to Hercules. You can't have it."

I said each word slowly and clearly and shook the purple mouse for emphasis. His eyes followed my hand.

Maybe I was crazy. Maybe Owen didn't understand one word I said. Maybe as far as he was concerned, I could have been speaking Italian or pig Latin. His eyes moved to my face and he gave me his best innocent/repentant look. I thought of it as his "I didn't do it and I'll never do it again" expression.

"How the heck am I supposed to discipline you?" I asked, sinking down onto my knees. Owen put a paw on my leg. I couldn't exactly stick him in the corner or tell him he couldn't go out in the yard. That wouldn't work with a normal cat, let alone one who could disappear whenever he felt like it. I knew some animal training experts advocated using a spray from a bottle of water to discourage bad behavior. Maybe I was treating Owen and Hercules too much like people, because my first thought when I'd read that advice was that I wouldn't shoot water from a spray bottle at Susan or Abigail at the library, so why would I do it to Owen or Herc?

"Don't do this again," I said, shaking a finger at him. I was very glad there was no one around to hear what I was saying. "If you do, those sardines in the refrigerator will magically disappear faster than you do."

Owen's eyes narrowed suspiciously, and he turned and looked toward the kitchen. I used to threaten to give Owen's kitty treats to the Taylors' German shepherd, Boris, but I'd made that threat one time too many without following through, and it had lost its effectiveness.

I reached over and stroked the top of Owen's head. "I love you," I said, "but sometimes you make me crazy."

"Merow," he said, wrinkling his nose at me. For all I knew, that was his way of saying, "You make me crazy sometimes, too."

I got to my feet, putting the little purple mouse in my pocket. "Are you hungry?" I asked as we went into the kitchen.

"Murp."

Cat for "I could eat."

Owen looked at the back door and meowed inquiringly. I'd told him Marcus was joining us for supper. Had he remembered?

"Marcus isn't coming," I said. I checked the slow cooker. It had just switched over from "cook" to "keep warm."

I turned back to Owen, who was sitting by the table looking at me. "He has a case," I said. I got a bowl down from the cupboard. It was all I needed. I'd set the table before I left. "Dayna Chapman's death wasn't an accident. It looks like someone might have killed her on purpose."

I heard a meow from the other side of the room. Hercules was poking his black-and-white head around the basement door.

"Hello," I said. "One, supper is almost ready. Two, Marcus isn't coming. Three, it looks like Dayna Chapman's death wasn't an accident. And four"—I pulled the purple mouse out of my pocket and set it on the floor, sending Owen a warning look that I hoped was sufficiently intimidating enough that he wouldn't so much as twitch a whisker in the direction of the toy—"this is yours."

Herc nudged the basement door open a little

more and started across the kitchen floor toward Owen and me.

"You know, Boris closes the door for Harrison," I said, taking the lid off the slow cooker. I liked Harry's big German shepherd, and I'd been impressed the first time I saw him close the back kitchen door in Harry Senior's small house.

Hercules made a face as though he'd just caught the scent of something bad, even though the aroma from the stew was filling the kitchen. Both he and Owen were smart enough to close any door in the house—although for Hercules it was easier to walk directly through a door—but being cats, they just didn't.

Herc picked up his mouse and set it next to his food dish. Then he came back over, sat down beside his brother and looked expectantly at me.

"Okay, you can both have a little chicken," I said. "But just a little."

The little black tuxedo cat licked his lips.

"Oh, and I almost forgot, Maggie sends her love," I said to Owen.

I swear he smiled.

I put a little chicken in each of their dishes and then filled a bowl with stew for myself. Since my only dinner companions were furry and were eating without using forks, I had no problem propping my feet on the chair opposite me and leaning an elbow on the table.

I wished Marcus was sitting in the chair opposite me. Things had been so good for the past three months. But we had a history of his cases coming between us. I didn't want that to happen with Dayna Chapman's death.

Hercules had finished his chicken. He came over, sat next to my chair and began to wash his face.

"Everyone is going to think it was Burtis," I said thoughtfully.

He paused for a moment, seemingly considering the idea. Then he resumed washing his face.

"I know his reputation," I said.

Burtis was the town bootlegger and as a younger man he'd worked for Idris Blackthorne, Ruby's grandfather, a hard and ruthless man who ran pretty much every illegal enterprise in a hundred-mile radius around Mayville Heights.

"Just because he could squash someone like a bug doesn't mean that he would," I said, as much to myself as the cats.

Owen lifted his head and looked around when I said the word "bug."

I exchanged a glance with Hercules.

"There are no bugs in here, Owen," I said. He looked over at me. "No bugs," I repeated. "It's just an expression."

He dropped his head over his food again.

Burtis had to have known that he'd be the main suspect if Dayna's death wasn't an accident. Maybe that was why he'd been encouraging me to get involved. I thought about what he'd said about the times I'd gotten mixed up in Marcus's cases. *"He isn't going to want you to stop being who you are."*

Owen had joined his brother and was carefully washing his face, too.

"Okay, so we're eliminating Burtis. Who else would want to kill Dayna Chapman? She hadn't even been in town for twenty-four hours."

They didn't have any more idea than I did. Aside from what I'd learned from Burtis, I really knew nothing about his ex-wife.

"Maybe it's time we learned a little more about the former Mrs. Chapman," I said to the boys.

"Merow," Owen said.

Okay, so he was in.

I looked at Hercules. "What do you think?" I asked. He was washing the white fur on his chest. He raised his head and looked in the direction of the hooks by the back door where I hung my jacket and briefcase.

My briefcase.

"Crap on toast!" I said, slouching lower in my chair. I'd left my briefcase with my laptop in my office. "Okay, as soon as I have my computer again we'll see what we can find online about Dana. In the meantime maybe we can use that other information superhighway."

Hercules frowned at me. Clearly he didn't know what I was talking about. Or he'd just noticed a knot in the fur on his tail. He started working on his tail, but I decided to believe it was the former anyway.

"The Mayville Heights grapevine," I said.

Marcus knocked on my back door a little after

nine thirty. I was curled up in the big chair in the living room with the cats stretched across my legs watching a movie. They weren't happy about having to move.

"Hi," I said as Marcus stepped into the porch and knocked the snow off his boots.

"I saw your light on. It's not too late, is it?" he said, leaning down to kiss me. The man could kiss. I tended to forget where I was and what I was doing when his mouth was on mine. I hoped the day never came when that didn't happen.

I smiled up at him and then remembered that he'd asked me a question. "No. We were just watching a movie on TV," I said, pushing my hair back off my face.

Marcus followed me into the kitchen. He draped his jacket on the back of a chair and then sat down. I was wearing a pair of old stretched-out sweatpants, heavy woolen socks and a baggy sweatshirt, and my hair was pulled back into a messy ponytail. I felt self-conscious for a moment. Then I remembered that Marcus had seen me covered in mud when the embankment behind the carriage house collapsed, and when I was half-frozen with a mild case of hypothermia, wandering the woods with a bleeding arm wearing only long underwear after making it out of a cabin just before the building exploded.

"Hi, guys," he said.

I realized he was talking to Owen and Hercules, who were looking around the living room doorway.

"Have you had any supper?" I asked, leaning my hip against the table.

He pulled both hands through his hair. "I had three cups of coffee and some beef jerky."

"That's not supper."

I heard a meow of objection from the doorway. "No, beef jerky is not supper, Owen," I said. I kissed the top of Marcus's head. "I'll warm you up some stew."

He reached for my hand as I moved past him. "You don't have to do that."

I smiled. "I know."

I got the stew out of the refrigerator, put a bowl of it in the microwave and poured Marcus a glass of milk. When I turned around he had a couple of "friends" sitting next to his chair.

"I said I would warm up some stew for Marcus, not you two," I said.

In perfect synchronization both cats leaned their heads to the right. Marcus noticed and did the same thing so all three of them were in their most adorable poses.

I leaned down toward the cats. "Don't encourage him," I stage-whispered.

Behind me Marcus laughed.

Once his supper was hot, I made myself a cup of hot chocolate and joined him at the table. Owen had a dab of gravy on his whiskers and I caught Hercules licking his lips, so I knew Marcus had snuck the two of them a bit of chicken and maybe part of a dumpling from his dish.

I folded my fingers around my cup and watched

Marcus eat for a minute. "You didn't find anything in Olivia's kitchen, did you?" I asked. "Or am I asking a question you can't answer?"

He set his fork down. "No, we didn't. And she insists she didn't put nuts of any kind in the chocolates she made for your party because of her own allergy."

"That was why she reacted to the chocolate that she ate at the theater."

Marcus frowned at me.

"Cashews and pistachios are in the same family."

"I didn't know that," he said.

I knew he'd file that little piece of information away in his head somewhere. It was like that with everything he learned.

He picked up his fork again. "Well, there were no pistachios in the kitchen where the chocolates were made, or any nuts, for that matter, or in her house, either, and she gave us permission to search both places."

I leaned over, grabbed the container of marshmallows from the counter and dropped two into my cup. "Not the kind of thing someone would be likely to do if they had something to hide," I said. "Did you talk to Georgia and Earl?"

"Uh-huh. Neither one of them uses nuts in anything."

"According to Abigail, Georgia makes anything with nuts at Fern's." I leaned back in my chair with my mug and took a long drink. "I don't think

I told you. Abigail helped pack the chocolate boxes."

Marcus finished half a dumpling before he answered, "I know. I talked to her and to Nic Sutton, who made the boxes."

"I wish people could have taken them home," I said.

"I'm sorry about that," he said.

I smiled at him. "It's okay."

My cup was empty, so I got up to make another cup of hot chocolate. I knew where the other half of the dumpling would go as soon as my back was turned. I poured more milk into my cup along with a big spoonful of the dark chocolate cocoa mix I'd gotten at the Farmers' Market and put the whole thing in the microwave. When I did turn back around, Owen was licking his lips, Hercules was washing his face and Marcus was spooning a carrot out of his bowl. It was cute how they actually thought they were fooling me.

I leaned against the counter while I waited for the milk to heat. "So the nuts weren't in anything Eric served or even with the coffee or the tea?" I asked.

Marcus reached for his glass. "No. We checked the kitchen at both places. Nothing."

"Wait a minute," I said slowly, turning to get my drink from the microwave. "You didn't actually say the nuts weren't in the chocolates. You said there didn't seem to be any way Olivia *could* have put them in."

Marcus looked at me, just the tiny hint of a smile flickering across his face. "You're right, that is what I said."

I sat down across from him again with my cup and the marshmallows. "So? What haven't you told me?"

He swiped a hand over his neck. At his feet both cats seemed to be listening intently. "All three of the chocolates in the box that Dana Chapman had were coated with pistachio oil. None of the other boxes that have been sampled had anything on the chocolates inside."

There was one piece of chicken left in his bowl. He pulled it apart with his fork and leaned over to give half to each cat, not even trying to hide what he was doing.

"So that's how you know somebody meant to kill Dana Chapman?"

Marcus nodded, wiping his fingers on his napkin. "Yes. I'm not telling you anything that won't be common knowledge in a few hours. In fact, maybe it already is."

He started to get to his feet and I stood up instead, reaching for his dishes with one hand and putting the other on his shoulder to tell him to stay put.

"The paper?" I asked. The *Mayville Heights Chronicle* was one of the few smaller newspapers in the state whose readership was actually on the rise.

"Yeah. Everywhere we went, one of Bridget's reporters was right behind us." He exhaled loudly.

"Sometimes I think it's impossible to keep anything secret in this town."

Dayna Chapman had been murdered. Murdered, just a few hours after she'd arrived back in town. Why, and by whom?

Maybe it was impossible to keep some things secret, but clearly not everything.

10

On Sunday, I caught up on all the chores I'd let go during the week and talked to my parents in Boston. I told them what had happened with the fundraiser and they were sympathetic, which made me feel better.

"I'll look back through my files and see what we've done for fundraisers over the years at the school," my mother promised. "If I come across any ideas that might work for you, I'll let you know."

She went on to tell me that her laptop was being repaired—something wrong with the space bar—again—probably having to do with tea or cheesecake was my guess. So I didn't tell her it looked as though Dayna Chapman's death hadn't been an accident. Mom normally read the *Chronicle* online, but without her computer she wouldn't be doing that, which bought me a few days before I had to tell her I was connected with a murder.

Again.

After lunch I made stinky crackers for Owen

and Hercules, and a pan of date squares for Rebecca and me to have with our tea.

When Rebecca arrived, she spent several minutes talking to the boys, who loved to see her even when she wasn't bringing them treats. Rebecca actually had conversations with the cats and didn't seem to think there was anything odd about it.

Even though there was no paper on Sunday, the news about Dayna Chapman's death was already circulating. Rebecca confirmed what little I'd learned from Burtis.

Dana had originally come to Mayville Heights on vacation with her parents. The only thing she'd seemed to like was Burtis. Her parents hadn't shared that enthusiasm. Dana had run away, coming back to Mayville Heights as soon as she was back home, and she and Burtis were quickly married.

No one was surprised that the marriage didn't last, but it seemed that many people were surprised it lasted as long as it did.

"And she never came back to visit?" I asked Rebecca.

"No," she said, adding a little sugar to her tea. "The boys didn't really spend a lot of time with her." She pressed her lips together for a moment. "Some people don't have what it takes to be a parent."

That was the closest to criticism I knew I'd hear from Rebecca. I sent her home with two date squares and a reminder about our Friday trip to Red Wing.

*   *   *

Ruby was waiting for me Monday morning as I pulled into the parking lot behind River Arts. I backed into Maggie's parking spot behind the former school, the way I usually did if I was there for some reason and she wasn't.

Ruby's collection of Christmas ornaments was packed in two wooden boxes sitting at one end of the big worktable in the middle of her top-floor art studio.

"Ruby, I can't take all of them," I said.

"Sure you can," she said with a smile. "I told you we're not using them at the store this year, and I have a collection that belonged to my grandmother that I use on my tree at home." She laid a hand on top of the closest crate. "There's a list inside both boxes so you'll have an idea of what there is. I'm warning you. There are a lot of different Santas."

"That's okay with me," I said. "I like Santa. I promise I'll take good care of them."

I noticed that the newspaper was spread over the other end of the long worktable. Ruby noticed me noticing.

"Dayna Chapman's death wasn't an accident," she said.

I shook my head. "It doesn't look like it."

She sighed softly, looked away out through the tall windows and then back at me again. "You didn't know my grandfather, Kathleen," she said, "and I don't exactly know how to describe him to you, except to say he had a flint-hard streak of ruthlessness in him."

I nodded, not exactly sure where the conversation was going.

"You know that Burtis worked for him."

"I do," I said.

She fiddled with the stack of bracelets on her left arm. "And you've probably heard the stories that Burtis took over part of my grandfather's business."

I nodded again.

Ruby stuffed her hands in the pockets of her jeans and scraped one sneakered foot on the floor. "A lot of people would tell you that Idris Blackthorne was a criminal, and I guess if you go by a strict definition of right and wrong, black and white, he was."

"In my experience the world isn't always black and white," I said.

That got me a smile and a slight nod. "As long as you played it straight and fair with my grandfather, you wouldn't have any problems. But if you lied to him or tried to cheat him, you had an enemy for the rest of your life."

It occurred to me that minus the illegal businesses, Idris Blackthorne sounded a lot like my mother.

"Burtis was friends with my grandfather until the day he died. In some ways he's like family."

"I don't think Burtis had anything to do with Dayna's death, either," I said.

Ruby's shoulders seemed to relax just a little. "I was hoping you'd say that," she said. "You know everyone isn't going to feel that way."

"I know," I said. "I also know that no matter what Burtis does for a living, fundamentally he has a lot of integrity."

She exhaled slowly. "You know how I told you I'd seen Brady having some kind of heated conversation with Dayna at the fundraiser?"

I nodded.

She crossed her arms over her chest, almost as though she was hugging herself. "I was worried about the backdrop. Afraid it wouldn't look good or hang right, so I kept checking on it in the beginning." She gave me a sheepish look. "I also saw— and heard—*Burtis* and Dayna. And they were fighting."

I studied her face. "You didn't say anything before." This just confirmed what Roma had told me.

She shook her head. "I didn't. Dayna is—was— Burtis's ex-wife. They fight and the next thing you know, she's dead. You know what people would think." She gave a slight shrug. "I know what it's like to be suspected of something you didn't do."

"I don't think it means anything," I said, jiggling my keys in my jacket pocket. "Burtis and Dana used to be married and she hadn't been back here in a long, long time. They probably had more than one thing to argue about."

Ruby shifted uncomfortably from one foot to the other. "I didn't hear much of what they were saying to each other, but I did hear Burtis say, 'It would be better if you were just dead.'"

I swallowed, hoping my face wasn't giving away the little pulse of anxiety I suddenly felt. "That doesn't mean he killed her, Ruby," I said. "When I was in sixth grade, Kevin Monaghan snuck into the girls' locker room, swiped my bra from my locker and draped it over the trophy case just outside the gym doors. I chased him down the hall, across the teachers' parking lot and onto the track."

I could still remember the mix of embarrassment and fury that had propelled my legs. "I was yelling that when I caught him I was going to drag him into the girls' washroom, stick his head in a toilet and flush until he drowned."

Ruby laughed. "Would you believe I said the same thing to Larry Taylor? I think we were in seventh grade, though. And substitute underwear for bra and flagpole for trophy case."

I shook my head. "Boys going through puberty really are an alien species," I said. "My long-winded point is you said it but you didn't actually do it."

She gave an offhand shrug. "Only because Agatha stopped me after the second flush."

I exhaled loudly. "Okay, bad example to make my point. But it's still valid—more or less. Most of us say things like I'm going to flush your head until you drown, or I wish you were dead, but we don't really mean it and we don't follow through."

Ruby nodded. "I get it, Kathleen. I really do. But what do I do if Marcus or Hope Lind asks me what I saw and heard the night of the fundraiser?"

"You tell them the truth," I said. "I know you and Marcus have had your issues, but he isn't going to jump to conclusions and neither is Detective Lind."

"Okay," she said. She smiled. "Thanks."

"I'd better get to the library," I said. I reached for one of the boxes and Ruby grabbed the other.

I noticed then that Ruby had one of the little chocolate boxes from the fundraiser sitting on her worktable. She followed my gaze. "There aren't any chocolates in it. It's one of Nic's prototypes. He asked for my opinion when he was working on the design."

It occurred to me that I knew nothing about Nicolas Sutton. I remembered that I'd seen him tweaking the way the little boxes had been arranged on one of the serving trays. Could he have tampered with the chocolates? Why would he?

"I didn't know the two of you were friends," I said as we started down the hall to the stairs.

"We're not, really," she said. "I just like his work. And we're both a little eclectic in our art. Nic's a found metal artist. He plays with paper a little—well, you know about that—and does some stuff with photography."

"How did he end up in Mayville Heights?"

Ruby stopped at the head of the stairs. "Why are you asking?"

"Curiosity," I said with a shrug. At least that was true. "Those boxes he made. I've never seen such detailed work with paper before."

"Yeah, he's really good," Ruby said as we started down the steps. "Maggie wants him to do some workshops when we get the space set up at the store." She shifted the box in her arms, balancing it on her hip. "I know he was living in Minneapolis. I don't know if that's home or not. He said he had some personal stuff and he wanted a new start."

"Mayville Heights is a good place for that," I said with a smile.

"So, things are good with you and Marcus?" she asked.

I nodded and I couldn't help smiling.

She smiled back at me. "Well, I think you're good for him. You know, my grandmother used to say, 'There's a cover for every pot.' Of course, then she'd say, 'But if you don't have a cover, you can use a big plate.'" Ruby laughed, her pigtails bobbing. "I have no idea what that means."

I grinned back at her. "Me either."

We put the boxes on the front seat of the truck and I thanked her again.

"I'll see you at class tomorrow night," she said.

At least we could start decorating the building for the holidays, I thought as I drove over to the library. I hadn't really found out anything about Nic Sutton and I realized how far-fetched it would be that he knew Dayna, had ended up in Mayville Heights and then had killed her.

I was grasping at straws because I really didn't know what else to do.

11

Marcus called about nine thirty. "Can you take a break in about half an hour?" he asked.

Mary and I were walking around the main floor of the building trying to decide on the best places for the new Christmas tree.

"I can," I said. "Are you coming over?"

"I need to ask you a few more questions about Thursday night," he said.

"I'll make a new pot of coffee."

"You two are adorable," Mary said after I'd hung up.

I made a face at her.

Marcus showed up exactly at ten o'clock, carrying two white cardboard boxes that I knew had come from Eric's. He was wearing his heavy dark blue hooded parka and there were a few snowflakes dusting his dark hair.

He handed me the smaller of the two and took the other one over to Mary at the circulation desk. "Happy National Pastry Day," he said.

Mary beamed at him and took the box. "Thank you. Happy National Pastry Day to you, too," she said.

I gestured at the second-floor stairs. "We'll be in my office," I said.

"What's in the box you gave Mary?" I asked once we were upstairs.

"The same thing that's in the box you're holding."

I used a fingernail to slit the tape on the edge, lifted the lid and breathed in the scent of cranberries and lemon. The box held two of Eric's cranberry lemon scones. Since I was wearing heels I didn't have to stand on tiptoe to kiss his cheek. "Thank you," I said. "And thank you on behalf of my staff."

He smiled. "You're both welcome."

"You made up National Pastry Day, didn't you?" I said.

He shrugged off his jacket and shook his head. "No, I didn't. Ask Eric. He's the one who told me it was National Pastry Day today." He hung the parka on the back of the closest chair. "I can't vouch for whether he made it up, though."

I got coffee for both of us from the staff room and we settled in the two chairs in front of my desk. "So, what did you want to ask me?" I said. His wavy dark hair was a bit overdue for a cut and I thought about threading my fingers in it and pulling him over for a kiss. *Pay attention*, I told myself sternly.

Marcus leaned back in his chair and stretched out his long legs. My train of thought almost got derailed again.

"First of all, tell me again what Dayna said to you."

I took a deep breath. "She said 'live.' I told her she was going to be okay. She said 'package,' which I think meant the box of chocolates. Then she stopped breathing."

He nodded. "The fundraiser was almost completely sold out in advance?"

I reached for one of the two scones. "There were maybe a dozen or so tickets left and Abigail had taken those."

"Did you know she'd sold them all?"

"No. Not until we got to the theater and I talked to her. On Thursday afternoon she picked up the chocolate boxes from Olivia, took them over to the Stratton and then went home to get ready, as far as I know. I'm guessing that Dayna happened to catch her at the theater. That was just luck." *Bad luck,* I added silently

I broke the end off my scone, popped it in my mouth and made a little grunt of happiness. I had a second bite and hoped Marcus didn't notice me licking the crumbs off my thumb.

He took a sip of his coffee. "Who decided when to hand the chocolates out to people?"

"I did," I said. "Everett was going to welcome everyone and make his pitch for donations. Then I was going to talk a bit about Reading Buddies. I thought if everyone had a little gift in their hand, it might put people in a giving mood."

He gave a slight nod. "So Taylor King and Mariah Taylor handed out the boxes."

I nodded over my coffee cup. "Yes, along with Olivia herself."

"Could you see Dayna?" He broke the end off his own scone and ate it.

"Uh-huh. She was just a table away from where I was standing, talking to Burtis and Lita." In my mind I could see the stage at the Stratton, filled with people. I could hear the jazz quartet and people talking.

"Did you see Dayna actually take a box?" Marcus asked.

In my mind I could see Olivia offering the tray and Burtis handing one tiny chocolate box to Lita and then giving the other one to Dayna.

"Kathleen?" Marcus was looking at me, eyes narrowed in speculation.

I took a deep breath. "Olivia offered the tray, but Dayna didn't take a box. Burtis handed one to her."

He gave another slight nod. "Then what happened?" He wasn't surprised.

"You already knew Burtis gave her the box."

"Yes," he said. He ate the last piece of his scone and followed it with a long drink of coffee.

"You talked to Burtis?"

He crumpled his napkin and dropped it in the garbage can. "I've talked to a lot of people—including Burtis."

"They had an argument—a difference of opinion, something—at the party, not long before Dayna had the chocolate that killed her," I said. I ate another bite of my scone and waited to see what Marcus would say.

What he said was "I know."

I brushed crumbs off my dark skirt. "Burtis told you himself." Before Marcus could say anything I held up one hand. "Can we just skip the part where you say, 'I can't tell you that,' and then I say, 'That's the same as a yes'?"

That got me the hint of a smile. "Okay," he said.

"Burtis didn't kill his ex-wife."

He set his cup on my desk. "Right now all we're trying to do is put together what happened on Thursday night. No one is focusing on Burtis, or anyone else, for that matter. Just the facts."

I shifted in my chair so I was facing him a little more directly. "Burtis wouldn't kill anyone," I said. "To me, that's a fact."

"You like him," Marcus said.

I nodded. "Yes. He's my friend. No different from Oren or Harry or Everett."

I leaned on the arm of the chair. "Seriously, Marcus, if Burtis was going to kill someone, do you see him doing it with a chocolate? A two-by-four, maybe. Or a sledgehammer. But doctoring a chocolate? There's too much subterfuge involved. It's way too indirect. That's not Burtis."

"He has had a couple of brushes with the law in the past," Marcus said, rubbing his thumb around the rim of his cup.

"I doubt either one of them had anything to do with someone's death," I said. "Anyway, what reason would he have had for killing Dayna? She'd been out of his life for more than twenty years."

He raked a hand back through his hair and looked away, out my office window, just a bit too soon. I stopped myself from putting my hand on his leg.

"Marcus, what aren't you saying?" I asked. "You know something about Burtis. More than just him arguing with Dayna and handing her that box of chocolates."

In the past we would have argued and he would have gotten up and left. Instead, he got to his feet and I did the same.

"This stays between us," he said, reaching out to brush a strand of hair back off my face. "It'll hit the paper tomorrow because it seems like Bridget has all the same sources we do."

"I won't say anything," I said.

Marcus folded his arms over his midsection and shrugged. "Burtis and Dayna Chapman were still legally married."

12

Marcus had to get back to the police station. He kissed my cheek and I repeated my promise to keep what he'd just told me to myself. The fact that Burtis and Dayna had still been married when she died didn't change my belief that Burtis had had nothing to do Dayna's death, but I realized it might matter to other people.

Harry Junior came in just after one o'clock. "Thank you for putting the sand down," I said, walking over to meet him by the main doors.

"You're welcome," he said, pulling off his heavy gloves. "I'm going to keep on that for a while. Thorsten has enough on his plate. There's a leak in the roof at the community center."

"Again?" I exhaled loudly. "He just got the last one patched." The community center roof was leakier than a wooden rowboat that had been left out all winter.

"Thanks for getting your book expert to look at

those old readers," Harry said. "We can use the money. I think there's more patch up there than there is original roof. Thorsten has someone coming to take a look tomorrow." He shook his head. "The whole building needs work. It's older than I am."

"Wow, that is old," I said, completely deadpan.

One eyebrow went up. "Better be careful, Kathleen, or I might just recommend you to head up the committee to renovate the community center."

"Do we have a committee to renovate the community center?" I asked.

Harry scratched his stubbled chin. "No. But I think we're going to need one." He gave his head a shake. "But that's not why I stopped in. The old man sent me to invite you to dinner tonight. I'm sorry about the short notice."

The only plans I had were dinner with Owen and Hercules and maybe a load or two of laundry after that. The short notice didn't really matter.

"He's been chewing on something all weekend," Harry said, rolling his eyes. "I don't have a clue about what's on his mind. I'm pretty sure he wants to talk to you. He sure as hell isn't interested in talking to me."

"I'd love to come," I said. "What can I bring?"

"Just yourself," he said. "About six o'clock."

"I'll be there." I smiled at him. "Are you joining us?"

Harry gave a snort of laughter. "Hard to tell, Kathleen. So far you're the only one who's been invited."

I showed Harry where Mary and I had decided to put the second tree and told him about Ruby's ornaments.

"I should be able to bring the tree first thing tomorrow," he said.

"Okay, we'll have the space ready," I said.

The rest of the afternoon was quiet, even for a Monday, which gave Mary and me time to rearrange things and bring the big tree stand up from the library basement.

Clouds were moving in over the water as I drove up the hill and my left wrist was aching, both signs that we were going to get some snow. Hercules was waiting for me on the bench in the back porch when I got home.

"This is a nice surprise," I said, leaning over to scoop him up. Not only did he dislike snow and rain, but he wasn't that crazy about cold, either.

"I'm home," I called when I stepped into the kitchen. I waited. No answering meow from Owen. "Either he didn't hear me or he's doing something he's not supposed to be doing," I said to Hercules as I set him down on the floor. I hung up my coat and set my hat and gloves by the heat. There was still no sign of Owen.

Herc stretched and followed me upstairs. I changed into jeans and a sweater and pulled my hair back into a ponytail.

"Merow?" he said, head cocked to one side as though he was asking a question.

"I'm going out for supper."

He seemed to consider my words for a moment

and then he turned and headed for the door. I knew what that meant.

"You can't come with me," I called after him. "I'm going out to the Taylors'."

He stopped in his tracks and made a huffy sound in the back of his throat.

I walked over to him. "Do you really see yourself having dinner with Boris?" I asked.

He looked up at me with half-lidded eyes. "Murrr," he grumbled.

"Yes, I know Boris is a dog," I said. "But that's not really his fault."

Hercules didn't look convinced.

"C'mon, let's go down to the kitchen and you can test the new batch of stinky crackers."

That seemed to cheer him up immensely and he headed for the stairs.

We found Owen in the kitchen, head almost on the floor as he peered under the refrigerator.

"What are you doing?" I asked.

He looked over his shoulder at me and gave a sharp meow.

"Don't tell me there are chicken parts under the fridge again?" I said. I got down on my hands and knees so I could look for myself. Just under the edge of the refrigerator, I could see a brilliant yellow feather.

"Give me a minute," I said, getting to my feet. I got my wooden mixing spoon, got back on the floor again and batted out a small yellow chicken on the first pass.

"Keep those things away from the refrigerator,"

I warned. "One of these days one is going to get stuck under there, beyond the reach of this spoon, and I'm not moving this great big refrigerator to get it."

Owen sniffed the catnip chicken suspiciously, then picked it up in his mouth. He looked at me, golden eyes narrowed, glared at his brother and stalked off to the living room.

Hercules watched him go and then shifted his attention to his bowl.

"Yes, I know I promised you stinky crackers," I said. I got fresh water for both cats, gave Herc a stack of the sardine crackers and left a little pile in Owen's dish.

"I won't be late," I said to Hercules. He was already into the crackers and all I got was a low murp, which might have been more about his enthusiasm for the crackers than an acknowledgment that he'd heard me—or even cared.

I laced up my low, heavy-treaded snow boots, pulled on my blue jacket with the hood and grabbed my purse, keys and gloves. I'd stopped and bought a couple of tallboys on the way home. As far as I knew, Harrison's doctor allowed him to have the occasional drink. I wasn't sure about Harry Junior, though. I could end up in the doghouse with him.

Harrison must have been watching for me, because he was waiting by the back door of his little house when I got out of the truck.

I stomped the snow off my boots, stepped inside and gave him a hug. "You look good," I said, stepping back to check him out.

As always, to me he looked like Santa Claus. The first time I'd met Harrison was when I discovered him in my backyard with Owen and Hercules while his son was mowing the lawn. For a moment I'd thought St. Nick was holding court in my blue Adirondack chair. Actually, Harry Senior reminded me of my favorite incarnation of Santa Claus, Edmund Gwenn in *Miracle on 34th Street*. Harrison had the same fluffy beard and the same warm gleam in his eyes.

Those eyes were smiling at me now.

"And if I looked like a steaming pile of horse manure, would you tell me?" he asked.

I made a face and shook my head. "No, but I probably wouldn't stand so close to you."

He laughed. The old man might have been in his eighties, but his laugh was deep and strong.

I felt a wet nose nudge my hand. I turned to see Boris beside me, looking up with his chocolaty velvet eyes.

"Hello, boy," I said, bending over to scratch behind his ears.

"Let me take your coat," Harrison said. He touched the dog's back. "Give Kathleen a minute to take off her things and catch her breath."

Boris immediately sat down. I gave Harry my jacket and he hung it over a hook by the back door. I put my purse over the top, stepped out of my boots and handed over the brown paper bag holding the two tallboys.

"You didn't have to bring anything," he said.

I smiled. "I know."

He unfolded the top of the bag and looked inside. Then he grinned at me. "Can't say I'm sorry you did, though."

"I'm not going to be in trouble with Harry, am I?" I asked as we stepped into the kitchen.

"That depends," a voice said behind me.

I turned to see Harry Junior standing by the woodstove.

"What did you do?" he asked.

"Nothing that's any of your business," his father said.

"How many tallboys are in that bag?" Harry asked me.

"You don't have to answer that, Kathleen," Harrison said as he moved toward the refrigerator.

I held up two fingers.

"Are you planning on sharing?" Harry asked his father.

"I might be," he said, setting the two cans inside his refrigerator. He turned around. "Then again, I might not."

I didn't even bother trying to stifle a smile.

Harrison made a shooing motion with one hand. "Take a seat," he said.

I sat down in the chair next to his, across from the fire burning and snapping in the woodstove. I couldn't help reaching one hand out to the flames. My hands had been cold all afternoon.

"Nothing's as warm as wood heat," Harrison said, easing down into his own chair.

I stuck out my other hand toward the fire.

"Cold hands?" he asked.

I nodded. "A little. Mary's making a pair of double-knit mittens for me. She says they'll keep my fingers warm."

Harrison nodded. "I have a pair of those. Hands are never cold when I wear them."

"That's because you wear them to church and you're so busy flirting one of your hands could be cut off with a chain saw and you wouldn't notice," his son said dryly.

"Ignore him, Kathleen," the old man said. "He's just jealous because he doesn't have a quarter of my appeal to the opposite sex."

"Oh, for heaven's sake," I heard Harry mutter.

Boris had come to sit beside me. He laid his chin on my knee and I began to scratch behind his ears. He gave an audible sigh and closed his eyes.

Harrison reached over and picked up an envelope that was on the small table beside his chair. I recognized the return address in a boxy black font in the upper left corner. It was from Henderson Holdings.

"Got this in the mail this morning," he said.

It had to be the refund for the fundraiser tickets. "Good," I said.

The old man gave me a look. "No, not good. Why in the name of all that's holy is Lita giving people their money back? I bought those tickets to help kids learn to read so they can go out and make something of themselves. Where I come from, when you have a fundraiser you don't give the money back. The end."

Boris lifted his head, looked over at Harrison for a moment and then went back to leaning on my leg again.

"Where I come from, when you don't deliver what you promised you give the money back. The end," I countered.

Out of the corner of my eye, I could see Harry Junior leaning back in his chair, an amused expression playing across his face.

"So what you're saying is you're not taking the check back?" Harrison had one hand on his cane and I half expected him to bang it on the floor to make his point.

"No, I'm not," I said.

To my surprise he smiled at me. "I guess I know you pretty well," he said. "So I pretty much knew that's what you'd say."

"Does that mean we're not going to argue about this?" I shifted my leg a little, which got me a look from the big German shepherd still leaning on me.

"It most decidedly does, seeing as how this envelope is empty." He waved it at me. "I took that check back down to Everett's office this afternoon and told him where to put it."

I glanced over at Harry, who had given up trying to stifle his smile.

"You're a sneaky old man." I mock-glared at Harrison.

"Guilty as charged," he agreed, struggling to get to his feet.

I made a move to stand up myself, but he waved me back down. "Sit," he said. "You're a guest."

He looked across at his son. "You're not."

The younger Taylor got to his feet. "Welcome to my world," he said softly as he passed me. The delicious aroma of apples, cinnamon and nutmeg filled the air as he opened the oven door and took a look inside.

"You're letting all the heat out," Harrison grumbled.

"Do I smell apple crisp?" I asked, leaning on the arm of my chair so I could see what they were doing.

"That you do," Harrison said, putting a blue glass pitcher of ice water on the table. "Mary Lowe's apple crisp." He smiled at me. "She likes me."

"That's because you flirt with her like the two of you are sixteen," Harry countered, using a kitchen towel to lift a heavy blue-and-white casserole dish out of the oven.

"Like I told you before, it's not my fault women find me irresistible," his father said, winking at me.

Harry just shook his head.

Harrison opened the fridge door again, studied the two cans of beer for a moment and then took them out and set them on the counter. He reached up into the cupboard next to the sink and lifted down two tall glasses.

"You don't have to use glasses on my account," I said.

"I'm not." He made a dismissive gesture with one hand. "None of us were born in a barn. And we've got perfectly good glasses. No reason not to use them."

He poured the beer into the glasses and set one at his place and one at his son's.

"Kathleen, my son needs a woman," the old man said as he moved around the table.

Harry's head came up and he looked over at his father.

"If I hadn't invited him over tonight, he would probably have had just a peanut butter sandwich for supper. When the kids are out he doesn't cook." He jerked his head in the direction of his son. "He thinks I don't know that."

Since I wasn't sure what to say, I didn't say anything.

"So do you have any suggestions?" the old man asked.

"I'll find my own woman, thank you very much," Harry said.

Harrison raised one eyebrow and gave me a conspiratorial grin. "We'll talk later," he said.

He looked over at the table. "If you want to wash up, looks like we're ready."

I gave Boris one last scratch. He made a soft noise that sounded a lot like a sigh.

"Go lie down," Harry said to the dog. He padded over and lay down next to the old man's chair, head on his paws.

I washed my hands at the sink and took the seat Harrison indicated at the table.

Over shepherd's pie and Mary's apple crisp—which was delicious, no surprise—we talked about the library and the problems with the roof at the community center. After Harry poured me a second cup of coffee, I leaned back in my chair, crossed my legs and fixed my gaze on the old man.

"So, why did you invite me to dinner?" I asked. "It wasn't just to tell me you'd already done an end run around me with that check."

"I can't just enjoy the pleasure of your company?" he said.

I folded one arm over my chest and behind me Harry Junior gave a quiet snort of disbelief.

I smiled. "You can," I said. "And I think you know I enjoy your company or else I would have said no to the invitation, but I also know when I'm being played like a five-string banjo."

Harrison laughed, which made his resemblance to Kris Kringle even more pronounced. "I figured you'd like to know more about Burtis and his ex-wife," he said.

I studied the old man. He might have been in his eighties, but he didn't miss anything. "Why do you think that?" I asked.

I wasn't going to admit he was right, even though he was. As I'd told Owen and Hercules, the Mayville Heights grapevine could be just as good a source of information as the Internet.

His expression grew serious. "Just because you and Marcus Gordon are keeping company doesn't mean you're going to sit around on your hands when your friends are in trouble." He studied my face for a moment. "Burtis Chapman is your friend, isn't he?" It was more of a challenge than a question.

That was really what it all hinged on. Was Burtis Chapman my friend? After a long moment I
nodded.

Harrison leaned against the back of his chair
and folded both his arms over his midsection, his
eyes fixed on my face. "Good," he said. "Then
you'd better get to work and find out who killed
his ex-wife before your fella arrests him."

13

We moved back to the chairs by the fire. Boris got up, stretched and padded out to the kitchen.

"So, what do you know about Burtis?" Harrison asked me.

I turned sideways toward him, pulling one leg up underneath me so I could see his face. "Not a lot," I said. "I know Burtis worked for Idris Blackthorne."

Harrison nodded. "The Chapmans didn't have a pot to piss in," he said. "Excuse my language. A pile of kids and not a lot of money. Burtis grew up poor and hard." He ran his fingers through his beard. "He quit school to work full-time for Idris and put food on the table for his younger brothers and sisters. That's not to say there weren't other jobs around here then—there were, good ones, but not if you didn't have an education."

I nodded.

"Everything Burtis has he worked for. I know

what people say, but most of his enterprises are legal."

Harry gave another snort.

"Well, close to," his father amended.

"Dayna came here with her parents, on vacation," I said.

"That's right." Harrison rubbed his hand absently over the chair arm. "She was seventeen. Pretty as all get out. Every teenage boy in town noticed her and every teenage girl wanted to run her out of town. You know how kids can be."

Boris wandered back into the room, nails clicking on the floor, and settled at the old man's feet, head against his legs. "I think the girl was smitten with Burtis the first moment she saw him, which was when she fell off the dock at the old marina and he fished her out of the water."

He narrowed his gaze at me. "Would it surprise you to know that Burtis wouldn't go out alone with her because she was just seventeen?"

I shook my head. "No, not really." As I'd told Maggie and Roma, Burtis seemed to follow his old code of ethics—like a knight during the crusades— or a Klingon warrior.

Harry Junior got to his feet, reached for my cup and inclined his head toward the kitchen—and the coffeepot—without saying a word.

I nodded. "Please," I said softly.

"It was late in the fall," Harrison continued, "right before Thanksgiving. Dayna's eighteenth birthday. She arrived in town on the bus and showed up where Burtis was working." He shrugged. "They were married four days later."

Harry handed me a fresh cup of coffee. "Thank you," I said. "I'm surprised. Burtis doesn't seem the type to be so impulsive."

"Probably the only time in his life he was," the younger Taylor said.

Harrison shifted again in his chair. Boris lifted his head and waited until the old man was settled again.

"They were happy. At least they looked like they were. Didn't last." He exhaled with a soft sigh. "After a time I think Dayna just got overwhelmed with the reality of bein' married. She had little kids, no friends or family, damn little money and a husband whose livelihood was a little sketchy. Not to mention parents who were pressuring her to come home."

I thought about what life must have been like for Dayna Chapman back then and felt a twinge of sympathy for her.

"One day she was just gone," Harrison said. "You can imagine the kind of loose talk that went around town."

I nodded.

"Burtis wouldn't talk about her and it wasn't long before people learned to stop fishing for information."

I took a drink, then balanced my cup on one knee. Harry made a good cup of coffee. "She never came back to see her children?" I asked.

Harrison smoothed a veined hand over his head. "Never. In the beginning Burtis took the boys to see her in the summer and a couple of times at Christmas, but pretty soon that stopped."

I took another sip of my coffee and saw a look pass between the two men.

"What aren't you telling me?" I asked.

Boris was asleep. Caught in a dream, he moved his back legs and made a low whining noise. With a bit of difficulty, Harrison leaned forward and patted the dog's back. The movement stopped. The dog sighed and settled back into sleep.

Harrison looked at me as he straightened up, and his mouth twisted to one side. His gaze moved to his son again.

"Dayna used to send gifts at Christmas and for the boys' birthdays. Dad's always been skeptical anything actually came from Dayna," Harry said, stretching his legs out in front of him.

I eyed the old man and after a moment his eyes met mine. "You think it was Burtis doing all that," I said.

He nodded and let out a soft sigh. "I may as well say it as think it. I do. Say whatever you want about the man, he's a damn good father."

Harry nodded his agreement. "He'd protect those kids with his life."

Harrison eyes locked with mine. "You can't fault a man for that," he said, and it seemed to me that there was a bit of a challenge in the words.

"No, you can't," I said.

"I don't want to see Burtis railroaded for something he didn't do."

I exhaled softly. "Neither do I."

Boris moved again then. His back feet scrambled as if he were chasing something and he yelped a couple of times.

Harrison leaned over again and gave the dog a couple more reassuring pats on the back. "He chases more things in his sleep than he does in real life," he said with a grin. "That reminds me, what about those two cats of yours? How are they?"

So we were changing the subject. "Spoiled," I said, smiling back at him. "I made sardine crackers for them yesterday and my house still smells like fish."

At the word "fish" Boris lifted his head, looked around and gave an enthusiastic bark. "Hush, Kathleen's not making treats for you," Harry said.

The dog's response was to drop his head down on his paws and look at me sadly. I thought about Owen doing the same thing. He and Boris had a few things in common.

I leaned over and stroked the top of the dog's head. "Next batch I'll send you some," I whispered. "I promise."

As if he knew what I'd said, he licked his lips.

I left shortly after that. Standing at the back door, I wrapped Harrison in a hug. "Thank you for supper and thank you for telling me about Burtis."

"My door's always open."

I smiled at him. "We're putting up another tree in the library tomorrow. Come and see it when you get the chance."

"I'll do that if someone will let me out of the house." His eyes darted sideways.

"That can probably be arranged," Harry said. "I'll be right back," he said to his father. "I'm just going to walk Kathleen to her truck."

We started across the side yard and I waited until I was sure we were out of earshot of the little house before I spoke. Harrison might have been over eighty, but his hearing was excellent.

"So, what did you want to tell me?" I said.

Harry looked at me and then he kicked a clump of snow across the yard. "What makes you think I have something I need to say to you?" he asked.

I pulled the hood of my jacket closer around my neck. "You were watching me on and off all night. Either you were struggling with whether you wanted to say something to me, or you were afraid I was going to steal the silver."

"Silver's locked up," he said, kicking another lump of snow that disintegrated when his boot hit it.

I stopped by the side of the truck. "So what is it?"

"I know it was one of the chocolates that killed Dayna Chapman."

I nodded. "It seems to be the worst-kept secret in town."

"Burtis handed Dana that box, Kathleen," Harry said. The words hung between us in the cold night air.

"I know. I saw him, too," I said.

Harry shifted uncomfortably from one foot to the other. "There's not that many years between Burtis and me. And we both had wives that decided they'd rather be anywhere else, so I get how he feels about his kids because I feel the same way."

I nodded, wondering what he was building up to.

"When he was young Burtis had this thing he'd do when he wanted to impress a girl. He'd pull a flower out from behind her ear. A little magic trick." Harry held out both hands. "A tulip, a rose, even a dandelion."

I saw his mouth twist sideways in a half smile.

"It worked every time." He scraped at a small chunk of ice with the toe of his heavy boot. "I think the old man's right. I think all those parcels and cards over the years for the boys that were supposed to be from their mother were really Burtis's doing. Not a whole lot different from surprising a pretty girl with a flower when you think about it."

I stuffed my hands in my pockets. "No, it's not."

"I can see why a man might not want his children to know that basically their mother hadn't really ever given a goddamn about them. And he might go to any lengths to keep them from finding out."

"Including kill her?" I asked.

Harry made a face. "Or make her sick enough to land her in the hospital."

I just couldn't see Burtis doing something like that. He was far more direct.

"I don't want to be thinking what I'm thinking, Kathleen," Harry said. "But it's kind of hard not to."

"I don't know how I can help you," I said.

Harry jammed his hands in his pockets. "You have a way of seeing past the things that don't matter. If you can see into the heart of this mess, then maybe you can keep some people from getting hurt who sure as hell don't deserve to be."

The conversation reminded me uncomfortably of the one I'd had with Harry when Agatha Shepherd died.

"Harry, I'm not the police," I said. I'd said that to him then, too.

He shrugged. "Maybe that's a good thing." He looked up at the night sky. "Looks like snow's coming," he said. He smiled. "Drive safely."

I nodded. "I will. Good night."

I got in the truck, started it and headed out the driveway. In the rearview mirror I could see Harry still standing in the yard.

I thought about what he'd told me as I drove home.

Had Dana abandoned her children even more than anyone knew? Had Burtis used a little misdirection and subterfuge to keep them from finding out?

With all her faults I'd never doubted the depth and ferocity of my mother's love for me or Sara and Ethan. I couldn't imagine what it would feel like to discover it was all a lie.

All I had was speculation, I reminded myself. And just because Burtis could seemingly make a flower appear from behind a young girl's ear didn't mean he could switch one chocolate box for another.

One thing that wasn't speculation was Burtis's love for his kids. But just how far would he go to protect them?

14

I'd had more coffee than I should have, so when I got home I made myself a cup of hot chocolate and sat at the table with it. After a moment I felt a cat wind around my leg. I looked down to see Owen's furry face looking up at me.

"Hi," I said.

He murped a hello in return.

I turned my mug in a slow circle on the table. "Burtis knows how to pull a quarter from behind your ear. Or a dandelion."

Owen looked blankly at me.

"Or in theory a little box of chocolates."

He still didn't see why that piece of information was important.

I thought about what I'd just said, that in theory Burtis could have switched the box of chocolates that he'd taken from Olivia's tray with another box that held three chocolates coated with pistachio oil.

"All he would have had to do was find out

Dayna was going to be at the fundraiser, then break into the office at the Stratton, steal one of the boxes of chocolates and put pistachio oil on them."

Even a small gray cat could see how preposterous that was.

I sighed. "Okay, that sounds stupid when I say it out loud."

Owen murmured his agreement, then jumped up onto my lap and nuzzled my chin to show he'd meant no offense.

I leaned back in the chair and stroked his fur. "This is crazy," I said. "I'm tilting at windmills."

He gave me a quizzical look.

"Tilting at windmills. Don Quixote."

Owen's expression didn't change.

"He's a character in a Spanish novel. I'll read it to you sometime," I said.

All that got me was an unenthusiastic "Mrrr."

I drank the last of my hot chocolate and stretched. Owen looked over at the counter and then back at me. That was his subtle way of saying, "How about a treat?"

"You get too many treats," I said.

He blinked. In Owen's world there was no such thing as too many treats.

"You need to get down," I told him, pointing at the floor. "I want to check my e-mail. Lise said she'd send me some photos. The band was playing in a club downtown over the weekend."

Lise was my best friend in Boston. My little brother's band, The Flaming Gerbils, was developing a bit of a following in the Boston area, helped along by a music video they'd made for their song "In a Million Other Worlds."

Lise's husband was a musician, a jazz guitarist, not grunge rock like the Gerbils, and Lise had been photographing his performances for years. She'd gone to see Ethan and his buddies on Saturday night and had promised to send me some photos.

Owen made grumbling noises, but he jumped down to the floor. I got my briefcase and set my laptop on the table.

I turned on the computer and Lise's e-mail pinged in my in-box. At the same time Owen launched himself back onto my lap. He put one paw on the edge of the table and studied the screen as I scrolled through the photographs.

They were fantastic.

"Look at this one," I said to Owen, touching the screen. Lise had caught Ethan in midleap onstage. I grinned as the cat leaned in, as though he actually was trying to take a closer look at the image.

My favorite shot of the nine photos was the last one, of Ethan again, seated on a stool with his guitar. I knew that had to have been during "In a Million Other Worlds." It was the only slow song the band did.

I leaned against the back of the chair, one hand on Owen, who still seemed to be studying the screen, as a wave of homesickness rolled over me. I was happy with my decision to stay in Mayville Heights. It really did feel like home, and people like Rebecca, Maggie and the Taylors felt like another family. But I missed Boston: Ethan and Sara, my mom and dad, Lise. We e-mailed, we talked on the phone, we texted—Sara and I had managed to Skype a couple of times. But I missed the little things—lunch with Lise, shopping with Sara, going to see Ethan and the band perform, watching my parents rehearse. I reminded myself that the twins were away from Boston now more than they were there, and even my mother had spent several weeks in Los Angeles during the fall on the soap the *Wild and the Wonderful*. No matter where my family was, it was hard to be away from them.

I thought about Dayna and what Harry had told me about his father's suspicion that the cards and parcels from her to her children had really been orchestrated by Burtis. Could that really be true? I didn't understand why she hadn't come back to see her children. Where she had gone and what had she done after she left Mayville Heights all those years ago?

Owen seemed to have gotten tired of looking at Lise's photos. He put a paw on the keyboard.

"Don't do that," I warned.

Owen hit another key and suddenly Google was open. He turned and looked expectantly at me. I had said I was going to see what I could find about Burtis's ex-wife.

What I found was nothing.

"How can someone leave no digital trail?" I said to Owen.

His response was to poke at the keyboard again, adding three a's and a q to Dayna Chapman's name.

"Owen," I started. Then I realized what the problem was: I was spelling her name wrong.

I kissed the top of his head. "You're a genius," I said.

He dipped his head in a display of *very* false modesty.

I'd been spelling Dayna Chapman's name without the y. It was with Dayna Morretti—y—and her maiden name that I struck pay dirt.

Six years previous Dayna had been a witness to a robbery at a Minneapolis pawnshop that had left the owner with a life-changing brain injury. I scrolled down through the online newspaper article, stopping when I got to the third paragraph. The pawnshop owner's name was Sutton. Nicolas Sutton Sr.

Owen and I looked at each other. It had to be Nic's father. It was just too big a coincidence.

15

Marcus and I had cat feeding duty out at Wisteria Hill in the morning. Roma had taken a couple of days off to go meet Eddie on the road. Marcus probably already knew about the robbery and Nic Sutton's connection—even indirectly—to Dayna, but I wanted to tell him what I'd learned.

It was just getting light when Marcus's SUV pulled into the driveway. I climbed into the front seat and leaned over to kiss him before I fastened my seat belt.

"I like this," I said as he backed out of the driveway.

"The bracing cold or going to feed the cats when it's still dark?" he asked. He was wearing his old navy parka and a red knit hat. He was as cute as a bug's ear, to use Mary's expression.

"Neither," I said, feeling my cheeks get warm. "I just meant that I like being able to kiss you." I suddenly felt awkward and tongue-tied. "I like that we're . . . us." I swallowed and looked out the windshield. I sounded like a love-struck teenager.

"You could have gotten in and kissed me any time you wanted to before we were us," Marcus said. "I wouldn't have minded."

I glanced over and saw his lips twitch as he tried and failed to hold back a smile. "You would have thought I was trying to get information out of you about one of your cases," I said.

We headed up the hill toward Wisteria Hill. "Wasn't that why you were always getting me coffee?" he asked, darting a quick sideways glance in my direction.

"No!" I said, a little more hotly than I'd meant to. Did he really believe that?

"I got you coffee because . . . because the first time you showed up to question me at the library, I'd just made a pot for myself. It would have been rude not to offer you a cup."

"Okay, so the first time was good manners. What about all the other times?"

"I wanted to talk to you."

"See?" he said, eyebrows disappearing under his red hat. "You were trying to get information out of me with a cup of coffee."

"You're so dense," I said softly, jiggling Roma's keys in one hand.

He looked confused. "About what?"

I felt my face get warm again. "I brought you coffee or made you coffee because I wanted an ex-

cuse to be where you were." It was the first time
I'd admitted it to anyone, let alone myself.

Marcus kept his eyes straight ahead, but he
took one hand off the steering wheel for a moment, felt for my hand and gave it a squeeze.

"I always drank slowly," he said after a minute
or so of silence.

I didn't say a thing, but he couldn't have missed
the grin that spread across my face.

Marcus turned up the long driveway and
parked the SUV in the cleared area by the house. I
used the key Roma had given me to get the cats'
dishes, food and water. Marcus took the water
jugs and the bag with the cans of cat food. I carried the dishes.

Harry had cleared a wide path from the driveway to the carriage house. As we headed around
to the door, I told Marcus about Smokey. Roma
had managed to entice him into the cage with
some shredded chicken. He had a long gash on his
leg that had gotten infected.

"I told Roma I'd stop by the clinic and check on
him," I said as Marcus held the side door open
and I ducked under his arm to slip inside. "She
said he was sleeping a lot. I thought it might help
to hear a voice he recognizes, at least while she's
away." I gave a little shrug. "It's silly, isn't it?"

He shook his head. "No, it's not. I think it's kind."

We put out the food and water and retreated to
the door the way we always did. Instead of leaning against the rough wood of the old building, I
leaned against Marcus and he wrapped his arms

around me. If there was somewhere better to be, at that moment I couldn't think of where it was.

After a minute Lucy poked her head out, caught sight of us and headed purposefully in our direction. I slipped out from under Marcus's arms and took a couple of steps away from him. Lucy stopped maybe four feet away from me. I knew she wouldn't come any closer and I didn't try to move any nearer to her.

She looked up at me and meowed. Behind her I could see the other five cats peeking out from where their shelters were. No one would head over to eat until Lucy did.

"Smokey's all right," I said. "He has an infection in his leg, but Roma is taking care of him."

I felt certain she understood. I only ever talked to Lucy when Marcus was around. I knew he didn't believe the small cat knew what I was saying. But even he couldn't explain why Lucy seemed to prefer me to all the rest of Roma's volunteers.

Lucy meowed again and then turned and headed to the feeding station. I moved back to Marcus and leaned against his side. He wrapped one arm around my waist and we watched the cats eating, looking for any sign of illness or injury. They all looked fine. When they'd finished eating and retreated to their shelters, we cleaned up, put out more fresh water and headed back to Marcus's SUV.

"Do you want to see if we can feed Micah?" he asked, pushing back the sleeve of his jacket to check his watch. "We have time."

"I would," I said, pulling my hat down over my ears a little better. "Roma said she's been coming to eat about every second day."

"I take it she hasn't had any luck with the cage," he said.

I shook my head. "No. She asked me if I'd try."

Marcus smiled and pulled off his gloves to help me get the food ready. "You're the Cat Whisperer. Maybe you can catch her."

I fished the two extra dishes out of the bag. He filled one with water while I opened the can of food and put it in the other bowl.

"Wait here," I said to Marcus, handing the bag of used dishes to him.

I put the food and water down in a small area Roma had shoveled out at the base of a large tree near the carriage house. Then I backed away, stuffed my hands in the pockets of my old brown jacket and waited. Two, maybe three minutes passed and I saw movement in the snow behind a tangle of bushes.

It was Micah.

At the same time I realized that Marcus was behind me, not over by the steps. I reached one hand behind me and caught his arm. The small ginger cat continued to creep slowly forward until she reached the food. She began to eat, watching us between bites.

"Don't stare at her," I whispered to Marcus.

"Why?" he asked softly.

"I don't want to spook her. You wouldn't like it

if someone stared at you while you were having breakfast, would you?" I took a couple of steps backward, which meant he had to take a couple of steps back as well.

He wrapped his arms around my shoulders and pulled me back against him. "Is it okay with you if I do this instead?" he teased in a low voice.

I looked up at him and nodded wordlessly.

We stood there while the little cat ate and I watched her out of the corner of my eye. When she finished she seemed to take a minute to study us and then she meowed softly.

"You're welcome," I whispered.

As soon as the cat was out of sight, I collected the dishes and added them to the other ones I was taking with me to wash.

"I'll take the empty cans with me," Marcus said, walking over to the steps to pick up the empty water jugs. "They can go in my recycling bin."

We got into the SUV and I retrieved the thermos I'd left on the floor on the passenger side. I poured a cup of coffee and handed it over to Marcus, then poured a second for myself.

He had peeled off his heavy gloves and the goofy red hat and now he wrapped his fingers around the plastic cup and smiled at me. "Thank you for this," he said. "It's colder than I thought it would be out here."

The warmth was soaking into my own fingers, thawing them out a little. I took a long drink of coffee and then shifted sideways. "There's something I wanted to tell you that I found about Dayna Chapman."

"What is it?" he asked.

"Did you know that she was a witness in a robbery about six years ago?"

He nodded, head bent over his cup. "The pawnshop. Yeah, I knew."

"The owner, the man who was shot, did you know his son is here in Mayville Heights?"

His blue eyes narrowed, just slightly, and the muscles along his jawline tightened. Again, it was barely noticeable. Most people probably wouldn't have noticed it, but I knew every angle of Marcus's face, every line.

"What makes you think so?" he asked.

I had another sip of coffee before I answered. "You didn't know," I said. "Did you?"

After a moment he shook his head. "Why are you so sure about this?"

"The owner's name was Nicolas Sutton Sr.," I said. "The guy who works for Eric, the new artist in the co-op, the one who did the chocolate boxes for the fundraiser, is Nic Sutton. He came from Minneapolis." I exhaled softly. "I might be wrong."

"I'll check it out," he said. "Thank you for telling me."

"Nic bumped into Dayna at the party," I said. "She gave him the brush-off. I didn't think anything of it until I discovered that they have a connection."

Marcus pulled his free hand back through his

hair. He did that when he had a lot on his mind. "Sometimes it's just a small world," he said. "But I'll check that out, too."

I checked my watch. "We should get going," I said.

He drained the last of his coffee and handed me the cup. "Thanks."

I wasn't sure if he meant for the coffee or the information.

"Can you get one of the cages from the clinic when you go to see Smokey?" Marcus asked as we headed down the driveway. "We could bring it up tomorrow and see if we can catch Micah."

"I can do that," I said. "I should bring something a little more enticing than regular cat food, though."

We spent the rest of the drive home debating the merits of cooked chicken versus sardines, settling in the end on the little fish, mainly because of the enthusiasm Owen and Hercules had for them.

Marcus pulled into my driveway, put the SUV in park and leaned over to kiss my cheek. "Have a good day, Kath," he said.

I smiled. "You, too."

"Let me know what you find out," he added.

I frowned uncertainly at him.

He held up one hand. "I know you're not going to stay out of this, so I'm not going to waste my time telling you to. If you come up with anything, call me. Deal?"

I nodded. It felt a little odd not to be arguing about this.

I slid out of the SUV and headed for the back porch with my thermos and the bag of cat food dishes. It seemed to me that I had two pretty much impossible tasks—capture a small and extremely skittish cat and figure out who killed Dayna Chapman. I had the feeling that catching Micah was going to be a heck of a lot easier than catching Dayna Chapman's killer.

16

I couldn't do anything with my hair, probably because it had been smashed down weird under my hat. I finally got it lying more or less smoothly in a ponytail. Hercules sat by the bed and watched. Owen, as usual, had disappeared somewhere.

Since I was running behind and more than a little frustrated by my hair, I decided to stop into Eric's for a breakfast sandwich and some soup to warm up for lunch.

"I'll talk to Maggie tonight at tai chi and see what I can find out about Nic," I said to Hercules as I pulled on my boots.

He gave me a blank look.

"I'm sorry. I forgot," I said. "I didn't tell you what I found online." I shook my head and reached for my woolen beret. "Nic Sutton might have known Dayna Chapman. I don't have time to bring you up to date. Ask your brother."

I leaned down and kissed the top of his head. "Have a good day," I said.

I locked the door and headed around the house for my truck thinking if anyone ever did hear me talking to the boys, they really would think I was a few marbles short of a game.

It was a busy morning at the library with both the seniors and the preschool story time. Harry had come in with the tree, a beautiful, bushy fir, about nine thirty. Abigail and I had helped him get it set in the stand, although Harry did most of the work.

"Would you like me to start with the lights after story time?" Abigail asked as we stood back to get a good look at the tree.

"Yes, please," I said. "The boxes are in my office. I have to take the budget estimates over to Lita, but I'll help you once I get back."

She smiled and bumped me gently with her shoulder. "I don't mind. I like decorating."

"Good," I said. "Come and do my house. All I have is a wreath on the front door and it's plastic."

She put her hands on her hips. "I'm pretty sure we can have you put in stocks down on the River-walk for that."

"It was a plastic wreath or the head of a Fred the Funky Chicken, and putting a yellow chicken head on my front door just didn't say peace and goodwill to me." I grinned back at her. "Seriously, though, I spent so much time on the fund-raiser, holiday decorations just kind of fell by the wayside."

Abigail nodded. "Have you decided what you're going to do about Reading Buddies?"

I twisted my watch around my arm. "Yes and no."

"Which means?" she prompted.

"It means by the time we take care of the expenses for the fundraiser, we'll have enough money to keep the program going until spring—if we're careful and creative. We can't really do anything with the holidays just a few weeks away, so I'll wait until January and then we'll start trying to come up with some new ideas for getting the money."

She nodded. "That works for me."

I looked at my watch. "I need to get over to see Lita," I said.

Abigail made a shooing motion with one hand. "Go ahead. I'll start on the tree first chance I get."

I smiled. "Thanks." I started for the stairs.

"Hey, Kathleen," she called after me.

I stopped and turned around.

"I'm serious," she said. "I'm good at decorating. I could come over this weekend and give you a hand."

As far as Christmas decorations went, my house looked as if it belonged to Ebenezer Scrooge. I nodded and pressed my palms together. "Yes. Thank you. I'll make brownies."

Lita had a fresh pot of coffee made when I got to Henderson Holdings. The fact that everyone in town seemed to know that I liked a good cup of coffee—or a not so good one—made me feel even more certain that I'd made the right choice when I decided to stay despite the occasional pangs of homesickness.

We went quickly through the budget estimates I'd put together. When we got to the bottom of the last page, I put my pen down and picked up my coffee. "Thanks for your help," I said to Lita. "I'll get the final copy to you by Monday."

"That's fine," she said. She seemed a little distracted. The bright red-and-silver scarf at her neck wasn't bright enough to hide the fact that she looked as though she hadn't gotten a lot of sleep.

"How's Burtis?" I asked.

Lita gave me an approximation of a smile. "All right," she said. "He told me the two of you had breakfast." She straightened the papers in front of her and then she looked up at me. "Kathleen, I think the police suspect him."

"Why?" I asked. "Has something happened?"

"They've questioned him twice."

"He was married to Dayna."

She gave me a tight smile. "I've lived here all my life, Kathleen. I know what people think about Burtis. And I know what they say behind his back."

"I think Burtis is stubborn," I said, choosing my words carefully. "And I don't think I'd want to play poker with him. But I know he didn't have anything to do with Dayna's death. I'm not the only one."

"Thank you," she said.

"Does he have a lawyer?"

Lita nodded. "Brady got him one. Someone he went to law school with who's practicing in Minneapolis."

Her expression changed, tightened just a little when she said Brady's name.

"Lita, is Brady all right?" I asked. "Dayna was his mother. It had to have been painful to lose her, even if they weren't really close."

She played with the scarf at her neck. "I think it might have been better if they were a little closer," she said.

I looked uncertainly at her.

"You saw her, at the café."

I nodded.

"She'd just gotten into town, I guess. She asked me where Brady's office was and I told her. I'm not so sure I should have. She went to see him." Lita took a deep breath. "Brady was very angry. I think more for his brothers than himself."

I thought about what I'd seen at the fund-raiser—Brady brushing his mother's hand off his arm. "You think he regrets what he said."

She sighed. "Or maybe he doesn't."

I thought about Brady as I walked back to the library. I didn't know him that well, but I liked what I knew. And no matter what she said, Maggie certainly did. He was a lawyer, though. Was it possible that Brady knew anything about his mother's connection to that pawnshop robbery?

Abigail had the lights up on the tree when I got back. "Thank you," I said. "We'll start on the ornaments after lunch."

I covered the phones and the circulation desk while Susan had lunch. I ate the soup I'd gotten at Eric's at my desk and spent some time online seeing what else I could find out about Dayna Chapman. The only thing that really caught my interest was the fact that her family was pretty much broke. Her father had died just six months ago and Dayna and her older sister, who lived in London, had inherited very little.

It felt a little uncharitable to be thinking it, but I wondered if that was why she'd come back to Mayville Heights after having been away for so long. Maybe it had to do with money, especially since Dayna and Burtis were still married.

Abigail and I worked at the tree on and off all afternoon. By the time it was time for me to leave, we had most of Ruby's ornaments hanging on the tree.

"It looks beautiful," I said to Abigail as I leaned against the front desk and surveyed our work.

She crossed her arms over her chest and looked at the big fir, nodding with satisfaction. "It'll be even better when I get the snowflakes."

"What snowflakes?" I said.

"The seniors from the morning reading group are going to crochet snowflakes for the tree. That's okay, isn't it?"

"Of course," I said. "But aren't we going to need a lot of snowflakes to go all around that tree?"

"Don't worry," she said. "You'd be surprised how fast some of them can crochet."

I brushed lint off the front of my sweater. "Wait a minute. Where are we going to get all the crochet thread?"

"Remember when Abigail was trying to teach me how to knit?" Susan said behind me.

I turned to look at her. A tiny snowman wired to something was poked into her topknot.

"I remember," I said slowly.

"Well, that didn't work so well," she said. "So I thought maybe crocheting, because you only have to think about one needle instead of two." She gestured with her hands.

"And?" I prompted.

"If I was supposed to knit myself a scarf or crochet a dress, then there wouldn't be a Land's End catalogue, would there?" she said with a shrug.

Abigail was trying not to grin and not really succeeding.

I smiled at Susan. "Since I pretty much used the same logic to justify one of Eric's breakfast sandwiches instead of a bowl of oatmeal and fruit, I'm going to agree with you."

She held out both hands. "Which is why you now have more than enough crochet thread for the seniors to make snowflakes. Don't you love it when a plan comes together?"

I laughed. "Yes, I do."

It was snowing when I headed home. All the way up the hill I thought, for maybe the twenty-fourth time, how glad I was that Harrison had loaned and then given me the truck.

I drove over to Roma's clinic, picked up the cat cage and checked on Smokey. Roma's friend and colleague David Thornton, who was covering for her, said that the infection in Smokey's leg wasn't responding well to the antibiotics. The old cat raised his head when he heard my voice and I talked to him for a while. After a few minutes he put his head down again and went back to sleep. I told David I'd be back in the morning to check on the big gray tom.

Hercules was waiting for me inside the porch "Twice in the same week," I said. "I'm flattered." He jumped down from the bench, made his way to the back door and meowed loudly and insistently.

"Give me a minute," I said, juggling my keys, my purse and my briefcase.

I got the door unlocked and as soon as I opened it Hercules was inside. He headed for the living room door, clearly a cat with a purpose. He stopped in the doorway, looked over his shoulder and meowed again.

"Hang on," I said. "I haven't even taken my boots off."

He gave me a look of impatience. I half expected him to start tapping one paw on the floor.

I set my purse and briefcase on the floor, hung up my jacket and stepped out of my boots. "Okay, what is it?"

Hercules turned around again and headed for the stairs. Whatever he was so insistent about was on the second floor of the house.

I followed the cat upstairs. He went directly to the bathroom, sat down beside the tub and meowed.

"What? You want a bath?" I asked.

He closed his jade green eyes for a moment and dropped his head in annoyance.

I looked in the tub. Herc's tiny purple mouse lay almost in the middle. There was a small patch of water just to the right of it. Given his intense revulsion for wet feet, I knew there was no way Hercules would jump in and get his mouse.

I leaned over, picked it up and set it on the floor in front of him. Gingerly he reached out one white-tipped paw and touched the little purple rodent.

"It's dry," I said. Hercules, being Hercules, didn't take my word for it. Very tentatively he touched his toy again.

"You wouldn't have to worry about that being wet if you hadn't dropped it in the bathtub in the first place," I pointed out.

He shot me a daggers look, picked up the mouse in his mouth and stalked out of the bathroom, muttering under his breath all the way.

I changed my clothes, brushed my hair and went down to the kitchen. No sign of Hercules or his brother. I stuck a bowl of pea soup with carrots and ham in the microwave and while it warmed I retrieved my laptop from my briefcase. I wanted to see what else I could find out about the pawnshop robbery that Dayna Chapman had witnessed. Was I right about Nic Sutton?

I couldn't find out much more than I already knew, so I stuck the name of the investigating detective—Leah Webster—in a search engine. There had to have been some kind of charges against the shooter.

I was hoping I could find an article about the court case. Maybe there would be photos. Instead all I discovered was a brief article that told me the shooter—who was a juvenile at the time—had taken a plea deal. I tried looking up Nicolas Sutton Sr. Again, I couldn't find any photographs.

I set the computer aside for a minute and concentrated on my bowl of soup. I looked around the kitchen. Hercules was miffed, but it wasn't like Owen not to be lurking by my chair to mooch a piece of ham. Then again . . .

"Owen, I know you're there," I said. "I can hear you breathing." I couldn't, but he didn't know that.

I waited.

Nothing.

"Fine," I said, focusing all my attention on my supper. "I can't share with someone I can't see." I counted under my breath, "One . . . two . . ."

He popped into sight on three. It wasn't as disconcerting as it had been the first time I saw the cat disappear and then reappear again, but I still had the sensation of being Alice in Wonderland tumbling down the rabbit hole.

I looked down at the floor. "Hello," I said.

"Murp," he replied.

I fished a bite of ham out of my soup with two fingers and set it on the floor so Owen could scrutinize it the way he did everything he ate. Then I pulled the laptop closer again and scrolled through more images. I had a few more minutes before I needed to leave for tai chi class.

I tried everything connected to the pawnshop robbery that I could think of. I was about to give up when at the bottom of a screen full of photos, I discovered something that I realized just might be very helpful. It was a photo of Detective Leah Webster taken at a first responders appreciation night at a Minnesota Wild game.

With her cousin.

Eddie Sweeney.

Marcus had said sometimes it was a small world. Suddenly, I was very glad he was right.

17

I shut the computer off and gave Owen the last two pieces of ham from the bottom of my dish. I rationalized it by telling myself how healthy Roma had said Owen was at his checkup the week before. Right before he bit her Kevlar glove.

"Eddie's related to the detective who investigated that pawnshop robbery," I told the cat as I put my dishes in the sink. "That might be a way to find out if I'm right about Nic."

Owen made a little grunt, which probably had a lot more to do with the ham than what I'd come up with.

"I'm leaving for class," I said.

I put on my boots and jacket, grabbed my heavy gloves and pulled on the striped hat Rebecca had knit for me. Then I grabbed my bag and went out to the truck.

When I got to the stop sign at the bottom of the hill, I realized I had enough time to stop at Eric's for a cup of hot chocolate. I hadn't had any dessert, I reasoned, and the only thing Mags would have at tai chi was tea. And if I got the chance to talk to Nic Sutton while I was waiting for my hot chocolate, that would just be a happy coincidence.

I headed for the restaurant, telling myself that if I could find a close parking spot, I'd take that as a sign to go in. There was an empty place directly in front of the café door. I smiled, thinking about Lise back in Boston, who would have said, "I don't believe in signs, but if I did, this would be one."

I pulled into the empty spot, tucked my keys in the pocket of my jacket, and reached across the seat to the floor of the passenger side for my bag where I'd tucked my wallet. It had fallen off the seat as I drove down the hill. I stepped out of the truck, sliding my hand in my pocket for the keys so I could lock the door.

They weren't there.

At the same moment Owen materialized on the driver's seat, standing on his back legs with his paws on the door, just below the window. My keys were on the seat by his feet. They must have slipped out of my pocket.

A split second too late I saw what was going to happen. I lunged for the truck door and Owen put one gray paw down on the lock.

I smacked both hands against the side window. The cat jumped and glared at me. I slumped against the front fender of the truck. How could Owen have managed to sneak into the truck yet again without me noticing? Either he was getting sneakier or I wasn't paying enough attention.

I exhaled loudly and watched my frustration hang in the air in front of me. Then I turned and put my face close to the driver's-side window.

"Open the door," I said, enunciating each word carefully.

Owen blinked his golden eyes at me. Could he even hear what I'd just said? Could cats lip-read? I wondered.

I took another deep breath, tapped on the window and then pointed to the door lock. "Put your paw right there," I said.

He yawned.

I tapped on the window again. "Owen, right there, put your paw right there," I said, a little more insistently than the last time.

He sat down on the seat, sniffed my keys and then began methodically washing his face.

He looked up at me once and I swear he was smiling.

He'd done it on purpose. He'd locked me out of my own truck on purpose. I knew how ridiculous that was. I also knew I was right.

"Open this door right now, you little fur ball!" I hissed.

He went back to his careful face-washing routine.

I leaned against the truck. Once again I had been bested by eight pounds of sneaky cat.

I turned my head to glare at him through the windshield. He didn't even twitch an ear.

"I know you can hear me, Owen," I said. "When we get home I'm going to gather up every sardine and every funky chicken and make a big bonfire in the front yard and—and—roast marshmallows out there."

I was lousy at making threats. Owen's whiskers didn't move and he didn't so much as flick his tail at me.

I narrowed my eyes at him. "I'm serious, mister," I warned.

I took out my phone. I tried Marcus, but the call went straight to voice mail. I sent a text to Maggie but didn't get a response, probably because class was about to start.

Rebecca was in class and so was Ruby. Roma was out of town.

I was about to call Harry when Eric stuck his head out the front door of the café. "Kathleen, is everything all right?" he called.

I walked around the front of the truck.

"No," I said. "I accidentally locked myself out of the truck and Owen is inside." I looked back through the windshield. I couldn't remember the last time he'd spent so much time washing his face. I held up my phone. "I'm going to try Harry."

"You won't get him," Eric said. "He stopped in for a coffee about ten minutes ago. He's at a meeting about the community center roof. You know Thorsten. Everyone's phone will be off."

I groaned and swallowed a word that my mother would have said a lady wouldn't use.

"I'm going to walk home and get my spare keys, then," I said, brushing snow off my jacket. At least it wasn't cold. "Could you keep an eye on the truck and Owen? He should be all right and I won't be that long."

Eric smiled and gestured to me. "Come have a cup of coffee and I'll text Susan. She might be able to come and run you up to get your keys."

I didn't really want to walk up the hill in the snow.

"Okay, thanks," I said.

I brushed the rest of the snow off me and followed Eric inside. I took a seat at the counter and he poured me a cup of coffee. "How did you get locked out?" he asked.

I made a face. "Keys fell out of my pocket and Owen hit the lock."

"I don't suppose you could coax him to hit it again and let you in?" he asked with a smile.

I pulled off my hat. "Only if you could somehow make a sardine materialize on the button," I said.

Eric shook his head. "That I can't do," he said. "But I can go get my phone. It's in my office. I'll be right back."

Nic was just coming back from making a circuit with the coffeepot. He looked from Eric to me. "Are you locked out of your car?" he asked.

"Truck," I said. "Yes. And my cat's inside." I shrugged. "Long story."

He set the pot back on its burner. "Is it new?" he said.

I shook my head.

"I can probably jimmy the lock and get you in, then," he offered.

"Really?" Eric said. He sounded skeptical.

"Yeah," Nic said. He grinned. "And before you ask, no, I wasn't a juvenile delinquent. My dad taught me. He had a pawnshop. He knew all kinds of stuff."

So I was right.

"What do you think?" Eric said to me. "I can still text Susan."

"It's worth trying." I looked at Nic. "The truck's old. You can't hurt it."

"Give me a second," he said. He took off his apron and pointed toward the kitchen. "Okay if I get a screwdriver from the toolbox in the storage room?" he asked Eric.

"Sure," Eric said. He looked at me. "I'll get my phone anyway, just in case."

"Thanks," I said.

He grabbed a couple of menus. A man and a woman—tourists, I was guessing—had just come in. Eric gestured at my coffee as he passed me. "That's on the house."

He headed for the customers and I took another long drink just in case I did end up walking up the hill.

Nic came out of the kitchen in a black jacket, carrying a long, flat-bladed screwdriver. "Show me your truck," he said.

I took him outside.

Owen had finally finished washing his face. He watched us walk around the truck with interest, but he made no move toward the door.

"What's your cat's name?" Nic asked as he lifted the driver's-side door handle.

"Owen," I said, making a face at the fur ball, who ignored me and watched Nic intently instead. "He is—was feral."

"In other words, don't try to pet him."

I nodded. "How did you know?"

He shrugged. "I volunteered with a rescue group in Minneapolis. There were three feral cats living in the alley next to my dad's pawnshop."

He pointed to the door handle hinge. "See this? You have to be very careful, but you stick the screwdriver in here . . ." He slipped it in an opening by the hinge. "You feel around for the rod attached to the lock mechanism and . . ." I heard a clunk. "That's it."

Nic opened the door, picked up my keys and handed them to me. He looked at Owen. "Hey, Owen," he said.

"Merow?" the cat said. He seemed a bit surprised to be called by name by someone he didn't know.

"I'll close this so he doesn't get out on the street," Nic said, shutting the door again.

"Thank you so much," I said, holding tightly to the keys.

He made an offhand shrug. "No problem. It's good to know I can still do that. It's been a while."

"I read the news story about your father," I said. "I'm sorry."

"Thanks," he said. He ran a hand over his

smooth scalp, wiping away the snow. "It took·a long time, but he's doing really great now."

I brushed snow off the side of the truck. "So you knew Dayna Chapman."

He nodded. "She was a witness. She was just walking by on the sidewalk when everything went down that night." He turned the screwdriver over in his hands. "You think the stories are true? You think someone killed her?"

I scraped my boot against the pavement. "Yes, I do," I said.

Nic rubbed his gloveless hand across his mouth. "I guess that makes me a suspect, then," he said.

18

He mumbled an oath under his breath. "The kid who shot my father? He has a new lawyer. They're trying to get the plea agreement tossed on some kind of technicality. The prosecutor thinks it actually could happen, so she's been looking at all the evidence again, talking to witnesses."

I wasn't sure why he was telling me all this. Maybe he hadn't had anyone to talk to about it all for a while.

"Including Dayna," I said.

He shrugged. "Not exactly. About six months ago she started hedging, claiming she couldn't remember certain things all of a sudden. I tried to talk to her, but when I went to her apartment she wouldn't come to the door. Then she dropped out of sight altogether."

He leaned his head to one side and studied my face. "I heard how you helped catch the person who killed that director who was here for the theater festival a few months ago, so I think maybe you'll get it."

"Get what?" I asked.

He continued to play with the long screwdriver. "I came here to see if I could find out something, anything that might give me a clue as to where she went. Hell, I thought maybe she might even be here. The fact that the co-op was here and I'm an artist? It just seemed like the perfect confluence of circumstances."

He blew out a breath. "When she walked into the theater Thursday night, for a second I thought I was hallucinating."

"You tried to talk to her."

"Waste of time," he said, making a dismissive gesture with one hand. The muscles tightened along his jawline. "She told me her son was a lawyer and that if I didn't stay away from her, she'd sue me. Then she just walked away."

"Do you have any idea why she suddenly changed her story?" I asked, leaning over to brush snow off the driver's side of my windshield.

"I figure somebody from that kid's family had to have gotten to her, but I didn't have anything to prove that. If I had, I would have gone straight to the prosecutor." He kicked a chunk of dirty snow from the front tire of the truck. "Dayna Chapman being dead doesn't help me," he said. "I didn't kill her."

I believed him. Nothing in his face, in his voice, in his mannerisms suggested he was lying. "For what it's worth, I believe you," I said. "But you should tell all of this to the police. Detective Gordon."

"Your boyfriend?"

I nodded.

He shrugged. "Okay. But Dayna Chapman getting killed might not have had anything to do with the robbery and my father getting shot."

"Maybe," I agreed. *Or maybe it did*, I added silently.

I thanked Nic for his help again and then climbed into the truck. Owen had had some time to perfect his innocent act.

"Not working," I said as I stuck the key in the ignition. "You are in so much trouble."

He looked over his shoulder toward the restaurant and gave a questioning meow.

"Yes, I found out a little more about Nic," I said.

"Merow," he said sharply. I glanced over at him next to me on the seat. He looked smug.

"No," I said. "There's no way you knew Nic could unlock this door and we'd end up talking. Not possible."

He gave me another self-satisfied look and then turned to watch out the windshield.

I drove over to tai chi, parked the truck and realized I was going to have to take the cat inside with me. The snow was easing up and I knew it would get colder.

Luckily there was a cloth shopping bag in one pocket of my old jacket.

I put the bag on the seat. "Get in," I said.

For once Owen didn't give me a hassle. I

grabbed him and my tai chi bag and got out of the truck.

The class was already in the circle and Maggie had started the warm-up. "You're late," she said. "Is everything okay?"

"I got locked out of the truck," I said, swiping a hand back over my hair. "Long story. And I, uh, kind of brought someone to class."

As usual, Owen's timing was perfect. He poked his head out of the bag and meowed hello.

Maggie waved at him. "Hey, Owen," she said with a smile.

He immediately began to purr so loudly everyone heard him.

"Is Owen planning on taking up tai chi?" Ruby asked. "Is that why you brought him?"

The cat tipped his head to one side as though he was considering the idea.

For once, I decided not to hedge. "Would you believe he can make himself invisible so I didn't see him get in the truck?"

Ruby laughed.

"Could I put him in your office?" I asked Maggie.

Owen made a sour face. He definitely knew what the word "office" meant. And he didn't like it.

"Would you like to stay for the class?" Maggie asked him.

"No," I said firmly.

"Merow!" Owen said at great volume.

"He won't hurt anything, Kath," Maggie said.

"Yeah," Ruby chimed in. "He doesn't want to be stuck back in the office all by himself."

Rebecca caught my eye and just smiled.

Owen—who knew how to play to an audience—tipped his head and gave them his most abjectly lonely look.

"Don't encourage him," I said with a sigh, but it was already too late. Maggie dragged over a chair, setting it just beyond the edge of the circle. She patted the seat and looked at me.

"You're still in trouble," I hissed as I set Owen down on the chair. I had a little bag of organic cat kibble in my other jacket pocket. I fished it out and made a pile of it on the chair.

I straightened up and turned around. "Everyone, please don't try to pet him," I said. "Owen was feral and he doesn't like being touched."

Owen was looking at Maggie with kitty adoration as she pointed out the different flavors in the little heap of dry food in front of him.

"Not even by Maggie," I added.

Maggie gave Owen a big smile and moved back to the circle. I slid into place next to Taylor King.

Mags worked us hard. Owen stayed on the chair and seemed to be watching us with interest, although most of that interest was focused on Maggie. By the time we'd finished the complete form at the end of the class, there were damp patches of sweat on my T-shirt.

"Hey, Kathleen, your push hands are getting better," Ruby said as she came to stand beside me. She used the edge of her baggy tee to wipe the sweat off her neck.

Taylor was still standing next to me. Her red

hair was coming loose from the messy bun she'd pulled it back into. She reached one arm over her head and looked in Owen's direction. Maggie and Rebecca were talking to him.

"Kathleen, what would happen if someone did try to pet your cat?" she asked. "Would he really not like it?"

Ruby laughed. "Oh yeah, he'd really 'not like it,'" she said before I could answer. She stretched one arm across her body and pushed gently on it with the other hand. "Kathleen was hurt last winter and while the paramedics were taking care of her, a police officer tried to pick him up." She gestured at Owen, who at the moment really did look like a sweet cuddly ball of fur sitting on that chair.

"What happened?" Taylor asked.

"Owen has claws and he knows how to use them." Ruby grinned at me. "I'm surprised they didn't put little kitty shackles on him for assaulting a police officer."

I smiled then because I couldn't help thinking about Marcus. He'd come to Owen's defense that day after I passed out. *He* was pretty much the only reason Owen hadn't ended up as a guest of animal control for the night.

I pulled my shirt away from my sweaty body. "Before I forget, we have the tree almost decorated," I said to Ruby. "Come see it when you get a chance." I turned to Taylor. "I know you like vintage things. Come see our tree at the library. We're decorating it with Ruby's collection of Christmas ornaments."

Taylor smiled. "I'd like that. I will."

Ruby bent from the waist and put her hands flat on the floor. "I'll try to come see the tree tomorrow," she said.

I walked over to Maggie. "It's snowing. Do you need a ride?"

She shook her head and pulled a hand over her neck. "Thanks, but I have to stop at my studio."

"Time to go home," I said to Owen. I leaned over and picked him up. "Say thank you to Maggie."

"Mrrr," he said, looking up at her, eyes narrowed almost into slits.

"You're very welcome," she said.

I leaned over and hugged her. "Thanks, Mags," I said.

"You can bring Owen to class anytime you want to as far as I'm concerned." She gave me a teasing smile. "I'm pretty sure he was doing cloud hands with us. You should get him to help you with yours."

I made a face at her. "Okay, I'm taking my cat and going home," I said. Then I turned and headed for the door. Owen twisted in my arms so he could look back over my shoulder.

"Hey, Kath, don't forget about lunch tomorrow," Maggie called after me.

I waved two fingers at her over my shoulder to let her know I'd heard and I hadn't forgotten.

It took me a while to get my coat and boots on and get down the stairs. Rebecca had to say goodbye to Owen, and then Ruby and finally Taylor wanted to see him. If talking to the cats meant I was crazy, then pretty much everyone I knew was crazy, too.

Finally we got back to the truck. Owen yawned and stretched out on the passenger side. Being charming was tiring, it seemed. I really wanted to be mad at him, but indirectly he *had* gotten me the information I'd wanted from Nic Sutton—although I wasn't sure how it was going to help. I didn't believe Nic had had anything to do with Dayna's death. What would he have gained?

I rolled my neck from side to side. I was tired. And hungry. I hadn't gotten the cinnamon roll I'd wanted from Eric's.

I looked over at Owen curled up on the seat. If I went back for one, was I setting myself up for getting locked out of the truck again? I wasn't completely convinced that my keys had "accidentally" fallen out of my pocket earlier. I decided I'd drive around the block and see if I could find a parking spot close to the café. Then I remembered that was what had gotten me into trouble in the first place.

"Do you know what Einstein allegedly said the definition of insanity was?" I asked Owen. He lifted his head and yawned again. Clearly he didn't care. "Doing the same thing over and over and expecting different results."

I stopped at the stop sign and had flicked on my blinker to turn left when I saw Maggie walking up the sidewalk in the opposite direction from River Arts and her studio, as if she were headed to Eric's

Place herself. The collar of her coat was turned up against the cold and a long multicolored scarf was wrapped around her neck.

And Brady Chapman was at her side, their two heads bent together in what looked like an intense conversation. It also looked as if they were a lot more than friends.

19

Marcus picked me up in the morning and I set the cat cage on the backseat of his SUV before I got in.

"Do you think this is going to work?" I asked as I slid onto the passenger seat.

"I think if anyone can catch this cat, you can."

I rolled my eyes. "You sound like Maggie," I said.

"You really do have a rapport with all of the cats," he said as he backed out onto the road. It was cold but the sky was clear. It was going to be a nice day.

I patted the bag I was carrying. "I think that rapport might just be the fact that I smell like sardines a lot of the time."

He shot me a quick look and smiled. "No, you don't," he said. And the look in his eyes made my heart beat faster.

As we drove out to Wisteria Hill, I told Marcus what I'd learned from Nic Sutton the night before.

"He's right," Marcus said. "The prosecutor was looking for Dayna Chapman. She'd stopped cooperating with them."

"Do you think he's right about the why?" I asked, putting the bag of cat dishes at my feet on the floor of the SUV. "Could someone from the shooter's family have gotten to Dayna?"

As soon as the words were out, I realized that was probably a question he couldn't answer.

"I'm sorry," I said. "You can't answer that."

He shook his head. "It's okay. It's not exactly a secret. They don't know why Dayna suddenly became so vague and evasive. If somebody from that kid's family got in touch with her, no one seems to know who it would have been. The kid's parents are dead. So are his grandparents. His girlfriend disappeared after he was arrested. All he has is a sister who seems to have pretty much washed her hands of him."

I leaned my head back against the headrest. "So that's probably just another dead end?"

"It looks that way."

"Are you going to arrest Burtis?" I asked.

Marcus didn't say anything.

"*That* you can't tell me."

He shook his head. "I'm sorry. You know how this works. I can't."

I did. I also knew that was closer to a yes than a no.

We fed the cats first. Once again Lucy came over to me and I told her all about my visit with Smokey.

Marcus put the empty water jugs and the dirty dishes back in his SUV. He got the cat cage and set it up in the same place under the big tree where we'd put the food the day before. I put two sardines on a little plate I'd brought with me and set it inside the cage at the back. Once Micah went inside and stepped on the pressure plate, the door would drop down and we'd have her without her being hurt. I knew she'd be frightened, but it was the safest way we had at the moment to catch her and I hated the thought of the little cat roaming around in the snow a lot more than I disliked the cage.

Marcus and I backed up all the way to the side steps of the house and waited. After a couple of minutes I thought I saw a bit of orange fur against the snow. I touched Marcus's arm. "Over there. Is that her?"

He leaned sideways and looked. "I think so," he said softly. We waited and in a few more moments we could see the little marmalade cat making her way through the snow.

She was so small and thin despite all the efforts Roma had made to make sure she was fed, and all I could think was *Go in the cage, go in the cage.*

We watched as she moved to the side of the wire crate first, whiskers twitching as she sniffed the sardines. She reached out and tried to poke a paw through one of the spaces, but the gap was too small. For a moment it looked as though the little cat was going to leave again. I felt Marcus's reassuring hand on my shoulder.

Then Micah walked around to the front of the cage and craned her head forward to look inside. "Go, go," I said just under my breath. I could see her whiskers twitching again. She could smell the sardines, but was that enough to entice her to go after them? It didn't look as though it was going to be.

"Do you still have those kibble things in your pocket?" Marcus asked in a low voice.

I'd only given Owen part of the bag at tai chi. I fished it out of my pocket now and handed it to him. "What are you going to do?" I said.

"I just want to try something," he said. "Is that okay?"

I nodded.

Marcus put the half-full bag of cat kibble in his pocket. He eased his way down the steps and moved to a spot about halfway to the cage. Then he bent down and put a few pieces of the dry cat food on the ground.

Micah watched him the entire time. I could tell from her body language that she might bolt at any moment.

Marcus didn't move. Neither did I. After a minute or two that seemed to stretch out forever, the cat took a step forward, and then another. Her gaze stayed locked on Marcus, but she continued to get closer and closer to him.

Finally, she reached the little pile of food. She grabbed two pieces of kibble in her mouth and backed away several steps. She ate them, watching him all the time. When he did nothing, she came back for the rest of the food, eating quickly, her small furry body tensed, ready to run if she needed to.

I didn't even see Marcus reach into the bag again. He slowly extended his hand and there were a few more bits of kibble on it. The cat's whiskers twitched. Her eyes narrowed. I was certain she was going to run for the shelter of the bushes and the blackberry canes. Instead she took a step toward Marcus. He kept his hand out, holding it steady, and she took another step closer. One more and she was close enough to reach the food. She did the same thing with the first bite that she'd done before; she grabbed it and backed away. Then she crept forward and ate the rest from Marcus's hand. It was the closest any of us had gotten to the little stray and I could feel my heart pounding in my chest.

When the few pieces of cat food had been eaten, I saw Micah hesitate. Then she licked Marcus's hand. She looked up into his face and he reached out with two fingers to stroke her fur. To my complete surprise she didn't run; instead she nuzzled his hand.

"You're a beautiful cat," I heard Marcus say. Oh so slowly he reached out his other hand. He had a chunk of kibble between his fingers and he fed it to her as his other hand continued to stroke her fur.

"Would you like another piece?" he said.

The cat made a soft murping sound, for all the world like what Owen and Hercules did when they were looking for a treat.

Slowly and carefully Marcus moved his hand back to his pocket. This time while Micah was eating he picked her up and got to his feet.

I expected the cat to turn into the same kind of Tasmanian devil—all claws and teeth—that Desmond, the clinic cat, had become when Marcus rescued him out here. Instead Micah licked his fingers again, then looked up at him and meowed.

He laughed. "Oh, you want more, do you? He reached into his pocket yet again and pulled out another bite. Then he walked over to me.

My foot had gone to sleep, I discovered when I tried to stand up. I wobbled and managed to catch my balance. The cat narrowed her eyes at me as she ate. She was probably wondering about the crazy dance I was doing.

"Hello, puss," I said.

Micah continued to stare at me, but she made no move to get away from Marcus.

"How did you do that?" I said to him.

He gave me a half shrug. "I don't know."

I gestured at the cat cage. "I'm going to get the sardines." I ran across to the cage, took out the plate of little fish, closed the trapdoor and raced back to Marcus. I held up the plate and the cat ate both fish, eyeing me curiously the entire time.

"Can you drive?" Marcus asked. "I'm not sure I should put her down."

"Sure," I said.

I retrieved the cage and stowed it in the back of the SUV. Marcus got in the passenger side and managed to get his seat belt fastened. Micah walked her way up his chest and looked over his shoulder. I kept waiting for her to panic, but she didn't.

"She likes you," I said as we started down the driveway.

He smiled. "I don't really know why."

"I do," I said, grinning at him.

Roma was at the clinic when we walked in.

"Hi," I said. "I thought you weren't back until tonight."

"Eddie had a team meeting and an extra practice, so I decided to come back early." She yawned. "I didn't plan for it to be this early, though."

She caught sight of Marcus then. She gestured at him with one hand. "What . . . ?"

I held up both hands. "She couldn't resist his charm," I said.

Roma smiled. "Good job, Marcus," she said. "I see your charm worked a lot faster on the cat than it did on Kathleen."

"Maybe I should have scratched under her chin and given her a treat," he said, raising his eyebrows at me.

Roma laughed. "Bring her into the examining room," she said. Then she grinned. "I mean the cat."

Roma checked Micah out carefully. I kept waiting for the little ginger tabby to panic and claws to start flying, but that didn't happen.

When Roma finished her examination, the cat walked to the end of the examining table and looked around. She was even nosier than Owen.

"Well, she's malnourished, she's missing the tip of her tail and something bigger than she is bit the back of her head, probably a couple of weeks ago," Roma said as she pulled off her blue gloves.

"That's horrible," I said.

"Otherwise she seems to be healthy. And she's definitely not feral."

"How do you know?" Marcus asked.

Micah was sitting down now, washing her face.

Roma reached for her tablet to make notes on her examination. "She's been spayed. She was probably a dump."

Marcus's face tightened and I felt a knot of anger in my own stomach. This wasn't the first time someone had dumped a cat out to fend for itself at Wisteria Hill.

"So, what happens now?" I asked.

Roma brushed her hair back off her face. "I'll get her up to date on all her shots. We'll make sure she doesn't have worms or fleas, and then she can, hopefully, find a new home." She eyed me. "Any chance you'd take her?"

I looked at the small orange cat carefully washing her face. "I don't think Owen and Hercules would take to having another cat around," I said.

She nodded. "I want to take Desmond out to Wisteria Hill when I move out there permanently. I don't think he'd handle that *and* another cat around very well."

"Maybe we could talk Maggie into taking her," I said with a grin.

Roma smiled back at me. "We could try."

I looked over at Marcus, who was deep in conversation with the cat. "Marcus, we should get going," I said.

He straightened up. "Are you going to put her in one of those cages?" he asked Roma.

"Yes," she said. "It's for her own safety." She held out her hands several feet apart. "They're big cages. You've seen them."

"I don't think she'll like it, locked up with all the other cats."

"Do you want to take her down to the police station for the day?" Roma asked. She kept a completely straight face.

"Could she at least stay in your office?" he said. "She's been wandering around Wisteria Hill alone for months. She's not going to like being in a cage."

I walked over to the window and looked out into the parking lot so I wouldn't laugh. I did like seeing this side of Marcus.

He could also be charming—and very persistent—when he put his mind to it and he quickly convinced Roma to keep Micah—in a cage—in her office. While he was talking he'd set his gloves and scarf down on the table and Micah had immediately stretched out on the scarf.

"She seems to like that," Roma said. "Okay if we keep it?"

"I have a scarf at home you can use," I said to Marcus, turning back around.

Marcus looked at Micah, who was kneading the soft wool with her paws. "All right," he said.

Roma, with his help, got the cat settled in her office.

"She's already got a home," she said softly to me as we watched Marcus put his folded scarf inside the cage for the cat to lie down on.

"I know," I said. "Marcus just doesn't know it yet."

20

I beat Maggie to Eric's Place for lunch by about five minutes.

"Sorry I'm late," she said as she shed her coat, hat and scarf and dropped into the chair opposite me. "We had a pile of last-minute Christmas orders at the shop this morning."

She put a hand flat on her chest, closed her eyes and took several slow, deep breaths. When she opened her eyes again, Claire was coming from the other side of the restaurant with everything for her tea.

"Thank you," Maggie said with a smile.

"Have you decided what you want?" Claire asked as she set a pot of hot water on the table.

I nodded. "I'll have the Wednesday soup and the Wednesday bread."

Claire nodded approvingly. "Good choice."

"I'll have the same," Maggie said.

"It should just be a few minutes," Claire said. She headed back to the kitchen

Maggie started making her tea. "What did I just order?" she asked.

"Chicken noodle soup and honey sunflower bread."

She smiled. "Oh, good."

Once the tea was ready she leaned back in her chair and folded her hands around her cup. "How was your morning?" she asked.

"Good," I said. "Remember the little cat out at Wisteria Hill that Roma was worried about?"

Maggie nodded.

"Marcus caught her."

"You're kidding," Maggie said, eyes widening. "I thought you were Dr. Dolittle."

I shook my head as I took a sip of my coffee. "I guess I'm not the Cat Whisperer after all." I tucked a stray piece of hair behind my ear. "Oh, and Roma got back this morning."

Maggie added a tiny dab of honey to her cup and stirred. "If I'd known, I would have asked her to join us."

"I did and she couldn't," I said. "So, how was your morning aside from the extra orders?"

Maggie picked up her cup again. "Good, actually. Oren brought over some preliminary drawings. He thinks we should move the cash register over to the other wall and then we could make the demo space a little longer."

I tried to picture the inside of the co-op store. "That might work."

Maggie ran a hand back through her hair. "Kath, do you think when we finally get the work done in the store that it might be possible to work out something between the library and the co-op?"

"What do you mean?" I asked.

She wrinkled her nose at me. "I don't know exactly. Maybe a demonstration of a technique at the shop and then a talk at the library?"

I nodded. "That has potential," I said.

Claire arrived then with our soup and bread. We ate in silence for a couple of minutes.

"You said Vincent Starr offered to come back," Maggie said as she buttered a piece of the thick bread.

My mouth was full, so I just nodded.

"Maybe we could do something with him," she said. "Rare books can be worth a lot of money, can't they?"

"Depending on the book, yes," I said.

She dipped the end of her bread in her soup. "Maybe we could get Starr back at the library to talk about what makes one book more valuable than another, and then he could do some kind of appraisal. You know, like *Antiques Roadshow*, at the co-op." She'd dunked her bread two more times while she was talking and most of it was just a soggy lump in her bowl now.

"We could do that," I agreed. I set my spoon down.

Maggie was talking too much and had barely touched her tea. Something was up. "Or you could just tell me what the heck is going on."

She looked at me and sighed. "What's going on is I'm not very good at lying."

I nodded. "I noticed. And that's not a bad thing, by the way."

"It's Brady. I know I said we were just friends, but we're sort of turning into more than friends."

"Okay," I said carefully.

She looked at me a bit uncertainly. "You're not surprised."

I reached for a piece of bread from the basket between us. "I might have been just a little bit," I said. "When I saw the two of you like this"—I held up my thumb and index finger pressed together—"last night, walking down here, not toward River Arts. It looked like more than two people who are just casual friends."

She dropped her eyes for a moment. "I'm sorry," she said. "I really was going over to my studio. Brady sent me a text right after you walked out to get your coat." She slumped against the back of her chair. "Oh, Kath, I don't exactly know what happened. He's not my type."

"I don't think you can say that anymore," I said with a smile.

Her cheeks flooded with color.

"You never really said how the two of you got to be friends."

"Brady and I started talking at the reception after the opening night of the New Horizons Theatre Festival in the fall. I guess that's when we really started getting friendly."

She smiled when she said his name. Just the way I used to do with Marcus. In the almost two years I'd known Maggie, I'd never seen her do that.

"I don't remember seeing you with Brady at that reception," I said.

Maggie laughed. "That's because you and Marcus had finally realized that I and everyone else was right about the two of you. I could have been dancing with a gorilla in a tutu and you wouldn't have noticed."

I felt my own face get warm and I reached for my mug and took a drink. "Why were you asking me about Vincent Starr? This has something to do with Dayna, doesn't it?"

Maggie nodded. "Brady talked to his mother before the fundraiser."

"I know," I said.

"She told him she came back to town to see him and his brothers."

I narrowed my eyes at her. "You don't think so."

She shook her head and there was a touch of sadness in her green eyes. "I had Brady's ticket for the party and I stopped by his office to drop it off to him because I was going to meet him there. I wanted to get to the Stratton early and double-check the table arrangement."

I nodded without speaking.

"Brady was out by the reception desk talking to his mother when I got there. She took a pen and a piece of paper out of her bag and wrote down her cell phone number for him." Maggie took a deep breath and let it out. "She had a ticket for the Vincent Starr lecture in her bag." Her eyes met mine. "You told me it was sold out more than a week in advance."

I felt something tighten in my chest. "It was."

"You sent some tickets out by mail," Maggie said.

"Yes, we did."

"Dayna Chapman didn't come here to see her sons. She came here because Vincent Starr was here. That's what Brady thinks."

"Do you think she had some kind of rare book?" I asked. I'd reduced half a piece of bread to a pile of crumbs on the plate in front of me without realizing it.

Maggie shrugged. "Maybe. Brady said she told him that his grandfather had died not long ago. Maybe . . . maybe she ended up with a book that belonged to him and wanted to sell it quietly so her sister wouldn't find out."

"Does Brady know if his grandfather was a collector?" I asked.

Maggie shook her head. She picked up her teapot and then set it down again, realizing that she hadn't put any more hot water in it. "There's one more thing that happened when Dayna was at Brady's office. He said his mother dropped a piece of paper with an address on it and when he picked it up and asked her about it she grabbed it from him and told him it was none of his business."

I caught Claire's eye across the room and pointed at Maggie's little hot water pot. The contents were probably cold by now. I waited until she'd brought a new one and topped up my coffee as well before I spoke. "Mags, did Brady see the address?"

"He did," she said as she started the tea-making process again. "Tamera Lane. There's no street with that name anywhere around here or in Minneapolis." She stopped and looked at me across the table. "Kath, I don't want to do anything to cause problems with you and Marcus. But you're good at this. Please, could you ask a few questions? Brady's a good guy."

It felt as though the entire town wanted me to figure out what had happened to Dayna Chapman. I nodded across the table at her. "Okay," I said.

21

I was having dinner with Marcus, so it was easy to stop at Roma's clinic on the way out to his house to check on both Micah and Smokey again.

The old tomcat was doing much better. "I think he's out of the woods," Roma said. "But keep your fingers crossed." She smiled at me. "Aren't you going to be late for your dinner date?"

"How did you know I have a date?" I asked.

She gestured to Micah. The tiny ginger tabby cat was asleep in her cage on top of Marcus's scarf. "Marcus stopped by to check on her on *his* way home."

"He says he doesn't have time for a cat," I said.

Roma laughed. "Yeah, I don't think she knows that."

Marcus was tasting something from a pot on the stove when I got to his house.

"I don't care what that is," I said, unwinding

my scarf from around my neck. "I haven't eaten since lunch and I'm hungry."

"So if it's roadkill in cream sauce you'll eat it," he said with a smile.

I smiled back, unzipped my coat and tucked my gloves in one sleeve as I took it off. "If it's gum rubber boot in sauce I'll eat it."

He gave an elaborate eye roll. "Well, I wish you'd told me that before I made meat loaf."

"You made meat loaf?" I said. "I love meat loaf."

He smiled. "I know," he said, "and Hannah says hi."

I dropped onto a chair. "Hi back at her. When did you talk to Hannah?"

He ducked his head over the large pot that smelled a little like nutmeg. "This morning when I called her for her meat loaf recipe."

I laughed.

"She says she's going to write out some of her recipes and e-mail them to me."

"I'm looking forward to that," I said. I tucked one leg up under me. "How was your day?" I asked. "Have you figured out who killed Dayna Chapman yet?"

"No." He looked back over his shoulder at me. "Have you?"

"No," I said.

"But you know something."

"Kind of."

"Kind of yes or kind of no?" He got a wire rack out of the cupboard and set it on the counter.

"Could I wait to answer that until we eat?" I asked.

He turned his head to look at me again. "Why?"

I stretched my arms over my head. "Because if we have a fight, then I'm going to have to go home and have a peanut butter sandwich instead of meat loaf and I don't want to do that."

Marcus reached for the oven mitts. "Okay," he said.

"You were supposed to say we're not going to fight," I said teasingly.

He took the meat loaf out of the oven and set the pan on the wire rack. He turned the heat off under the pot on top of the stove and then he closed the space between us in two steps, leaned down, swept my hair behind my ear and kissed me. It would be clichéd to say my heart started fluttering. But it did. "We're not going to fight," he whispered against my ear.

Marcus went back to finishing supper and I sat there for a moment and tried to remember what we'd been talking about.

"Mmmm, that is so good," I said after the first bite of the meat loaf. The nutmeg I'd thought I smelled had been sprinkled in the turnip and carrots that had been cooking on the stove.

"I'll tell Hannah you liked her recipe."

I looked at him sitting across from me. He was an incredibly handsome man. He was kind and loyal and smart. He had integrity and cats loved him. And no one had ever kissed me the way he did.

I set down my fork. "I've been trying really hard *not* to get mixed up in this case."

"I know," he said. "And I know it's difficult because people you care about are involved." He closed his eyes for a moment. "Kathleen, I don't want you to be someone you're not. I really don't. It's just that—" His mouth worked as he tried to find the right words. "I remember what it felt like when you went over that embankment down by the river, and that was just a few months ago. And last year, when you came so damn close to getting caught inside when that cabin exploded in the woods." His blue eyes locked on to mine. "I don't want to lose you."

"You're not going to," I said. I leaned across the table to kiss him this time. I pressed my hand against his cheek.

He smiled. "Your sleeve's in your turnip," he said.

I smiled back at him. "Your elbow is in yours."

After we'd gotten our respective body parts out of our supper and cleaned the turnip and carrot off our clothing, I told Marcus everything I knew.

"It feels like some kind of Victorian melodrama," I said. "I can't shake the feeling this is all connected to that pawnshop robbery."

"I can't make a case on feelings."

I pushed my plate away. "I know," I said. "But you have to admit it's odd that Dayna stopped cooperating with the prosecutor's office, she dropped out of sight and the next thing she shows up here—somewhere she hasn't been in more than twenty years."

"It does seem a little too convenient to be a coincidence," he said. He got up and cleared the plates from the table. "Banana bread and coffee?" he asked, reaching for the kettle.

"You made banana bread?" I said.

He shook his head. "No. I bought banana bread. It's from Fern's. Georgia Tepper made it."

I shifted in my chair. "That means you went to Fern's to talk to Burtis and yes, thank you, I'll have a slice."

He laughed. "Okay, yes, I went to talk to Burtis over at Fern's. Not exactly on the record, but not exactly off it, either."

I rolled up my sleeve so the turnip stain didn't show. "Marcus, do you honestly think Burtis killed his ex-wife?" I patted my chest. "In here, and in your gut."

"I don't do gut feelings," he said, leaning against the counter and folding his arms over his midsection. "I need facts. I need evidence."

"You also have instincts," I countered. "What do they tell you?"

I looked at him without speaking.

Finally, he raked a hand back through his hair and gave me a wry smile. "Okay. My instincts tell me that Burtis didn't kill his ex-wife."

"So, does the evidence point to anybody else?"

"We're still investigating," he said. "We don't have all the evidence."

He was just a second too slow in answering.

"Who?" I asked.

"C'mon, Kathleen," he said, reaching for a knife to slice the banana bread. "You know I can't tell you that."

I thought about everything I'd learned so far about Dayna Chapman's death. I had a sinking feeling in my stomach. "Brady," I said.

Marcus's mouth moved, but he didn't say anything.

"It's Brady," I repeated.

Marcus let out a long, slow breath. "She was at his office, and they had words at the reception desk."

I shook my head. "It wasn't Brady."

"I didn't say it was," Marcus said.

I thought about the look on Maggie's face when she'd said Brady's name.

"We have to figure out who killed Dayna Chapman."

"We?" Marcus asked, his eyebrows going up.

I nodded. "Uh-huh. You and me."

I ate my banana bread while Marcus gave me his "this is a police investigation" speech.

When he finished I had a sip of my coffee before I answered. "Everything you said is right. But the fact is, people will tell me things that they won't tell you. Dayna Chapman's murder touches a lot of people I care about—Maggie, Lita and yes, Burtis." I took a deep breath. "I won't do anything stupid, but I'm not going to stop asking questions. If that's a problem you're just going to have to arrest me." I stuck both hands out in front of me, my hands pulled into fists, like I was waiting to be handcuffed.

Marcus studied me for a moment and then picked up his cup.

"Too melodramatic?" I asked after another moment of silence.

He nodded as he got up for more coffee. "Just a little."

We didn't talk any more about the case for the rest of the night.

Both Owen and Hercules were in sulky moods in the morning. Owen flicked his tail in Hercules's face and in return his brother swiped at it with one paw. A couple of yowls were exchanged before I banged my bowl of oatmeal on the counter, making them both jump.

"Both of you stop it," I said sternly. There was silence for a moment and then they both began to grumble under their breath as they sat crouched on the floor. "Hello!" I snapped. "Did I ask for comments from the peanut gallery?"

I pointed at Owen and flicked my finger toward the back door. "You! Time to go outside. I'll be out in a minute." I looked at Hercules, who did a lousy job at not looking guilty. "Go in the living room or go upstairs."

They hesitated, eyeing each other. I took one step toward them and they both moved, Owen for the porch and Herc for the living room door.

"Much better," I said. I didn't know if it was the shorter days or maybe the full moon, but both cats were acting crankier than usual. Of course, they could have been thinking the same thing about me.

After I finished my oatmeal, I went outside to

clear the steps and the path around the house. Harry had already been by to clear the driveway.

Owen bounded around happily in the snow chasing a dried leaf.

"Let's go," I called when I finished. He came across the backyard with a snow beard stuck to his face. "All you need is a red stocking cap and you'd look like Santa Claus," I said, leaning down to brush off the snow. He went ahead of me up the steps. Hercules was sitting on the bench in the porch. He jumped down and followed us into the kitchen, lifting one paw and shaking it in annoyance when he stepped on a tiny bit of snow that had fallen off his brother's tail.

I split the last of the bag of kitty kibble that was still in my old jacket between the two of them. Owen stopped to rub against my ankle and I bent to give him a scratch behind one ear. "Have a good day," I said.

Hercules had quickly eaten the dried chunks of cat food and now he was waiting by the door.

"Are you going outside?" I asked as I pulled on my hat and tucked some stray wisps of hair underneath it. He blinked at me, then craned his neck and looked at the porch door. That seemed to be as much of a yes as I was going to get. Hercules didn't like going outside much in the snow—or the rain or the mud. Usually he had a purpose. I wondered what it was this time. At least the locked door wouldn't be an obstacle to him getting back in again. That was the one advantage to his "superpower."

I let the cat go ahead of me and turned to lock the porch door. When I turned around again Hercules was already following the path around the side of the house. I didn't have a good feeling about that. By the time I got around to the truck, he was waiting by the driver's door.

"No," I said.

He looked at me. He looked at the door.

I bent down and picked him up. I expected at least an angry yowl. Instead he went limp in my arms.

"Passive resistance," I said. "It's not going to work."

I stuck him back in the porch and because this wasn't the first time this kind of thing had happened, I scooped up a couple of handfuls of snow onto the top step. I knew he'd walk through the door, but he wouldn't walk through the snow.

I was almost around the end of the house when I heard him. I stopped and turned around. Hercules was coming along the path, stopping to shake a paw every step or two, green eyes narrowed, ears pulled forward, complaining all the way. I went to pick him up again and as I reached for him he darted left, past me, and headed for the truck.

I turned the corner just in time to see him launch himself from a snowbank onto the hood of the truck. *He'd climbed up onto a snowbank?* He scrambled to get his balance and for a moment I thought he was going to slide down onto the front bumper. Then he managed to get upright and stable. He shot me a look of victory and walked through the windshield onto the dashboard. Then he shook himself and jumped down onto the seat.

I opened the door and looked at him. "Why do you do this?" I asked.

"Murp," he said, and it seemed to me that he almost shrugged.

"There's nothing going on at the library."

His response was to turn his head and look out the front window.

I reached past him and set my briefcase on the floor on the passenger side. "This doesn't mean you've won," I said as I climbed in.

He very wisely didn't point out that I was wrong.

Surprisingly, considering all the back-and-forth with Hercules, I actually got to the library early. I slung my briefcase over my shoulder and carried the cat in my arms because I didn't have a bag to put him in. I hoped like heck that no one would see me. Pets did not belong in the building and I'd already heard more than one joke about bring-your-cat-to-work day.

I took Hercules up to my office and set him down. He immediately jumped up onto my desk. When I set my laptop down beside him, he put one paw on top and meowed loudly.

I looked at my watch. "Okay, we have a few minutes to see what we can dig up about that pawnshop robbery."

I was still convinced it was the key to Dayna Chapman's murder. It seemed that Hercules was as well.

The previous librarian, Ingrid, had subscribed to a news service package for libraries. It had turned out not to be that popular with library patrons and when it expired at the end of January I wasn't going to renew our subscription, but since we still had access for a few weeks I decided to log in and see what I could find on the Minneapolis robbery. All I came up with was a short newspaper article about the sentencing for the young man who had shot Nic Sutton's father. There was one photo of him being led out of the courthouse in handcuffs. At the time he was only eighteen and his slight build and strawberry blond hair made him look even younger.

The paper clearly hadn't deemed the story to be very important. They hadn't even sent their own photographer to court. The photo was credited to Edwin Jensen, a blogger who covered crime and policing stories in the Minneapolis area. He called himself an "independent journalist." He might have been independent, but he also seemed to have a bit of a bias against the Minneapolis Police Department. On the other hand, he also had an uncanny ability to be able to find out that a crime had happened and be the first on the scene. His blog had tens of thousands of readers.

"What do you think?" I asked Hercules. "Is it worth a look?"

"Merow," he said decisively.

A click on Edwin's name sent us to his blog. Deep in the archives we hit pay dirt. Jensen wasn't much of a writer, so his stories were always photo-heavy. There were probably two dozen shots posted from the night of the pawnshop robbery, many just slightly different versions of one another. I found one of Dayna Chapman standing talking to a police officer. POLICE TALK TO WITNESSES, the caption said. There was another similar shot with the same caption, and another after that. The only reason I took a closer look at the third image was that Hercules had stuck his head in my way and I'd had to lean closer to the screen. I recognized the face, I realized. But it wasn't Dayna Chapman in the photograph. It was Olivia Ramsey.

22

I slumped against the chair back. "What the heck?" I said.

Either Hercules had gotten bored or he'd decided his work on this planet was done, because he was sitting on my desk washing his face.

"We have to talk to Olivia."

"Mrr," he said. It might have been a yes. It might not have been.

I straightened up and pulled the laptop closer. Buried in a post from three days later, I learned that a teenage witness named Livie West had actually come past the pawnshop after the robbery and shooting had happened. She'd stopped to help with first aid for Nic's father—and was being hailed as a hero—but she'd been too late to see anything. The only real witness was Dayna Chapman.

"Livie West," I said, standing up and walking around my desk. "Olivia was using a different last name."

I had to talk to her and I needed a reason. I didn't want to just barge in and start asking questions.

I looked at my desk, where Hercules was still washing his face, and realized I had the perfect excuse right there: the thank-yous from the board to everyone who'd worked on the fundraiser. I'd brought them back from my meeting with Lita so I could add my own personal thanks.

"I could deliver Olivia's thank-you in person," I said. I looked at my watch. But first I had to see if Susan and Abigail were downstairs.

I looked at Herc. "Please, please, please stay in here," I said. He jumped down onto my chair and sent it spinning lazily in a circle. Hopefully that would keep him entertained for a while.

It was eleven thirty before I could get away from the library. I'd hoped to sneak Hercules down the stairs and take him home after I stopped at Olivia's, but there were just too many people around. I left the cat curled up asleep on my desk chair and crossed my fingers he'd stay there.

Olivia was in the kitchen that Decadence Chocolatier shared with Sweet Thing and the Earl of Sandwich, packing truffles into silver boxes with white embossed snowflakes on the lids.

"Those are beautiful," I said.

She smiled. "Thank you."

I held up the envelope with the board's thank-you. "This is just an official thank-you from the library board," I said.

"You didn't have to do that," Olivia said. "My truffles didn't exactly help you."

"That's not your fault."

She peeled off the thin plastic gloves she was wearing and took the envelope, turning it over in her hands.

"Kathleen, there's something I haven't told anybody," she said.

"What is it?" I asked.

She stared down at the floor for a moment. "Dayna Chapman wasn't exactly a stranger to me."

It was the last thing I'd expected to hear. "What do you mean?"

Olivia sighed, then looked at me again. "Six years ago I was living in Minneapolis. I was heading home from the comic book store on a Tuesday night and there was a man, lying on the sidewalk bleeding." She stopped and took a moment to compose herself. "He, uh, it turns out he owned a pawnshop. There was a robbery and he . . . he was shot."

"You must have been terrified," I said.

She gave me a half smile. "You know, I wasn't. I was on the first responder crew at school. I just started first aid. Someone had already called nine one one. Five minutes and the paramedics were there and it was over."

"Dayna was another witness," I said.

"She was the only witness." Olivia reached over to straighten a row of chocolate boxes on the workspace in front of her. "I got there after everything had happened. I didn't see a thing. The police took us back to the police station and once they figured out that I didn't know anything that could help them, they drove me home." She shook her head. "That was the only time I'd ever seen Dayna until last Thursday afternoon."

Afternoon? "You saw Dayna before the reception?"

Olivia dropped her gaze again. "I know I should have said something."

"Why didn't you?" I stuffed my hands in the pockets of my jacket.

"I was scared." She traced the snowflake design on one of the boxes with a finger. "She was here. We had a connection because of a crime that happened years ago and then she died after eating one of my chocolate truffles."

"You didn't tell the police."

She shook her head. "I didn't tell anyone. And I figured no one would make the connection because now I go by Ramsey, which is my stepfather's name, but back then my last name was West. It was stupid, I know."

"Olivia, what did Dayna want?"

"She wanted me to talk to the prosecutor's office. She wanted me to be a witness if there was a new trial. She said she couldn't do it." She exhaled slowly. "I didn't even recognize her at first. I told her I couldn't testify because I'd gotten there too late. I hadn't seen anything." She looked up at the high ceiling overhead for a moment. "She wanted me to lie. I said no."

Just then Georgia Tepper came in from the front of the old house.

"Ask her," Olivia said. "She was here."

"Ask me what?" Georgia said.

"Tell her about Dayna Chapman being here."

Georgia hesitated.

"It's okay," Olivia said with a shrug. "I'm not keeping it a secret any longer. I shouldn't have done that to begin with."

"Liv was scrubbing down that table," Georgia said, gesturing to the large workspace in front of us. "Mrs. Chapman—I didn't know who she was then—was standing right about where you are. I heard her say, 'All you have to do is lie.'"

Olivia looked at me. "I know it was stupid not to say I knew her from the start. I'll call Detective Gordon and tell him everything."

"I think that's a good idea," I said.

When I got back to the library, Hercules was still dozing in my chair in a patch of sunshine. I sat on the edge of my desk and leaned over to stroke his fur. He made an inquiring little "murp" sound that I decided to interpret as a question about how my visit with Olivia had gone.

"Would you believe Olivia told me she knew Dayna Chapman before I had a chance to ask her?"

The cat tipped his head from one side to the other as though he was pondering the coincidence.

"Interesting timing," I said. Before I could say

anything else, there was a knock on my door. I turned Hercules to face the window and hurried over to answer it.

Susan was standing there with a look of exasperation on her face and her updo skewered with two pencils. "Problem," she said. Her glasses had slipped partway down her nose.

"What is it?" I asked.

"We plugged in the tree lights, there was a fairly loud popping sound and now none of the outlets are working in the computer room, so obviously none of the computers are working, either."

"Is anything on fire?" I asked.

Susan shook her head. "No, but I did see sparks come out of the outlet."

I rubbed the space between my eyebrows. "That's not good," I said as I closed the door behind me.

Susan pushed her glasses up her nose. "Yeah, I didn't think so, either," she said.

The limit of my electrical knowledge was switching the breaker on and off in the basement, and that didn't fix the problem. I called Lita. She promised she'd have Larry Taylor over before the end of the day.

"I don't think those boneheads who worked for Will Redfern wired things right in the first place during the library renovations," she said in a voice edged with annoyance. "And I can say that because at least two of them are my cousins."

I kind of agreed with her. This wasn't the first time Larry had had to come to fix something Will

Redfern's boys hadn't done quite right. I thanked Lita and hung up.

Even without the lights turned on, the tree looked beautiful. Since the building didn't seem to be in danger of catching on fire, I decided there wasn't really anything else to do but put a big COMPUTERS TEMPORARILY OUT OF ORDER sign on an easel at the entrance to the computer space, and hope Larry could stop by sooner rather than later.

And he did. Unfortunately it was just as I was going to take a late lunch and drive Hercules home.

"I guess you're going to have to stay for the rest of the day," I told him. It didn't seem to bother Hercules at all.

I kept an "emergency" box of dry cat food, a water dish and a small covered kitty litter pan hidden in a box in the locked closet in my office. The boys had ended up at the library more than once, and even though we had a strict no-pets policy, they seemed to think the rules didn't apply to them.

Larry discovered the electrical problem was a faulty set of lights and a breaker that had been recalled by the manufacturer. While he worked in the basement, Abigail began the tedious job of taking the lights off the tree without removing all the ornaments.

Marcus came into the library about midafternoon. There was a woman with him and as soon as I got a good look at her I realized I knew her. Or more specifically I knew who she was: Leah Webster, the investigating officer in the pawnshop robbery.

"Everything comes to he who waits," I said softly.

"Tolstoy?" asked Susan, who was passing behind me with an empty book cart.

"Close," I said. "It was actually Skeletor from *He-Man and the Masters of the Universe*. Tolstoy said, 'Everything comes in time to him who knows how to wait.'"

"Good to have that cleared up," she said dryly, her lips twitching with amusement.

Marcus had reached us by then. "Hi, Kathleen," he said. He was wearing a dark woolen topcoat over his tweed sport coat, with a blue shirt and a blue-and-gray tie. I remembered that he'd had to go to court this morning.

"Hi," I said, smiling because any other response would have been extremely inappropriate.

"This is Detective Webster," he said.

I held out my hand. "Hello," I said. "I'm Kathleen Paulson. Welcome to the library."

She smiled back at me as she thanked me and I could see the family resemblance between her and Eddie. They had the same shape mouth and the same smile.

"Detective Webster came to consult on a case and her car won't start," Marcus said. "Thorsten said it looks like she just needs a new battery."

"I'm a bit of a history buff," Leah Webster said. "I've heard about your library's collection of documents. I figured I'd take my chance to take a look at them." Her dark eyes narrowed. "You have two diaries from when this area was first settled, don't you?"

"As well as some correspondence and the personal papers of the town's first mayor all scanned into our computer system." I made a face. "Unfortunately our computers aren't available at the moment."

Marcus raised an eyebrow.

"Faulty breaker," I said. "Larry Taylor is here." I turned back to Leah Webster. "But we also have most of the information loaded on the hard drive of a new computer that we're going to use just for genealogical research. If you don't mind being upstairs in our very messy workroom, you could look through what we've downloaded so far."

"I don't want to put you out," she said.

"You wouldn't be. We usually don't have patrons up on the second floor, but since you're a police officer I think we can make an exception."

"I appreciate this," Marcus said, and the gleam in his blue eyes told me the words were more than just a social nicety.

"I do, too," Detective Webster said, her enthusiasm obvious in the wide smile she gave me. "I had no idea you had such an extensive collection."

I nodded. "From what I've been told, it was the pet project of the head librarian two librarians ago. We have a student intern who's been photographing everything, bit by bit, and putting the images on a series of CDs and now on this new computer. The idea is that people will be able to see the documents without necessarily having to handle them. Eventually, we may be able to work out online access."

I held up a hand. "I'm sorry. This has kind of become my pet project, too."

Detective Webster shook her head. "You don't need to apologize. It's nice to meet someone else who has a love of history."

I gestured toward the stairs. "I'll get you set up."

"I'll call you when I know more about your car," Marcus said.

She nodded. "Thank you."

I took the detective up to the workroom, turned on the computer and showed her the simple cataloging system Mia and I were using to keep track of the images.

"I'll poke my head in later," I said. "If you have any problems I'll either be in my office, which is the first door at the top of the stairs, or I'll be downstairs. And any of the other staff members can help you."

She smiled again. "Thank you so much, Kathleen."

"You and Eddie Sweeney are cousins, aren't you?" I asked.

She nodded. "Yes, we are. How did you know?"

"I saw a photograph of you with him somewhere. And you have the same smile."

The smile got larger. "I'm guessing you know Roma Davidson, then," she said.

"She's one of my closest friends."

Her gaze was already being pulled to the waiting computer screen. "Everyone who knows Eddie is hoping for a happily-ever-after ending there," she said.

I nodded. "So is pretty much everyone who knows Roma." I gestured at the computer. "I'll let you get started."

Marcus was waiting for me downstairs. "Susan said you had a problem with the lights on the tree," he said.

"A short, which is how we found out about the defective circuit breaker," I said. I had the urge to reach over and straighten his tie, but there were a lot of people around, so I put my hands in my pockets instead. "Detective Webster seems nice."

He smiled, shaking his head at the same time. "I know you know who she is, Kathleen."

"Did she help you?"

"No comment," he said, adjusting the scarf at his neck. "I need to get going. Promise me you won't question her."

I held up three fingers. "I promise I won't question her," I said solemnly. "Librarian's honor."

"There's no such thing as librarian's honor," he said, fastening the buttons of his coat.

"Yes, there is," I said, trying not to grin too widely at him. "It's part of our oath along with promising to shush people and to read a book a day."

He shook his head. "I'll see you later."

I waggled my fingers good-bye at him.

Lita called about half an hour later. "Did Larry make it yet?" she asked.

"He did, thank you," I said. "He's almost finished."

"Great," she said. "Do you have a minute to talk about Reading Buddies?"

"I do," I said, perching on the edge of my desk because Hercules still had my desk chair.

"You know I sent all the refund checks out."

"I do. And I know you got some of them back."

"All of them," Lita said.

"What?" I asked. I had to have heard her wrong.

"Every single one of them has been returned, several with a second check as a donation."

I had to swallow the lump at the back of my throat before I could speak. "I . . . I don't know what to say," I said.

On the other end of the phone, Lita laughed. "I do," she said. "I'm really glad you decided to stay." She gave me the total so far. "Can you make the program work with that?"

"Yes," I said. It would be tight after we'd paid the expenses from the fundraiser, but Abigail and I could be creative.

"I'll let Everett know," she said. "Good job, Kathleen."

I hung up the phone and looked over at Hercules. "I love this place," I said.

"Mrrr," he agreed before going back to his nap.

I went back downstairs and did a quick tour of the main floor. Abigail and I had put together half a dozen different exhibits about rare books—including our predictions on which current best-sellers we thought might be collectors' items one day—and we'd decided to leave them out for a few more days. Oren Kenyon came in as I was rubbing fingerprints off the front of a display case with the edge of my sweater.

"Hello, Kathleen," he said, pulling off his heavy woolen hat, which made his gray-blond hair stand up all over his head. He reached in the pocket of his jacket and handed me a folded chamois. "Try this."

I took the square of sheepskin and made quick work of the smudges on the glass-fronted case. "Thanks," I said, handing it back.

He tucked the chamois in his pocket again. Then he looked around the space, and a smile spread across his face. "I spent a lot of time here when I was a boy. It's one of my favorite places in town."

"Me too," I said, smiling at him.

"I'm glad that children still come here. I'm glad that you came up with the Reading Buddies program. So, this is for you." He put his hand in his other jacket pocket, pulled out an envelope and held it out to me.

"Oren, what is this?" I asked, even though I was pretty sure I knew. I recognized the envelope. It had come from the bank down the street.

"Open it please," he said.

The flap of the envelope wasn't sealed, so it only took a moment to pull out the check I'd guessed was inside. "Oh my word," I said softly when I saw the amount.

"Before you say you can't take it, you should know I wouldn't have that money if it weren't for you."

I looked blankly at him.

Oren shifted from one foot to the other. "Kathleen, do you remember the party for the library's one hundredth birthday?"

I nodded. It had been a gorgeous, warm day this past spring. The entire town had turned out to celebrate the renovations to the one-hundred-year-old Carnegie Library.

"What does the library's centennial have to do with this check?" I asked.

"My father's sculptures were on display here."

Oren's late father, Karl Kenyon, had been a jack-of-all-trades, just like his son, but what he'd really wanted to be was an artist. Karl had created some incredible metal sculptures. I'd seen them for the first time in Oren's workshop, just a few months after I arrived in Mayville Heights, and I'd been awestruck at the man's talent. Oren had agreed to let us showcase some of his father's pieces during the celebrations at the library. People had been amazed at the huge metal eagle, with a wingspan of over six feet, soaring over the computer room. I smiled at the memory. That had been a good day.

"The curator of the Museum of Contemporary Art in Chicago was here the day after the celebration. She was on vacation with her family. She wants to put two of my father's sculptures in an exhibit in the spring."

"Oren, that's wonderful," I said, grinning at him. I would have hugged him, but we weren't those kind of friends and I didn't want to make him any more uncomfortable than he already seemed.

"That check is the deposit on what they're going to pay me." His fingers played with the knitted hat in his hands. "I want it to go to the Reading Buddies program, Kathleen. My father's art wouldn't be getting seen by people if you hadn't convinced me to let you put it on display here." He looked around again. "And who knows what would have happened to this building and all the other programs if you hadn't been here?"

I'd been hired to supervise the renovation and upgrading of the library for its hundredth birthday. A few months ago I'd signed a new contract with the library board to stay on as head librarian. Even though I'd ended up in town because I was running away from my life in Boston, Mayville Heights had become home.

"Oren, if I hadn't taken the job, someone else would have," I said. "You don't owe me anything."

I looked at the check again. It was a lot of money. It could buy a lot of books for the Reading Buddies program. Still, I felt uncomfortable taking so much money from Oren. It wasn't as if he was a wealthy man.

"*You* came to Mayville Heights, Kathleen,"

Oren said. "*You* made all of this happen. Please take the money."

I could tell how determined he was by the set of his jaw and the conviction in his voice. If I said no, I suspected, Oren would just take the money over to Everett's office.

I folded the check in half again. "All right," I said, smiling at him again. "Thank you. You made my day."

Oren smiled back at me. "You're welcome." He looked at his watch. "I have to get over to the hotel."

I nodded and after a second's hesitation reached over and gave his arm a squeeze. "This means a lot."

He ducked his head. "I'm glad I can do it," he said. Then he turned and headed for the main doors.

Reading Buddies could expand. I had more than enough money now to cover the expenses. I had the urge to jump up and down and clap my hands, but I settled for going to find Abigail so I could share the news. Finally, something was going right.

Leah Webster spent an hour and a half looking through the photographs, fortified with a cup of coffee and a date square, before Thorsten arrived with her car. I didn't ask her a single question about the pawnshop robbery or the shooting of Nic Sutton's father. I was beginning to think it didn't have anything to do with Dayna's death after all.

I gave Leah my e-mail address in case she had any questions and wished her a safe drive back to Minneapolis. I was about to head back up to my office when Simon Janes, Mia's father, came through the front door. He smiled and headed toward me. His walk had a bit of a swagger that matched his personality.

He didn't waste any time on social niceties. "This is for you," he said, handing me a heavy buff-colored envelope.

"What is it?" I asked uncertainly. It seemed to be my day for people handing me envelopes.

"Why don't you look and find out?" he said.

I slit the end of the envelope. The check inside fell to the floor. I bent to pick it up and couldn't quite believe my eyes. It was made out to the Reading Buddies program and the amount would keep us going for the next two years. In just a day I'd gone from thinking I might have to cut back the program to being able to make every one of my plans happen.

I looked at him, speechless, for a moment. "I, uh . . . thank you," I finally managed to get out.

"You're welcome," he said. "But you really should thank Mia."

"I will," I said.

"It's enough to expand your program and keep it running for a while?"

I nodded.

"Your fundraiser was a disaster," he said bluntly. "When I said that to Mia she called me an ass."

I wanted to laugh at Mia's accurate assessment of her father, but given the fact that I was holding a very large check with his signature on it, I didn't.

"She's not really an assertive person," Simon said with a smile. "The only rebellious thing she does is dye her hair outlandish colors. After she called me an ass she told me I could easily fund your program and I should. I decided she was right."

"I appreciate that," I said.

I still thought Simon Janes was a bit obnoxious, but the check in my hand was softening my opinion of him.

"Spend my money wisely, Ms. Paulson," he said. "I'll be interested to see how your program goes."

"You're welcome to check in anytime," I said. I waited until he was gone; then I walked over and waved the check in Abigail's face.

"Is it real?" she asked.

"As far as I know," I said. "Between the money from Oren and this, we can do everything we talked about."

"Is it all right if I jump up and down and squeal?" she asked.

I grinned. "I'd be disappointed if you didn't," I said.

When I eventually got back up to my office, Hercules was sitting in the middle of my desk with a very self-satisfied look on his face, and two tiny tendrils of paper stuck to his tail that told me he'd been in the workroom. It was where we kept the paper shredder.

That meant there was an excellent chance that the piece of paper at his feet had been stolen—from Detective Webster.

23

"What did you do?" I asked, glaring at him. He lifted one white-tipped paw and set it down on the piece of paper.

"You stole that from the detective, didn't you?"

He sat up a little straighter, obviously proud of himself.

"I told Marcus I wouldn't ask her about the case."

"Merow," Hercules said, looking down at the piece of paper and then back at me.

"Okay, so stealing something from a police officer"—I glared at him—"isn't quite the same as asking her questions, but it's still wrong."

The cat's expression didn't change. This wasn't the first time Hercules had swiped a piece of paper from someone connected to one of Marcus's cases. In the previous cases it had actually helped me eventually figure out who the killer was.

I crossed the room, leaned back against the desk and picked up the piece of paper.

"I think this makes me an accessory after the fact," I said.

His response was to lick his paw and take a couple of swipes at his face.

"Somehow I don't think the fact that you're cute is going to help me," I said.

Hercules leaned against my arm as I looked at the page that he'd "borrowed" from Detective Webster. It was a list of items stolen from the pawnshop.

I looked down at the little tuxedo cat. There was something about his expression that made me think if he could talk he would have said, "See? Do you get it?"

The problem was I didn't. I looked at the list again. What was I not seeing? Hercules thought this was a clue. Both Owen and Hercules somehow knew what was a clue and what wasn't. I would have admitted Herc's ability to walk through walls and Owen's to become invisible before I would ever have admitted that to anyone. It still felt uncomfortable to admit it to myself.

The list of stolen items was surprisingly short, I noticed, several diamond rings, a couple of watches . . . and two rare books.

"Dayna Chapman had a ticket to Vincent Starr's lecture," I said to Hercules.

The wheels were turning in my brain. "Could Dayna have somehow been involved in that robbery?" I asked Hercules.

Something was there in the back of my mind, poking at me like a broken spring in a chair. I put my finger on the titles of the two stolen books. A first edition of Steinbeck's *East of Eden* would have been worth maybe fifteen hundred dollars. The first edition of *The Hobbit*, a little more—probably between three and four thousand. Neither book was going to make anyone rich.

I replayed what Maggie had told me about Brady's conversation with his mother. And then I had it. I looked at Hercules.

"I should be mad at you," I said, "because you're going to turn into a feline delinquent. But I think I have an idea of what Dayna was up to." I looked at my watch. I was done for the day in about fifteen minutes. "We're going to have to make a little side trip before we go home," I said, reaching for the phone.

Maggie answered her cell on the third ring. "Hi, what's up?" she said.

"I need to ask Brady a question about that conversation he had with his mother," I said. "Could you set that up for me?"

"You figured something out."

I stretched my legs out in front of me. "I'm not sure," I said. "That's why I need to talk to him."

"I'm sitting here outside his office right now," Maggie said. "We were going to have an early supper before class."

"I can be there in about twenty minutes."

I pictured Maggie pulling a hand through her blond curls. "Okay, I'll see you then," she said.

*   *   *

When I walked into Brady Chapman's office, his receptionist smiled at me. "You can go on back, Ms. Paulson," she said. "Mr. Chapman is expecting you."

Brady was standing in his office doorway with Maggie. "Hi, Kathleen," he said. "Maggie says you might have figured something out. What is it?"

"Tell me about the piece of paper with the address on it that your mother dropped," I said.

"That isn't going to help," Brady said. "The street doesn't exist. Not here. Not in Minneapolis or Red Wing, either."

"Tamera Lane," I said. "Right?"

Brady nodded.

I pulled a pen and a pad of paper out of my bag. "Like this?" I wrote the address across the middle of one page.

Brady shot Mags a puzzled look. "Yes," he said.

I exhaled loudly and tapped the paper with one finger. "That's not Tamera Lane," I said. "It's Tamerlane. All one word, and it's not an address; it's the name of a very, very valuable book."

"How valuable?" Maggie asked.

"The last one sold at auction in 2009 for more than six hundred thousand dollars," I said.

24

"Good dog!" Maggie exclaimed.

"You think my grandparents owned a copy of this book?" Brady asked, pulling a hand over the back of his neck.

"I don't know," I said. I couldn't tell him that I thought his mother might have had something to do with stealing the book. First of all, it was a big leap to think that Nic Sutton's father had had a copy of a very old and rare book and that it had been stolen, and yet he hadn't said anything about it to the police and his insurance provider. And second, I couldn't tell Brady that I suspected his mother had been involved somehow in that pawn-shop robbery. It would have been cruel, especially since I didn't have any proof.

"I need to tell Marcus about this," I said.

Brady shrugged. "That's okay."

His mind was somewhere else. *Replaying that visit with his mother,* I wondered.

He loosened his tie. "Thank you, Kathleen," he said.

"I'll see you at class," I said to Maggie.

"Thanks," she said, wrapping me in a hug. "There's more, isn't there?" she whispered against my ear. She studied my face when she let me go and I nodded, almost imperceptibly, but I knew from the way Maggie pressed her lips together that she'd seen.

I touched her arm. "I'll see you later," I said.

I called Marcus as soon as I got home. I told him I thought the address Dayna Chapman had dropped wasn't an address at all and explained about the value of the book. *Tamerlane and Other Poems* was Edgar Allan Poe's first published work, and a 2009 sale of a first edition had been big news. Well, at least among librarians and book collectors. I could tell from the tone of his voice that he wasn't convinced.

Maggie must have been watching for me, because she came over to me as soon as I stepped into the studio. "Did you talk to Marcus?" she asked.

I nodded.

"What did he say?"

"I don't think I convinced him that Dayna had written down the name of a rare book and not a nonexistent street," I said, adjusting the drawstring waist of my workout pants.

"What didn't you say to Brady?" she asked.

"Mags, don't ask me that," I sighed.

Her eyes narrowed. "Why?"

"Because . . . because I'm way out on a limb. Because I don't want to say anything that might hurt Brady when I don't have any proof. And because I don't want you to have to lie to him."

She swallowed and nodded. "Okay."

I gave her arm a squeeze.

I'd left the truck parked on a side street about halfway between the studio and Eric's Place. After class I walked over to the restaurant. I knew there was a good chance Nic would be there, and I needed to see if he knew anything about his father having a copy of *Tamerlane*.

He was just delivering a tray full of food and I waited at the counter. "Hi, Kathleen," he said. "What can I get you?"

"A large hot chocolate with marshmallows to go, please."

"Just give me a minute," he said as he disappeared into the kitchen. He came back with a tall take-out cup, the top rounded over with a pile of the Jam Lady's handmade marshmallows.

"May I ask you a question about your dad's pawnshop?" I asked as I snapped the take-out lid on the top of the cardboard cup.

"Sure," he said with a shrug. "What did you want to know?"

"There were two first editions stolen in the robbery."

He nodded. I noticed a tiny flush of color in his cheeks.

"Did your dad get a lot of rare books in the shop?" I asked.

Nic fingered the knot in the strings of the long apron tied at his waist. "A few. In a pawnshop you never know what's going to come through the door."

"Like a very rare, very valuable book that might have some questionable lineage?" I asked. That was about as diplomatic as I could word things.

Color flooded his face. He looked down at the floor for a moment. "I don't know," he finally said. "Not for sure. But it's . . . possible." His mouth twisted to one side. "My grandfather started that pawnshop. Not everything he did was on the up-and-up. Some of his customers still brought my dad business. He didn't turn it down." His eyes narrowed. "Why do you ask?"

"I'm trying to figure *why* someone would have wanted to kill Dayna Chapman. Maybe then I can figure out who did."

25

I would have slept late in the morning since I didn't have to go in to the library until noon, but Owen poked his furry gray face over the edge of the bed and meowed at me about six thirty.

"Go away," I mumbled.

He put his paw over my nose. I knew this was another one of those battles that I'd lose, so I got up.

Both cats were still in crabby moods. Hercules managed to upend Owen's dish and Owen kept crowding Hercules away from his. Frustrated, I finally snapped my dish towel in the air. That got their attention and made a very satisfying whipping sound. I glared at them. "I don't know what's up with you two, but cut it out," I said.

I picked up Owen's dishes and set them on the floor over by the sink. I moved Hercules's breakfast closer to the back door. I could see them darting looks at each other while they finished eating, but other than that it was peaceful.

Roma called just after eight o'clock. "What do you think about having supper in Red Wing before we go shopping for Rebecca's dress?" she asked.

"I'd like that," I said. Maybe a change of scenery would help me figure out what I was missing about that pawnshop robbery. "Want me to check with Rebecca?"

"If it's not too much trouble," Roma said. I could hear a smile in her voice.

"You sound extra happy," I said. "Has Eddie gone AWOL from the team?"

She laughed. "No. Ollie called me last night. She's coming for Christmas!" Roma's daughter was a biologist and a commercial diver. "And don't let me call her Ollie when she's here. That was her nickname when she was two."

"My mother still calls me Katydid," I said. "But I'll try to keep you out of trouble."

Roma said she'd pick me up at the library at five thirty and we ended the call.

I was about to call Rebecca when I heard the sound of a cat squabble from the kitchen. Hercules was next to his water dish, eyes narrowed, ears flattened. Owen was by the basement door. He didn't look nearly as wary as he should have. Hercules rarely got angry, but when he did it was a bad idea to get in the way of his fury. Of course, usually the person he was angry with was Roma and usually there was a needle and Kevlar involved.

"What's going on?" I said.

Hercules stopped glaring at his brother long enough to look at his water dish. His little purple mouse was lying in the middle, doing the dead mouse float.

Hercules loved that little mouse. He never would have dropped it in his water dish. On the other hand, Owen had been coveting the toy since the day Rebecca bought it for his brother. Hercules didn't usually go for toys, which meant until the purple mouse had arrived, all the toys in the house were the property of Owen.

I looked at him sitting by the door. I had no proof, of course, but there was something defiant in the way he sat there, head up, tail flicking around.

I took a step closer to him. "Owen, did you do that?" I asked, pointing at the water dish with its little purple corpse. He met my eyes for a moment and then he turned to study the side of the refrigerator. Okay, so he was a cat and not a person, but that looked like a guilty conscience to me.

"That mouse belonged to your brother," I said. "That was mean."

His gaze flicked back to me for a moment and then something behind me caught his eye. He gave a yowl of outrage. I turned around to see Hercules coming from the living room with one of Owen's yellow funky chickens in his mouth. He set it on the floor, put a paw on the body and pulled off the head. Then he looked directly at Owen and started chewing.

It was a really stupid idea for revenge. Hercules was pretty much indifferent to the charm of catnip and I knew the bits that were flying into the air as he shook his and the chicken's head were going to make him sneeze. Which in a moment they did.

The first sneeze launched the yellow chicken out of his mouth. It arced across the kitchen in a perfect curve and splashed down next to the purple mouse.

There was a sudden silence in the room. Owen made his way over to the water dish. He poked the limp chicken head with one paw. Hercules joined him. He looked sadly at his mouse, but he didn't poke it. That would have meant getting his paw wet.

"That serves you both right," I said.

I went into the living room and called Rebecca, relaying Roma's idea of supper when she answered.

"Oh my word," she said. "I forgot completely that we were going to Red Wing."

"Is it a problem?" I asked.

She sounded distracted.

There was a brief silence and then she sighed softly. "Kathleen, have you ever been out to Marsh Farm?" she asked.

"Is that the beautiful, big house between here and Red Wing where they have weddings in the summertime?"

"That's it," she said. "It's usually closed all winter, but Everett has rented the entire place because we didn't have an engagement dinner and now he's decided we need to do that before we get married."

"Oh," I said.

"I hope you don't have any plans for next Saturday night," she added.

I sat down on the footstool. "Is there anything I can do to help?"

"Thank you, dear, no. Maggie's out there right now seeing what we'll need for centerpieces and things like that. And then I have to drive out there myself because now it seems that Everett has come up with a seating plan that Maggie is going to need to see."

"Do you need to talk to Maggie for anything else?" I asked.

"No," Rebecca said. "I don't care about seat covers and party favors. All I want to do is get married. I should have listened to you when you suggested I tell Everett that I didn't want all this hoopla."

"You love him," I said. "You didn't want to hurt his feelings. So let me do something for you. Where's this seating plan? Do you have it?"

"Lita's going to bring it up in a few minutes."

"Call her and tell her to drop it off here," I said. "Please. Then Roma and I will pick you up about quarter to six, we'll find a dress in Red Wing and things will end the way they do in all stories of true love: happily ever after."

Rebecca actually laughed. "Having you become my backyard neighbor is one of the best things that's ever happened to me."

"Me too," I said.

"You're a darling girl," Rebecca said. "Thank

you. I'll call Lita. She should be there in about fifteen minutes."

"I'll see you tonight," I said.

I had more than enough time to get the vacuum
cleaner out and vacuum up the bits of catnip on
the kitchen floor. What on earth had Hercules
been thinking, assuming that cats thought through
what they were going to do? He didn't even like
catnip, but he was willing to eat it just to get back
at Owen.

It was as if one domino had been knocked over in
my brain and suddenly another and another were
following. Hercules was a cat, a very smart one with
some very unusual abilities, but a cat nonetheless.
And he'd eaten a catnip chicken to make a point.
Was it possible that Olivia Ramsey had eaten a chocolate she knew she was allergic to, just to eliminate
herself as a suspect in Dayna Chapman's death? If
Marcus had been here he would have laughed and
said I was being sent off on a tangent by my feelings.
I didn't have a single fact. Why on earth would Olivia Ramsey want to kill Dayna Chapman?

Then another domino fell over. Roma's daughter's name was Olivia, too. Ollie had been her
baby nickname when she was two. She could just
as easily have been called Liv. The way Georgia
had called Olivia Ramsey "Liv."

Dayna had said "live" and "package" to me.
Both Marcus and I had assumed she was trying to
say she wanted to live and she was allergic to
something in the little package of chocolates. But
what if "live" was really "Liv," short for Olivia?

I scrambled up the stairs for my laptop, brought it back downstairs and went to Edwin Jensen's Web site. I scrolled through the photos looking for any with Dayna and Olivia together. I couldn't find any, but as I studied the images of Olivia, I noticed something. In the first two shots of her giving first aid to Nic Sutton's father, there was something on the ground beside her. Olivia had said she was coming from the comic book store. But it didn't look like a plastic bag. It looked like a small, padded envelope.

It looked like a package.

Package.

Liv. Package.

No. That was crazy.

I scrolled through the other photos of Olivia as quickly as I could. She wasn't carrying any padded envelope in any of the later pictures.

"Olivia Ramsey killed Dayna," I said out loud. "Why?"

I had to call Marcus. I started for the living room, but there was a knock at the back door. That had to be Lita.

It was.

"I'll take this out to Maggie," I said. "Thanks for bringing it out to me."

"Thank you for helping Rebecca," Lita said. "And Brady said you may have come up with something that will help figure out who killed his mother."

"I hope so," I said.

I took the list into the kitchen. There was lots of

time to take the seating chart out to Maggie, then come back and convince Marcus that I knew who had killed Dayna Chapman, but didn't know why.

I put on my coat and boots and was about to leave when it occurred to me that I should call Maggie to make sure she didn't leave for any reason before I got to Marsh Farm.

"Hey," I said when she answered her phone. "I have a seating chart from Everett that I'm about to bring out to you, so don't leave."

"Kath, could you bring Owen with you?" she asked.

"Um, yes, I guess I could," I said. "Why?" I was pretty sure I knew the answer to my own question.

"Because I think I just saw a mouse on the stairs."

Maggie was afraid of mice. She wasn't that crazy about hamsters, gerbils or guinea pigs, either.

"Go wait in your car," I said. "The furry cavalry is on its way."

I reached over to the counter, grabbed the bag of sardine treats I'd made just a few days ago and gave it a shake. It was the fastest way to get Owen's attention. His gray head peered around the living room doorway before I got my boots laced.

"Road trip," I said. "Maggie needs us."

I left a few crackers in his dish for Hercules and took the rest with me.

I tried Marcus before I pulled out of the driveway, but the call went straight to voice mail. I didn't leave a message. My theory was a bit too complicated to explain in just a few words. I figured fifteen minutes to drive to Marsh Farm. Fifteen for Owen to do his thing and for me to act as cleanup crew and fifteen more to drive back. At the most I'd be back in an hour and then I could try Marcus again.

I wasn't even close to right.

26

Maggie's Bug was parked in the circular driveway in front of the main entrance to Marsh
Farm, but she wasn't in it.

"That's a good sign," I said to Owen. There was
a small silver truck in front of her Volkswagen.

I'd brought the cat carrier bag with me, and
Owen climbed inside without argument.

Marsh Farm looked nothing like any farm I'd
ever seen. The house was bigger than Wisteria
Hill—three floors instead of two. It was shingled
with blue-gray cedar shakes and had many large,
multipaneled windows. The wine-colored front
door was unlocked and I stepped into a beautiful
foyer with cream-colored walls and an elegant
crystal chandelier overhead. A wide staircase led
to the upper floors. The treads were dark polished
wood with an Oriental carpet runner in shades of
burgundy and cream. Behind the stairs I could see
a huge window and above it there was a massive
oil painting of a Victorian-era woman on a horse.

"Maggie, where are you?" I called.

"Back here," she answered.

"That was helpful," I said to Owen.

I got a snippy meow in return. Owen didn't like any criticism of his ladylove.

Maggie's voice had come from the left side of the big house, so I went in that direction. The huge front room looked as though it had been a parlor of some kind. It led into a smaller room, which in turn led to the kitchen, which was where I found Maggie and Olivia Ramsey.

"Oh, uh, hi, Olivia," I said. "What are you doing out here?"

"She came to check out the kitchen for Georgia," Maggie said. She leaned toward the cat carrier. "Hey, Owen."

He murped a hello back at her.

"Where is it?" I asked.

Maggie gave a little shudder. "The second set of stairs up to the third floor."

"I offered to go take a look," Olivia said.

"But I thought it would be safer if she stayed down here. With me," Maggie hastily added.

"It's okay," I said, giving her what I hoped looked like a reassuring smile. "Owen and I will go see what's going on." What I really wanted was to grab Maggie and get out of there, but I didn't want Olivia to know I was onto her.

I let Owen out of the bag on the second-floor landing. "Go for it," I said.

I could see something gray and furry about five steps from the top. Owen crept slowly from tread to tread. Suddenly, he stopped. I held on to the strap of the cat bag, ready to swing it if something decided to make a run for it in my direction.

Owen was already on the step with whatever the furry animal was. He grabbed it in his teeth and started back down to me.

Great. It wasn't dead. I really hoped Maggie wasn't waiting down by the front door. As Owen got closer to me, I realized whatever he was carrying in his mouth definitely wasn't dead. Because it had never been alive. The cat stopped at my feet and looked up at me.

"What is that?" I said. He dropped his find on the floor and then swatted it with one paw. It rolled about six inches.

I leaned over for a closer look. It was a fur pompom, probably from a hat or a fur coat.

"Good job," I said.

He preened appropriately.

Maggie and Olivia were still in the kitchen.

"Did he get it already?" Maggie asked.

"Yep," I said, holding up the little ball of gray fur. "You were menaced by a pompom."

Maggie had her arms folded over her chest, shoulders hunched, and now she gave me a sheepish look.

"Well, that's embarrassing," she said. She looked at Owen, who was standing just to my right. "But you're still my hero."

He smiled at her. I swear.

I handed her the seating chart Lita had given me. Maggie looked at it and frowned. "I don't think this is going to work," she muttered. Then she looked up at me. "Would you like to see the room Everett wants to use?" she asked.

"I would," I said.

Olivia was opening cupboards and making notes on a small pad.

"We'll be back," Maggie said.

Olivia nodded over her shoulder. "Okay."

I scooped up Owen and put him back in the carrier bag before he had a chance to disappear into another room or disappear altogether.

Maggie took us back through the two rooms I'd passed through, to another large space on the other side of the huge house. It was actually two rooms, separated by a set of leaded-glass sliding French doors.

"This is beautiful," I said

She nodded. "I know. But it's a lot fancier than what Rebecca had in mind."

"Everett seems to have lost *his* mind when it comes to this wedding."

Maggie pulled out her phone. "I'm going to take some pictures of the room on the other side. I think it might be the better choice."

Maggie snapped several shots of the other room and then stopped dead in the center of the space. "I'm supposed to meet Oren in about forty-five minutes," she said, rubbing her forehead. "I completely forgot."

"You have lots of time to get back to town," I said.

"I know. But Olivia needs to take some measurements in the kitchen and make an inventory of some of the equipment for Georgia." She looked around uncertainly. "I'll try Oren's house. Maybe he's still there."

Oren Kenyon was one of the few people I knew who didn't have a cell phone.

There was no answer at Oren's.

Maggie put her phone in her pocket. "Kath, I hate to ask, but could you stay here with Olivia and then lock up?"

I nodded. "Go," I said. I could fake it with Olivia for a few more minutes.

I followed Maggie back to the kitchen, where she explained to Olivia what was going on. A small blowtorch was sitting in the middle of the large island in the center of the room.

"Are you sure you don't mind staying?" she asked me. "Georgia really needs to figure out her dessert menu and get back to Everett about the price. She's working at Fern's this morning, so I said I'd come out and look at the kitchen for her."

"It's not a problem," I said.

"Why do you have a blowtorch?" Maggie asked, gesturing at it.

Olivia smiled. "Would you believe it was one of the things Georgia asked me to look for? She uses it to caramelize the top of crème brûlée."

Maggie smiled. "I didn't know that. Then again, I've never made crème brûlée." She handed me the keys and gave me a hug. "I owe you lunch at Eric's for this," she said.

Olivia had gone back to looking in cupboards and writing in a wire-bound notepad.

"I'm just going to look around a little," I said to her. It made me a bit uncomfortable being in the same room with her, given what I believed she'd done. But then again, there was absolutely no way she could know what I suspected. Once I was in the front parlor again, I pulled my phone out of my pocket, thinking maybe I'd see if I could reach Marcus.

"Put the phone away," Olivia said behind me.

I turned around to look at her. I hadn't realized she'd followed me.

She was holding the blowtorch except now it was lit, a tight blue flame coming out of the end.

"What are you doing?" I said.

She smiled, but the gesture was cold. "Protecting myself."

I frowned. "From me?"

Olivia shrugged and looked around. Then she took a couple of steps toward me. I backed up toward the foyer. She knew, I realized. She knew that *I* knew what she'd done.

"You've been looking at Ed Jensen's Web site," she said. "You've been spying on me."

Behind me Maggie's voice said, "Olivia, what are you talking about?"

I swung around. Maggie was standing just inside the big front door. "I forgot my phone," she said, walking over to me. She looked at Olivia. "Why are you carrying that blowtorch? What's going on?"

I swallowed down the lump in my throat. "Nothing's going on, Mags. But you'd better get going or you'll be late for your meeting." I tried to keep my voice even and calm.

"Not so fast," Olivia said.

I put the strap of the cat carrier over my head so the bag was resting against my hip. "I don't understand," Maggie said, her forehead wrinkling into a frown. "Kathleen wasn't spying on you."

I stepped in front of her so I was between her and Olivia and the blowtorch.

"Edwin Jensen has some kind of software on his computer to monitor visitors," I said.

Olivia nodded. "He has the coolest tracking widget. He could tell someone from Mayville Heights was looking at the pictures he took the night of the robbery, and"—there was a disconcerting cunningness to the smile she gave me—"he could also tell which Web site that person arrived at the blog from." She arched an eyebrow at me. "When Edwin told me it was a news service for libraries, I knew it had to be you poking around."

"That's why you confessed to me that you knew Dayna. You knew I'd been checking you out."

"You're right," she said. "Pretty smart of me, wasn't it?"

I took a step backward. Maybe I could keep her talking and we could make it to the door. Even though I was in sock feet and Olivia was wearing boots, I felt pretty sure I could outrun her in those heels she had on, and I knew Maggie could.

"How did you get him to help you?" I asked.

"I played the helpless victim," she said. "I told him an old boyfriend wouldn't leave me alone." She shrugged. "I had to do him a couple of times, but it was worth it."

I swallowed down the sour taste at the back of my throat.

"I don't understand," Maggie said. "*You* killed Dayna Chapman? But you ate one of those chocolates. You could have died."

Olivia shook her head. "No. I had that all worked out." She looked at me. "I did improvise the part where you got my autoinjector. That was pretty good." She turned the blowtorch and studied the blue flame. "I really wish I didn't have to kill you. You know, I came up with the whole plan in the library. I did all my research into that old book on your computers and I borrowed every single Edgar Allan Poe book you had. That's how I got the idea that I was going to have to eat one of those chocolates, too."

" 'The Purloined Letter,' " I said.

Maggie looked lost.

"It's a Poe short story," I explained. "About a hidden letter. Poe's detective finds the letter when the police can't because it's been hidden in plain sight with some other mail." I didn't take my eyes off Olivia. "Who would look for a valuable, stolen letter in with the everyday correspondence? Just like who would think anyone would deliberately eat a chocolate that could kill them?"

Olivia turned the blowtorch back around so it

was facing us again. "Uh-huh," she said. "Since I almost died, too, why would anyone suspect me?"

She looked pleased with herself.

"You were the lookout the night of the robbery," I said. I nudged Maggie backward another step, hoping I'd get an opportunity to shove her toward the front door.

"And no one was supposed to get hurt," she said. "If that old man had just opened the safe when Jake told him to, everything would have stayed on track."

"You knew the book was there." I eased my right hand toward the pocket of my jacket. Could I get my phone and hand it back to Maggie?

Olivia suddenly leaned forward and flicked the torch at me. "Hands where I can see them," she said. She straightened up. "Yes. We knew that old book was there. A friend of Jake's saw it. Leo figured if the old man had some crappy old book in his safe, it had to be worth something. Turns out he was right."

"How did Dayna find out?"

She shook her head in frustration. "The stupid-ass prosecutor let Dayna look at the pictures from the night it all happened. She noticed the parcel I'd had just disappeared."

"She knew you had something valuable."

Olivia was moving her fingers back and forth, just beyond the edge of the blowtorch flame. She didn't even look at me. "I knew she'd be bleeding us dry for the rest of our lives. I didn't really have a choice." She glanced at me for a brief second. "I told Dayna she should come for the rare-book lecture so we could find out how much that Poe book was worth. Thank you for setting that up, by the way. It made it so easy to get her to come here." She smiled at me. "Now that we've finished the recap for anyone who tuned in late, move away from the door."

I stayed where I was and reached behind me to grip Maggie's arm.

"There's no point in trying to make a run for it," Olivia said, gesturing at my hair with the flaming torch.

I could feel the heat as she flashed it by my face. Still I didn't move. Our best chance to get away from Olivia was to get close enough to the door to bolt for the yard. Unfortunately, we were about halfway between the stairs and the door.

She made a sour face, took several steps to her left and with her gaze still locked on my face used the blowtorch to set the semi-sheer, floor-length curtains on the big window behind the stairs on fire. The flames shot up the thin fabric.

"Next time that'll be your friend's hair," she said. "Move away from the door."

I gave Maggie's arm a reassuring squeeze and stepped away from her.

"No," Olivia said, emphatically. "Her too." She took a step toward Maggie.

I looked at Mags, hoping the fear that was squeezing all the air out of my chest wasn't showing on my face.

"Up," Olivia said, gesturing with her free hand. I knew going up those stairs was a bad idea, but I couldn't chance her setting Maggie's clothes on fire.

The elaborate staircase went up six steps to a small landing. Then it turned ninety degrees for another four steps before making one more ninety-degree curve up to the second floor.

I could feel the heat from the burning curtains. I looked around for any sign of a sprinkler system, but I didn't see anything. Owen moved in the bag against my hip. Through the top mesh panel I could see him crouched down inside, ears flattened against his head. I needed to keep Olivia distracted long enough to open the top of the bag the rest of the way so hopefully Owen would do his disappearing act, jump out and somehow have a chance at getting away.

I slid my hand up the nylon fabric so it was resting on the top of the bag. "How are you going to explain the fire?" I asked.

Maggie started to cough. The foyer was filling with smoke. Whatever those filmy curtains were made of gave off a foul, chemical smell that mixed with the smoke.

Olivia brushed her hair back from her face and swiped at her eyes. She continued to move toward us. I had to start up the first turn of steps to stay ahead of her.

"I think I'll blame it on Maggie," she said. She looked at Mags and shrugged. "I'm sorry. I really only want to kill Kathleen, but you're kind of a package deal." She turned her attention to me. "You'll tragically lose your life trying to save your friend. I'll tell everyone how brave you were."

We were about halfway up the stairs now, facing the wall of flame behind the stairs. The fire had made it up to the curtain rod and as I watched, it jumped to the huge oil painting on the wall above the windows. It crackled and snapped, fueled by the oil paint and dry canvas. The smoke was heavier and I pressed one hand to my mouth. Next to me Maggie had another coughing fit.

Olivia gestured at the cat carrier with the blowtorch. "Give me the cat," she said.

I pressed the bag against my hip. Owen hadn't yet realized the top was open and he could jump out. "No," I said.

Olivia's eyes narrowed with anger. "You want the poor thing to die in here? What's the matter with you?"

She leaned over so the flame was just inches above the elegant Oriental carpet runner.

"Give me the cat," she repeated.

What else could I do? Maybe I could get us all out of this. My hands were shaking, but I eased the strap of the cat bag off my shoulder. Olivia held out her hand.

"Sorry," I whispered to Owen, and then instead of handing over the carrier I threw it at her. As the bag arced down over the few steps between us, Owen somehow launched himself up and out. Eyes wide and angry, and fur going every which way, he landed three steps below me and darted between Olivia's legs.

It was enough to knock her off balance on those high heels. She fell backward, dropping the blowtorch. It ignited the edge of her faux leather pants. Whatever they were made of was highly flammable.

Flames shot from her ankle to her hip in seconds. She screamed, hands flailing, which only succeeded in setting her sweater on fire. I flung myself on her, smothering the fire with my body and my heavy woolen coat. Above me Maggie sank onto a riser. She tucked her face in her elbow and looked at me. I tried to get my breath, but it was almost impossible, as there was so much smoke now.

Olivia moaned in pain, tears streaming down her face. Her fake leather pants had melted more than burned, and there were patches of the fabric layered onto the burns on her leg.

The blowtorch had fallen on the landing, and the Oriental carpet runner was already on fire.

Maggie had stumbled down around the turn of the stairs. "We've gotta get out of here!" she said. She coughed, bending almost double.

Olivia was shaking and whimpering. She was going into shock, I realized. The fire had spread now from the huge framed oil painting to the wallpaper. The woolen carpet was smoldering, making even more heavy dark smoke.

"Grab her shoulders," I yelled to Maggie. Talking started another coughing jag, but I managed to grab Olivia's feet. Maggie caught her under the arms and we got her around the turn and down the few stairs.

Then I heard a wrenching groan as if the house itself were in pain. The massive oil painting behind the stairs seemed to shudder and then, almost as though in slow motion, it broke from the wall and fell forward.

"Maggie!" I screamed.

Out of reflex she jumped backward, pulling Olivia with her. The momentum from the falling picture knocked me backward as well, up the stairs. Beside me Owen yowled as the carpet, which had been mostly smoking before, now began to really burn.

Olivia gave an agonized moan of pain.

"Kath!" Maggie screamed, struggling to get to her feet. The burning canvas was wedged on its side like a wall of flame between us.

"Get out!" I yelled at Maggie. "Go!"

She hesitated.

"Go!" I screamed. "Get yourself and Olivia out and go!"

Wheezing, she pressed her face into her elbow. "I'll come back for you," she shouted when she could breathe again.

"No!" I hollered. "Just get out and call nine one one."

The flames were licking their way closer. Owen was beside me on the stairs, crouched low, ears flattened, hissing in anger or in fear, I wasn't sure which. I waved Maggie down the stairs.

She gave me a last panicked look and began to drag Olivia down the steps.

I grabbed Owen and the empty carrier bag, pressed the crook of my elbow against my mouth and nose and began to climb. I knew it was a very bad idea, but I had nowhere else to go.

There were four large rooms on the second floor of the old house. Every one of them was locked. I grabbed the doorknob of the closest door with both hands and tried to make it turn. I shook it. I took a step back and kicked it. It didn't give. I tried to force the door open with my hip, but it was heavy solid wood with raised panels. It didn't move. None of them did.

The fire continued to lick its way up the carpet runner.

"We don't have a choice," I said to Owen. I started up the staircase to the third floor.

The air was actually a little better on the top floor of the old house, but I knew that wouldn't last very long as the thick, noxious smoke rose through the stairwell. The doors on this level were locked as well. I was coughing most of the time and wheezing when I wasn't. I put all my fear into kicking the doorknob to the room at the far right end of the hall, and by some miracle the door opened. I slipped inside, pushed the door shut with my hip and set Owen down on the floor. I doubled over, hands on my knees, and coughed. When I stood up again at least it was easier to breathe.

There was very little smoke in the room. Owen looked at me wide-eyed.

"We're going to get out of here," I said, swiping a hand across my face.

The room we were in was set up as a sitting room with several elegant chairs grouped in front of a high, multipaned window. I couldn't get it open, and even if I had, we were three floors up. It was too high to jump.

I sank down on to the floor and Owen climbed into my lap and nuzzled my chin. I stroked his fur. "We can do this," I said, my voice shaky. "We've gotten out of worse messes."

I remembered being trapped in that tiny cabin in the woods the previous winter, locked in a dark, cramped basement with a leaking propane stove above us. We'd gotten out just before the cabin exploded and I'd walked through snowdrifts up to my knees. But we'd survived.

Smoke was rolling in under the door. "Hang on," I said to Owen.

I pulled off my coat and jammed as much of it as I could into the crack between the bottom of the door and the floor.

The floor was warm. I felt the gleaming hardwood all around the area of the door. It was very warm. The fire had to be below us, working its way up the walls.

"We have to get out of here now," I told Owen.

The cat turned to the long window. I walked over and looked out over the backyard. It was too far to jump. We'd never survive the leap.

Then I saw it—a small balcony just slightly to my left and one floor down. Was it possible?

Could I somehow drop onto those few square feet? From the balcony it was maybe a twelve-foot drop to the ground, less if I landed in one of the banks of plowed snow. I might end up with a broken leg, but the odds were better than if I jumped from here.

It would have been better if the balcony were larger or directly underneath the window instead of off center from where I was. I tried to calculate how far off it was. My hands were shaking.

It was too much of an angle. I couldn't jump. "What if I miss?" I said to Owen. He looked at me for a moment; then he walked across the room and climbed into the cat carrier. Was that his vote of confidence?

I couldn't let Owen die and he couldn't get out without me. I rubbed away tears I hadn't known I was even crying. "Okay," I said. "Let's do this."

I picked up the closest chair, took two running steps forward and flung it through the window. It smashed the glass and fell to the ground. Cold air swirled into the room. It felt wonderful.

There was a poker by the fireplace. I used it to clear away the broken glass and the bottom part of the window.

I held on to the wide trim and looked out, careful not to get too close to the edge. The balcony looked a long way down.

"We need something to hold on to," I said to Owen. The four-poster bed was covered with a rose-patterned quilt. I flung back the edge. Yes! It was also made up with sheets. I hauled them off the bed, used my teeth to start an edge and tore both of them into long strips.

The area of warm floor was spreading. I knew I was running out of time. I knotted the ends of the sheets together, hoping this would work as well as it did in every prison escape movie Maggie had ever made me watch.

I was tying the makeshift rope to one leg of the big four-poster when I heard voices outside. I held on to the sheet and edged my way to the window again.

Burtis Chapman's big black truck was in the backyard almost directly below the balcony. Marcus got out of the passenger side and climbed onto the roof. I watched as he steadied himself, jumped and almost fell into the bed of the truck. He was trying to reach the balcony, I realized. He was coming to get me.

The tears started again and I brushed them away. Marcus got hold of the railing on the fourth try. He pulled himself up and over onto the balcony.

I zippered the top of the cat carrier and put the strap over my head. Then I made a loop in the end of my knotted sheet rope. Holding on to that, I went back to the window. Marcus was looking up at me. I'd never been so glad to see his face.

"You have to jump," he yelled.

I nodded. The balcony where he was standing seemed like such a long way down. Every part of me was shaking.

Marcus held out his arms. "Hang on to the window ledge," he shouted. "Swing your legs to the right and let go. I'll catch you."

I did the math in my head. It was about fifteen feet from the window ledge to the balcony below. Marcus was over six feet tall. Given my own height, I'd only be about eight inches from his arms.

Eight inches felt like eight feet.

"I'll catch you," he shouted. "I swear to God I'll catch you."

I heard something collapse behind me in the hallway. A wall, maybe? The stairs?

I was out of time. I shifted the cat carrier around onto my back and grabbed my bedsheet rope. Then I got down on my hands and knees and backed out the open window. My arms could only hold my weight for a few seconds, but that was all I needed. I swung my legs to the left and let go of the makeshift rope.

And fell . . .

Right into Marcus's waiting arms. I knocked him back against the French doors, but he didn't let go of me. And I didn't let go of him.

"You all right?" he said. He felt my arms, touched my face with his fingers. I nodded. I couldn't seem to find any words.

"We have to get off this balcony," he said.

Below us Burtis was standing in the bed of his truck. Marcus helped me over the railing.

"You sure you're okay?" Burtis asked, concern making tight lines around his mouth and eyes.

I nodded. "I'm okay," I said before another bout of coughing made it impossible to speak.

Maggie was standing by the tailgate of the truck, tears sliding down her face. Burtis helped me down and she wrapped me in a hug.

"I'm okay, Mags," I said. "It's okay. It's okay."

Owen made a loud meow of protest.

Maggie let me go, swiped at her face and tried to smile at me but couldn't quite get there. I pulled the bag over my head and undid the zipper. Owen poked his head out and looked around. His eyes seemed a little loopy, but otherwise he looked okay.

Behind me Marcus jumped down into the bed of the truck. Ric Holm and his partner were coming across the snow to us carrying their first aid gear. I could hear sirens in the distance.

I was still shaking, but I was safe.

I was safe.

27

Olivia was charged with the premeditated murder of Dayna Chapman, as well as two counts of attempted murder and one of arson for the fire at Marsh Farm.

It turned out that Marcus had been at the Chapman place, talking to Burtis, when Maggie called him. Burtis had followed Marcus out to the old house, both of them breaking every speed limit.

Maggie spent the night in my spare bedroom after an afternoon in the ER to make sure we hadn't inhaled too much smoke. Roma checked Owen over carefully from ears to tail. Aside from a little singed fur, he was fine.

"I didn't go out there on purpose to confront Olivia," I told Marcus as we waited at the clinic for Roma to finish her examination.

He put his arm around my shoulders. "I know that," he said. "Maggie told me."

"So you're not angry."

He kissed the top of my head. "All I am is very, very grateful."

I leaned my cheek against his arm. "Me too."

Marcus spent the night on the living room sofa. He showed up with his pillow, his toothbrush, Eric's meat loaf and mashed potatoes and a look on his face that told me he wasn't going to take no for an answer.

When I woke up in the morning, Maggie was curled up in the big wing chair by the window with Owen snoozing on the floor at her feet.

"Maggie, why aren't you still asleep?" I asked, sitting up and raking my hands through my hair.

Her expression was serious, lines etched around her mouth. "I'm sorry," she said.

"For not sleeping longer?" The back of my throat was dry.

"For not coming back to get you. I keep thinking what would have happened if . . ." She let the end of the sentence trail away, and her eyes filled with tears.

"Oh, Mags," I said. "I should be apologizing to you. I'm the one who almost got you killed. The entire staircase was on fire. There was nothing you could have done."

She gave me a stricken look. "I don't know what I would have done if anything had happened to you."

I felt the sting of unshed tears in my eyes and I blinked them back. "Me too," I said. "But nothing happened that couldn't be fixed." I went to get out of bed to hug her, but my legs were tangled in the blankets. I did a crazy flailing dance and fell onto the floor as Owen meowed loudly and bolted into the closet.

When Marcus appeared in the doorway, Maggie and I were on the floor in a heap of sheets and blankets hugging, laughing and crying all at the same time while Owen peered, wide-eyed, around the closet door.

"Oh, good, you're awake," Marcus said. "There's coffee."

For some reason that just made Maggie and me laugh harder.

When the two of us went downstairs we found Rebecca and Brady Chapman at the table having coffee with Marcus. Hercules was sitting beside Rebecca's chair eating what looked like a bowl of scrambled eggs.

I looked at Marcus. "I couldn't find the cat food," he said.

Rebecca came around the table and hugged both of us. "I'm so glad you're both all right," she said.

"I'm sorry about Marsh Farm," I said.

She held up a hand and shook her head. "It doesn't matter. All Everett and I care about is that neither one of you . . ." She looked around me to Owen, who was standing in the living room doorway probably wondering why there was were so many people in the kitchen at breakfast. ". . . or you," she said, smiling at the small gray cat, "are all right."

Which is why exactly six days later I found myself standing in the living room at Wisteria Hill, which had been transformed into a winter wonderland. Maggie, with a little help from Abigail, had strung white lights around the windows and the fireplace. One of Harry Junior's trees stood in the corner decorated with the snowflakes that were eventually going to be hung on the library tree and the Christmas ornaments that were usually on Ruby's personal tree. The mantel was trimmed with pine boughs, red ribbon and fat cream-colored candles inside glass hurricane lamps.

Everett and Rebecca were getting married. After the fire at Marsh Farm Rebecca had told Everett what she really wanted: a simple wedding surrounded by the people she loved the most. Roma offered her living room, where Rebecca and Everett had met for the first time. It was perfect.

Everett's granddaughter tapped me on the shoulder. "Ready?" Ami asked.

I smiled at her and fingered the small box wrapped in shiny silver paper with a red-and-green bow. "I'm ready," I said. I nodded at Maggie as we passed her.

Roma was waiting at the bottom of the stairs. Like Ami and me, she was carrying a small wrapped present.

Ami tapped on the door of the bedroom at the top of the stairs.

"Come in," Rebecca called.

She beamed, clasping her hands together when

she saw the three of us. "You're all so beautiful," she said. We were all wearing tea-length, cream-colored dresses—different styles—all with red sashes tied at the waist.

I put a hand on my chest. "You're the one who's beautiful," I said.

She truly was. There was a glow to Rebecca. That was what love looked like, I realized. And the rose-colored dress from Abel's that she'd tried on the first night Roma and I took her shopping looked perfect on her. The only alteration it had needed was to be shortened a little, and Ella King had done that in an afternoon.

Rebecca noticed the boxes in our hands. "No," she said shaking her head. "You don't believe in that something old, something new superstition, do you?"

Ami looked at Roma and me. "I told you she'd say that." She turned back to Rebecca. "It's not superstition, Rebbie. It's tradition. Deal with it."

Rebecca smiled at her. She loved Everett's only grandchild as if she were her own.

Ami handed her the small square box she'd been holding. "This is borrowed," she said.

Rebecca undid the ribbons and unwrapped the paper. She pulled the top off the box and lifted the lid. For a long moment she stared at the contents of the box and then she lifted out a small silver heart-shaped locket.

Ami smiled. "Do you remember that?"

Rebecca's eyes were bright and I noticed she

swallowed hard before she answered. "I didn't know you still had it," she said softly.

Ami looked at Roma and me. "Rebbie gave me that on my first day of middle school. She said I was about to start one of the best adventures of my life." She turned back to her soon-to-be-official grandmother. "You're about to start one of the best adventures of your life." They hugged each other and I had to swallow down the lump in my throat.

"I'm next," Roma said. "Mine is blue." The box she handed Rebecca was long and flat. Rebecca laughed when she saw what was inside—a lacy blue garter. She slipped off her high-heeled shoes and stepped into the garter, sliding it up her leg until it was just above her knee. She hugged Roma. "Thank you," she said. "I think Everett will like this."

"I really don't need to hear this," Ami exclaimed, clamping her hands over her ears.

We all laughed.

"My turn," I said. I felt the unexpected prickle of tears as I gave Rebecca my package. "This is something new."

Rebecca undid the paper and the ribbons and opened the small jewelry box. "Oh my word, these are lovely."

I'd gotten her tiny silver heart earrings as close to a match as I could find to Ami's locket.

"Thank you, my dear," she said as she wrapped me in a hug. "This day wouldn't be happening without you," she whispered.

"Just be happy," I whispered back.

Rebecca pulled out of the hug and turned to the mirror to put on the earrings. They looked as good as I'd hoped they would when I bought them.

"Thank you," she said. "And I don't mean to sound ungrateful, because I wasn't expecting this tradition." She smiled at Ami. "But isn't it something old, something new, something borrowed, something blue? Unless you were thinking I'm the old."

"You are not old," Ami said firmly. She glanced at Roma and me, and with exquisite timing there was a knock on the door.

"Come in," Rebecca called.

The door swung open and a man about my age stood in the doorway. He was wearing a dark gray suit with a blue shirt and a blue-and-gray tie. He had blue eyes, shaggy salt-and-pepper hair and Rebecca's smile. "Was someone looking for something old?" he asked.

"Matthew!" Rebecca exclaimed.

He covered the space between the door and his mother and lifted her up into a hug.

"How? How?" Rebecca said as she touched his face and ran a hand through his hair.

Matthew Nixon smiled at his mother. "I don't know if you've noticed, but Everett Henderson doesn't exactly take no for an answer."

"He wanted you to have the wedding of your dreams," I said.

"Oh, I am," she exclaimed, throwing her arms around her son again.

Ami looked at me and grinned. I saw Roma surreptitiously wipe away a tear. I had to blink back a couple myself.

It was the most beautiful wedding I'd ever been to. Rebecca's favorite people were my favorite people, too—Roma, Maggie, Harry Taylor Senior and Junior, Marcus, Brady Chapman, Mary and her husband. And Oren Kenyon played the piano.

Rebecca's brother, Stephen, the best man, walked with the maid of honor, Ami. He was a taller version of his sister with kind gray eyes. Harrison Taylor escorted Roma, and I walked in with Burtis Chapman.

"Thank you for everything you did for my boys," Burtis said as we waited for our cue to start walking.

"You're welcome," I said. "Thank you for helping save my life."

He smiled. "Anytime, girl," he said.

And after so many years of waiting to be together, Rebecca and Everett were finally married, fittingly, it seemed to me, in the place where they had fallen in love more than fifty years before.

After we'd toasted the happy couple, Rebecca walked over to Marcus and me. She handed me the bouquet of daisies that she'd carried.

"What's this for?" I asked.

"Tradition—and Ami—says I should throw this, but I'm not because I want you to have it." She looked at Marcus. "Don't wait too long for your happily ever after," she said. Then she turned and walked back to her new husband.

"They're pretty," Marcus said, gesturing to the flowers. Then he leaned down and kissed the top of my head. "And I like the sound of happily ever after."

I smiled up at him. I liked the sound of it, too.

ABOUT THE AUTHOR

Sofie Kelly is an author and mixed-media artist who lives on the East Coast with her husband and daughter. In her spare time she practices Wu-style tai chi and likes to prowl around thrift stores. And she admits to having a small crush on Matt Lauer.